RISKY BEHAVIOR

Rich Goldhaber

A LAWSON SERIES NOVEL

This is a work of fiction by the author. All of the names, places, characters and other elements of this written material are products of the author's imagination, are fictitious, and should not be considered as being real or true. Any similarity to actual events, locations, organizations, or persons, living or dead, is entirely coincidental.

All rights to this work are reserved. No part of this book may be used or reproduced in any manner whatsoever without the written permission of the author, except in the case of brief quotations as part of articles and reviews.

Copyright © 2013 Rich Goldhaber

ISBN-13: 978-1489522146

ISBN- 10: 148952214X

ACKNOWLEDGEMENTS

The author would like to once again thank a wonderful group of friends, family, and supporters who have been helpful in fine-tuning this literary work, as well as the following individuals who deserve special recognition.

Miriam and Luis Blanco have provided help with editing and critical comments, and their efforts are greatly appreciated.

Don Tendick's thoughtful critique of the story has enhanced the quality of this novel.

Kathleen and Lu Wolf have once again added great value to this novel with their thoughtful comments.

Jeanne, my Editor and Chief, and wife, made many contributions, all of which have improved this book's plot.

ALSO BY RICH GOLDHABER

The 26th of June

Succession Plan

Vector

Stolen Treasure

For: my parents, Rose and Al, who are hopefully looking down from above with some sense of pride.

Risky Behavior

Chapter 1

It was one of those frequent transitional fall days in the city of Chicago. You know the kind. The aroma of freshly cut lawns and the beauty of vibrant fall colors had been replaced with dull grey leafless trees and bronze-tinted dormant grass. The arrival of a cold front carried by a stiff northwest wind all but ruined what started out as a beautiful day. In short, it was football weather.

Bobby Fowler huddled with the varsity football team waiting for Coach Simpson's pre-practice speech. At six-foot-five and 225 pounds, he towered over most of his teammates. The entire team could have given the coach's speech. It was always the same; too little intensity, failure to tackle on defensive, and lack of blocking on offense.

Coach Simpson blew his whistle and walked to the front of the assembled group. His pallor matched the overcast sky as he began his speech. He uncharacteristically stopped in mid-sentence and looked upward as if searching for Devine assistance. He staggered slightly, suddenly grasped his left arm, grimaced in obvious pain, and fell to the ground.

Assistant Coach Wilson rushed to Simpson's side and then called 911. The team gathered around their fallen leader in silent fear. Most looked on not understanding the gravity of the situation, and had never witnessed death up close and personal. Unfortunately, Bobby understood exactly what was happening. He broke away from the team and sat down on the nearby bleachers. He buried his face in both hands, and began to cry.

Bobby knew the coach had experienced a massive heart attack, the same type his mother had died from almost five years before. He had been there when it happened along with his father. At first, Bobby thought his mother was choking on her dinner, but then, she too had grabbed her left arm and had fallen off her chair. She had looked chalk-white, as she lay unconscious on the kitchen floor. While his father administered mouth-to-mouth resuscitation, Bobby had called 911, but by the time the medics arrived, it was all over. His mother was gone and almost a year of grieving followed.

Seeing the medics arrive and the coach being taken off the practice field on a gurney had once again surfaced all those terrible memories; and now, Bobby looked at his fellow teammates, who were all visibly shaken by what they had just witnessed, and felt certain Coach Simpson was going to die.

With the ambulance's siren wailing its melancholy sound of despair, Assistant Coach Wilson, with tears in his eyes, quickly called an early end to the practice and ran off the field toward his car parked in the teacher's parking lot. Everyone knew he would be following the ambulance to nearby Oak Park Hospital.

Bobby changed back into street clothes in the locker-room. It was the first time he could ever remember being able to hear the air-conditioning system pushing fresh air into the sweat-filled room. The only other sound came from the old grey metal lockers being slammed shut. Everyone was deep in personal thought, trying to sort out what had just happened.

The wind had pushed the front eastward and a chilly blue sky had once again returned to the city. Bobby threw his full backpack onto the backseat of his father's white Lexus and headed home. He turned left onto Lemoyne Avenue and saw a navy-blue BMW parked in his driveway. He parked on the street and climbed the stairs leading up to the front veranda. The mahogany front door was ajar. His stepmother, Gloria, was always harping on not leaving the doors open. She claimed it was an invitation to any would-be burglar. Why any robber would venture into a house in broad daylight with a car parked in the driveway was beyond his ability to comprehend. It was just another example of his stepmother's preoccupation with ridiculous issues.

Bobby guessed his older stepsister Janet probably left it open, and the car no doubt belonged to her latest boyfriend. He grinned, thinking she might be making out. He approached the front door quietly, hoping to catch them both in some heavy action in the family room.

Peeking in the front door, he listened for any sounds, but as he looked around the first floor, he quickly concluded they must be upstairs in her room. Her door was probably shut, but maybe he'd get lucky and be able to catch them in the act. His pledge of silence would certainly be worth a considerable amount of indebtedness, a significant bargaining chip for future transgressions on his part.

He silently placed his backpack at the bottom of the staircase. Carefully avoiding the creaking third step from the bottom, he moved slowly up the carpeted wooden staircase. Near the top of the stairway, he looked left down the hallway at his stepsister's room. The door was wide open. Maybe he could take a picture with his iPhone. An actual picture of Janet caught doing it would certainly add to his negotiating position.

Bobby crept along the upper hallway and approached her room. He listened for any sounds of sexual pleasure. He began hearing subdued squealing, but the sounds were not coming from Janet's room. Instead, the noise seemed to be coming from the master bedroom. Was she really stupid enough to actually be screwing in her mother's bedroom? Yes, she would definitely pay a steep price for his silence.

He reversed his direction and moved cautiously toward the opposite end of the hallway. Near the master bedroom, he suddenly considered the possibility of his father's unexpected return from Afghanistan, but quickly dismissed the possibility. He had Skyped his father only yesterday, and his father had used the code word Nana's birthday. That meant he was about to leave on another reconnaissance mission.

No, he was definitely going to catch his stepsister in the act. He grinned in anticipation of what he was about to see. He readied his iPhone camera and slowly opened the bedroom door. He leaned forward and inched his head into the room.

What Bobby saw would haunt him for the rest of his life. The late-afternoon sun shining through a bedroom window highlighted the king size bed. Amidst an assortment of scattered clothing, Bobby's nude stepmother lay on her back, legs spread, moaning softly, with her arms and legs wrapped around a man who Bobby knew all too well. Her partner was his stepmother's ex-husband, Ray Bussard.

Bobby's heart raced from a surge in adrenalin. The stench of raunchy sex filled the room, a smell Bobby would never forget. He stood frozen in time, at first captivated by witnessing a live sex act and then repulsed by what he had just witnessed. He stared in utter disbelief for several seconds and then retreated into the hallway His first reaction was to barge into the bedroom and confront his stepmother and lover, but then uncertainty and fear took over, and he slowly and quietly backed down the stairs. He grabbed his backpack, left the house, started his car, and drove down the street. He wanted to put as much distance as soon as possible between himself and what he had just witnessed.

Losing track of time, he drove aimlessly around the neighborhood and finally parked his car on the street just outside the Burger King on North Avenue. Bobby closed his eyes and clutched the steering wheel until his hands turned white from the loss of blood. He finally left the car with his backpack and sat down on the curb to gather his thoughts. Out of anger, he began pounding the backpack with his fist, but finally realized the stupidity of this action. Instead, he buried his face in his hands and cried softly.

His father was serving a tour of duty in Afghanistan, and he had just witnessed his stepmother screwing her ex. He had always disliked this woman, believing she had caught his father at a time in his life when he was seeking companionship after losing his wife. Now, he knew his initial reaction had been right all along, and this slut was in the process of destroying both his father and their family.

Anger and absolute disdain for this woman filled his heart. The question was what to do about it? He collected himself and tried to consider the alternatives. He regretted not taking a picture with his iPhone. If he confronted her now, she would probably deny anything ever happened, but he knew what he had seen. There was no doubt in his mind; he saw her screwing Ray Bussard; saw her cheating on his father, and he knew something had to be done.

This was almost too much for him to process. Every time he tried to think of what to do, he could only picture his stepmother enjoying herself, spread-eagled on his father's bed, moaning passionately. His mind oscillated between his cheating stepmother and thoughts of his own mother probably turning over in her grave.

Why not just kill the bitch? He laughed to himself as he thought about the pleasure in seeing her die. His father kept a gun on the top-shelf of his closet. He knew how to use it. She certainly deserved to die. The more he thought about his stepmother and what she had done, the more he wanted to end her life; but how could he do it without being caught? The moral implications of killing her never crossed his mind, and her death would certainly fit the crime.

As he thought about what to do, one thing kept reemerging; somehow, he needed to end the marriage between this evil woman and his father. Telling his father about what he had seen, wouldn't solve the problem, because he wouldn't be able to do anything until he returned in five months after his National Guard Ranger unit stood down from active duty. If he told him now, his father would go ballistic, and his life might be compromised on the battlefield from this personal distraction. Bobby certainly didn't want the possibility of his father's death resting on his shoulders.

He knew he would have to figure this out by himself. He, and he alone, needed to take responsibility for the decision; but that still didn't answer the question of what he should do. Whatever he did, he knew the endgame needed to put an end to the marriage. If he could just make that happen, then he and his father could once again live together in happiness.

Bobby sat on the curb for hours trying to understand what to do. He lost track of time and finally realized it had gotten dark, and a light rain had been falling for some time. A nearby streetlight cast a dark shadow in front of a young man searching for an answer to a difficult question. Rain mixed with tears dripped from his nose. He wiped his face on his coat's sleeve and looked at his watch. He was late for dinner. He had no idea how he could possibly face his stepmother but knew he had to pretend nothing had happened. He climbed back in his car and drove back to his house knowing the solution to this complex problem would eventually present itself, and then he would do whatever needed to be done.

Chapter 2

Freddie "the Raccoon" Moran squinted in the bright sunlight as he left the Joliet Federal Lockup's main gate. He had just served his seven-year sentence for illegal possession of firearms and was now out on parole as a free man. He walked into the visitor's parking lot, and a group of reporters quickly surrounded him. Video cameras were rolling, and several microphones were thrust into his pockmarked face.

The Raccoon had become a local celebrity. He was a known contract killer who worked for anyone capable of paying his steep fees. For years, he had successfully evaded prosecution. Possible government witnesses had always disappeared before trial, and now, no person in their right mind would consider testifying against the Raccoon.

A perky female news reporter he had seen on channel nine asked, "Mr. Moran, how does it feel to be out on parole?"

His face broke out into a wide grin. He pointed both his hands up to the sky as if invoking heavenly support. "It feels good to finally be vindicated."

"But Mr. Moran, you were found guilty."

"No way was I guilty. I was framed by the Government. But I don't want to talk about that no more. I just want to go about living a normal life."

Freddie Moran walked away from the crowd of reporters and got into a taxi that had been waiting for him. He waved to the press as the yellow cab pulled away. He gave the driver an address in Chicago and settled back for the one hour ride into the city.

His sister had been taking care of his condo just off Lake Shore Drive, and he was looking forward to enjoying his newfound freedom. The problem was he didn't know what he was going to do. He had only one marketable skill, expert assassin.

The taxi arrived at his building, and he saw his older sister pacing outside. Bundled up in a heavy black winter coat and wool scarf, she waited for his arrival. They embraced as only close family can, and hand in hand, they took the elevator up to his second-floor unit.

"Freddie, it's good to see you again as a free man. I was always so sad looking at you behind that glass window."

"I missed you Ruth. You have no idea how bad things were in there. It's good to finally get out."

"Jim has a job for you if you want it. All you have to do is show up. Please don't get caught up in this other stuff. If you get caught, they'll send you away for a long time. I know you can turn your life around, and Jim is giving you a second chance."

"I appreciate his offer, but I don't know how I could possibly fit into his construction business. I wouldn't have a clue of what to do. It's just not me."

Ruth started to cry. She looked him in the eyes. "Please, just give it a try."

"Okay, I promise I will. I owe that much to both of you. I'll stop by Jim's office tomorrow."

Ruth gave him a warm hug, put on her coat, and started to leave. "I filled the fridge and pantry for you. Let me know if there's anything you need. Love you!"

"Love you too; thanks for everything."

Freddie, a man whose ruthless reputation was legendary, broke down and began to weep. He had served his time and now he was a free man. A person doesn't know how important freedom is until they lose it. Freddie thought back to his years in prison; the demands from fellow inmates for oral sex and sodomy. It was a world beyond description where gangs ruled the cellblock, and the other prisoners just tried to survive. He wiped away his tears and tried to compose himself.

He walked to the fridge and looked inside. Ruth had bought his favorite beer. He picked up a bottle of Samuel Adams Boston Lager and looked at it with reverent anticipation. He hadn't had a beer in almost seven years. As silly as it sounded, he had dreamed of this first bottle of beer for all that time, and he wanted to relish the moment. He didn't want a glass. His dream had always been to pull it straight from the bottle. He brought the open bottle up to his nose and smelled the nectar. It was indeed a gift from the gods.

He sat down by the TV in his favorite seat and savored the first sip. It was all he had dreamed of and then some. Sipping it slowly to maximize the enjoyment, he contemplated his life.

He had gotten mixed up in his early teens with a gang of crazies who were into acts of violence. He killed his first person when he was just sixteen years old. It had been an accident, but the kid deserved it. For weeks afterward, Freddie Moran had experienced a profound sense of pleasure from the act. Over time, he kept recalling the thrill of that moment, and when a gang-war erupted over turf, Freddie volunteered to eliminate the leader of the rival gang. He relished in planning the hit, and after taking out the leader with a single shot to the head, he was held in celebrity status by his fellow gang members. The acts of violence became more frequent and ritualized and ultimately became the dominant part of Freddie's life.

As the years went by, he realized he could make a good living killing people. The local mafia wanted to hire him on a permanent basis, but he preferred to operate as an independent. As his reputation grew, he received more contracts than he could handle. He became very selective in who he agreed to kill. He actually began to believe he was doing the community a service by preventing the most undesirable characters from completing future acts of violence.

Now, however, with seven years to contemplate his true value to society, he realized he had been nothing more than a paid murderer, and certainly not a superhero protecting the good citizens of Chicago. Perhaps those years behind bars had really changed him. One thing for sure, he knew if he didn't change, it would only be a matter of time before he was charged with murder and put away for life.

Over the years, he had accumulated several million dollars from contract fees, all stashed away in overseas accounts. He knew he could easily live off the interest and maintain a comfortable lifestyle for the rest of his life. The real question was whether he could conquer his compulsive need to kill. The act of planning and executing murders always yielded an endorphin high lasting many days. If he was going to kick the habit, he was going to need to find something to replace the excitement of the kill, and he doubted the construction business would serve that purpose.

He opened a second bottle of beer and turned on the TV He looked at his watch. It was time for the news, and he wanted to see if his interview would make the local headlines. He switched to WGN and waited for the perky reporter to appear on the screen.

Halfway through the newscast, the lead commentator gave the lead-in to his interview. "Today, after nearly seven years in prison, Freddie "the Raccoon" Moran was released from Joliet Federal Prison. As many of you will probably recall, the Raccoon was implicated in a number of contract killings. He gained almost celebrity status because his alleged victims were some of the most violent criminals in the city. Leslie Aronson interviewed the Raccoon earlier today."

And there he was, being interviewed on TV. He suddenly felt a surge of pride. The lead commentator had actually praised his work. Perhaps he could best serve society by continuing on with his many good deeds.

Chapter 3

Bill Fowler sat with his buddy Don Burke on a narrow mountain ledge overlooking the Khyber Pass. It was located in the northeastern part of the Spin Ghar Mountains. In earlier times, it was known as the Silk Road and was a major trade route between Asia and Europe. Today the road linked Afghanistan and Pakistan and remained the primary entry point into Afghanistan for Al Qaeda and Taliban fighters.

Bill's Ranger unit was charged with monitoring activity and intercepting these undesirables. Terrorist movements were reported back to Headquarters. CIA drones were then vectored to their area and deadly missiles launched if the Rangers confirmed the travelers were indeed terrorists. They couldn't interview the suspects, so the criteria established were very simple. If they were men, and if weapons could be identified, then it was assumed they were bad guys, and the drone operators fired their missiles. The problem, of course, was every male above the age of ten carried a weapon and almost always kept it in open sight. It was a badge of manhood they all wore proudly.

A Black Hawk S-70i helicopter had inserted them into the mountains two nights earlier, and it took another day to find the perfect little hiding place. During the day, they placed a large camouflage drape in front of their hideout to prevent their position from being discovered. At night, they felt comfortable moving further out on the ledge and viewing the entrance to the pass with their night vision equipment.

Don was manning a night vision telescope mounted on a tripod while Bill ate his evening meal, a ready-to-eat dinner identified as beef stew. It had the consistency of mush. Thankfully, it couldn't be seen in the moonless night. The evening's dessert consisted of six crackers filled with some sort of cheese and a bottle of water to wash down the entire 1500-calorie gastronomic delight.

Bill and Don had been doing these two-man reconnaissance missions twice a month since their deployment, each one lasting a week. Spending 24/7 with the same person for a week could lead to problems, but luckily both men had quickly reached a high level of compatibility. With little to do other than talk, both men felt comfortable in sharing their innermost thoughts. Each acted as the other's personal psychiatrist.

"Anything coming down the pass yet?"

"Nope, I think it's still too early. I'm guessing we won't see any action for another hour at least. Have you given any more thought to what you're going to do about your wife?"

"Things are getting worse. A couple of months ago one of the guys I play tennis with told me Gloria was getting pretty familiar with a couple of the tennis pros. She tends to go for the younger guys. I'm sure she's fucking everybody. If it's not a pro, then it's somebody else."

"So what are you going to do about it? You've got to do something."

"I talked to her about a divorce before we left, but she told me if there's a divorce, she's going to take me to the cleaners, and I believe her. Sometimes I'd just like to take my gun from the closet and take care of business. You know what I mean?"

"Sure, but you get the chair for that kind of stuff. If you're going to do something like that, you've got to make sure it looks like an accident. Hey wait; something's coming down the road."

Bill immediately picked up his night vision goggles, and watched as a couple dozen men and two donkeys loaded with supplies entered their field of vision. Don, with the more powerful equipment confirmed they were all carrying assault rifles. They were still almost a mile away but making slow steady progress as they moved along the winding road.

Bill called Headquarters. "Opera House, this is the Two Tenors."

"This is Opera House; go ahead Two Tenors."

"We've got about two dozen bad guys with weapons moving down the road. Recommend you vector a drone to our GPS coordinates."

"Can you light up the target?"

"Roger that; have the pilot contact us on this frequency when he reaches our area. What's his ETA?"

"We're vectoring in Grumpy. The ETA is sixteen minutes, repeat sixteen minutes."

"That's a roger Opera House; sixteen minutes."

All of the drones working with Don's and Bill's Ranger unit were named after the Seven Dwarfs. They were still waiting to work with Happy and Doc. While Don continued to follow the caravan with his night scope, Bill set up the laser-targeting device. Everything was ready by the time Grumpy arrived on the scene.

"Two Tenors, this is Grumpy; do you read."

Grumpy, this is Two Tenors; we read you loud and clear."

Two Tenors, I am at your GPS coordinates; are you ready to light up the target?"

Bill turned on the laser targeting system and directed the narrow beam of invisible light at the center of the terrorists who were now almost past their position. "Roger that Grumpy. The target is lit up. You are a go; repeat, you are a go."

"I have acquisition Two Tenors. I will release in five, four, three, two, one, release. The package is away and running true."

Bill kept the laser trained on the group and prepared for the fireworks. Grumpy was probably releasing from ten thousand feet, far enough away from the impact point to remain undetectable. Bill did some quick calculations in his head and decided impact would occur in about twenty seconds.

The smart-bomb hit right on target at twenty-three seconds, and lit up the night sky. The intense glare from the explosion viewed through their night-vision equipment would have blinded the rangers if they had not closed their eyes just prior to impact. Ear-plugs had prevented their eardrums from rupturing as the blast reverberated along the canyon walls. A large crater centered on the road replaced most of the jihadists as well as the two donkeys. The few men who had been at the front and back of the caravan were lying along the road, but their lack of movement demonstrated the widespread destructive power of the smart-bomb.

"Grumpy; this is Two Tenors; your package was delivered with precision; maximum effect achieved. Thank you and goodnight."

"Roger that Two Tenors; over and out."

"Two Tenors, this is Opera House. Will you execute plan Acey or Ducey?"

Acey and Ducey referred to two different post-strike strategies. Acey meant they would stay at their present location and complete additional target acquisition over the next few days. Plan Ducey assumed their present position might be compromised, and they would relocate to a new position to complete their mission.

Bill, who was senior, replied, "Opera House, this is Two Tenors. We will execute Acey; repeat, we will execute Acey."

"Roger that Two Tenors. Continued good hunting; over and out."

Both rangers continued their vigilance for the next hour while the smell of cordite drifted slowly up to their position. Don slept while Bill took over surveillance of the road.

As the sun crept over the mountain range to the east, a line separating night from day quickly dipped down into the valley below their perch. Bill scanned the road with binoculars and noticed a small group of men entering the north end of the valley.

"Don, get up; we've got company."

Don quickly woke up and grabbed his own pair of binoculars. Six men spread across the full width of the valley, with their weapons raised, moved cautiously toward the impact area They had obviously seen and heard the smart-bomb's impact during the night.

Bill said, "Let's pack everything up. If we need to leave in a hurry, I want to make sure we're ready to go."

Both men finished packing their backpacks just as the small group arrived at the impact crater. After inspecting the dead remains of their fellow terrorists, they immediately began searching the mountains looking for the enemy. These Mujahedeen knew full well there was better than a fifty-fifty chance American soldiers located in the mountain overlooking the road had directed the smart-bomb that had killed their cohorts.

Bill knew their position was well camouflaged, but these soldiers were familiar with the terrain and adept at detecting a military presence. If they were discovered, he knew it would happen in the next few minutes.

One of the Mujahedeen soldiers shouted and pointed to their position. He ran off the road and began climbing the lower part of the mountain leading up to their hiding place. He wouldn't be able to reach their position without climbing equipment, but would be able to get close enough to confirm their presence.

The soldier disappeared from view, and neither Bill nor Don were about to risk sticking their heads out past the camouflaged drape. Suddenly, they heard shouts and the unmistakable sound of a RPG being launched from below. The grenade struck the mountain just above their ledge and exploded on impact. Scattered stone shards filled the air and ripped apart their camouflage drape.

"Let's go!" Bill screamed.

Bill grabbed the remains of the drape and both men moved quickly along the ledge. A misstep now would result in certain death, but they needed to move quickly to avoid what both knew would be a second barrage of RPGs and small arms fire.

As expected, bullets began striking all around them, and then they heard another RPG being launched. The grenade exploded near them as they reached a narrow trail leading up and over the top of the mountain. If they could just reach the crest of the mountain, they would be safe, but they still had another fifty feet to climb before they reached safety. Two more RPGs struck simultaneously near the trail, and Don clutched his left arm. This is where their physical endurance training would pay off. With over one-hundred pounds of equipment stuffed into each backpack, they held onto nearby rocks to help them advance up the narrow gap in the mountain.

They finally reached the crest, fell to the ground, and rolled to the protection of the backside of the mountain. After removing their backpacks, Bill inspected Don's wound. A grenade fragment had sliced into his arm, just above the elbow. It would need stitches for sure, but no bones or arteries were damaged. Bill used his knife to cut a strip of cloth from the camouflage drape and used it to tie a tourniquet above Don's wound. "That will have to do for right now. I'll sew you up as soon as we get to a more secure area."

Don said, "That was close. Where to now Kemosabe?"

Bill took out his map and located their position. "Let's move further to the south. That will put us closer to our extraction point."

Bill unpacked his satellite radio and after setting it up called Headquarters. After explaining the situation both men headed off toward the safety of the next mountain range. It was just another day at work.

Chapter 4

Dr. Sally Lawson arrived home from work after another long day in the Emergency Room at Northwestern Hospital in Chicago. She ran the Department of Emergency Medicine, but she still preferred spending countless hours fixing up patients rather than dealing with the bureaucratic nightmare of budgets and other meaningless paperwork.

She pulled in the driveway and parked her car in the back of the lot near the detached garage. She emerged from her car wearing blue surgical scrubs and a pink backpack. Her dark-brown ponytail bounced from side to side as she headed next-door to see her friend Bobby Fowler.

It had been two weeks since Bobby's encounter with his stepmother and her ex-husband, and he was shooting hoops by his garage. Nothing unusual about that, but Bobby was uncharacteristically quiet. Normally, whenever Bobby was practicing his shots, he never failed to challenge Sally to a game of Horse. "Hey Bobby, what's with you? No game of Horse or Twenty-One?"

Bobby was lost in thought and didn't hear Sally's friendly challenge.

Something wasn't right. Sally wasn't a psychiatrist, but it was obvious Bobby had a major problem and wasn't acting normal. She unlocked the backdoor, placed her backpack on the kitchen table, and proceeded to pour two glasses of lemonade. With one in each hand, she walked up to Bobby and presented him with one of the glasses. "No thanks Doc, I'm not thirsty."

"Come on Bobby, let's sit down. I need your help with something."

Over the years, Sally and Bobby had established a rather close relationship. After Bobby's mother died, Sally had been one of his surrogate mothers until Bill had remarried. They were still close, and as Bobby's hormones began surging, he was always asking Sally about how to win the heart of his latest girlfriend.

Bobby reluctantly followed Sally onto the Lawson's deck, and both sat down on two of the chaise lounges facing each other. "What's up Doc?"

"Well, I've got this friend, and he and I have been really close for years. He has some kind of problem, I just know it, but he won't talk to me about it. He knows I'll help him anyway I can, but I guess he just doesn't want to offload any of his problem onto my shoulders. What should I do?"

Bobby quickly understood what Sally was driving at. "I don't want to talk about it, okay."

Bobby started to stand up, but Sally gently held him down. Bobby, normally I wouldn't press this, but I've always thought of you as my younger brother. You've shared a lot of things with me, and I've noticed you haven't been your usual self for a couple of weeks. Something's up, and I can tell, it's something important, something really important.

Sometimes it helps to talk over a problem with a good friend. That's what good friends are for. What's going on?"

Silence followed; painful silence. Bobby fidgeted, squirmed, took a sip of his lemonade, looked down at the ground, and finally looked directly at Sally. She could see tears forming in his eyes and knew that unless she changed the subject, Bobby would soon breakdown and she wanted to avoid that embarrassment for her good friend. "What's going on with Beth what's her name? Do you still have the hots for her?"

Bobby's face turned red as she knew it would. Sally got close to him and whispered in his ear. Bobby looked at her in disbelief. "We haven't done anything. She's just a good friend."

"Good, because I told you if you're going to do anything, make sure you've got protection."

Bobby turned serious and looked her straight in the eyes. "Look Sally, you're like my best friend, and I've shared things with you I've never told any other person, but I can't tell you about this. It's just too personal and too important."

"Okay, I can accept that, but I can tell whatever it is that's troubling you, is pushing you toward a bad place, a place where people become depressed and do things they later regret. I just want to make sure whatever it is you're worried about, you make it right with yourself, and the sooner the better. So let's change the subject. What's going on at school?"

"Coach Simpson died of a heart attack two weeks ago. It happened at football practice. He just clutched his left arm and collapsed to the ground, just like Mom. I knew he would die, and the whole thing reminded me of her death."

"Is that what's bothering you?"

"No, it's just something that happened at school, and I felt bad for his family, and the whole thing reminded me of when Mom died."

"Bobby, it's been almost five years since she died, and the way it happened has been burned permanently in your unpleasant memory bank. It's never going to go away. Maybe the thing to do is whenever you see something that brings back those bad feelings to immediately think of some nice memories of your mother. It might help."

"I'll try, but it's hard."

"You know when I was going to Purdue my parents died in an automobile accident. I had a lot of terrible memories just like you. In fact, I dropped out of school for a semester."

"How did you get back to normal?"

"It's funny; I was living in a condo. One day I witnessed an accident. I pulled two passengers from their car and administered first aid. From that moment on, I knew what I wanted to do. I went back to school, finished my B.S. degree in Nuclear Engineering, and went on to Medical School."

"Do you still have memories of that accident?"

"Sure, but like I said, I try to remember the good things, not just the accident. How are you doing on the college applications?"

"I still want to go into computer science. Are you still willing to write a recommendation letter for me?"

"Sure, I promised I would. Are you still active in that Computer Club?"

"Yep, it's fun."

"What do you guys do there?"

Suddenly Bobby was lost for words. He squirmed in his seat "Stuff," he said, "just stuff."

Sally knew the look. "Stuff, what kind of answer is stuff? Come on level with me. Are you guys doing any hacking?"

"A little bit, but nothing bad. There're some really smart guys there. They've even developed some neat viruses."

"Promise me Bobby. You will not get involved in any of that. If you get caught, you'll screw up the rest of your life."

Dan's car pulled into the driveway before Bobby could answer. Dan left his car, found Bobby's basketball on the grass, and began shooting baskets. Bobby, seeing his chance to escape Sally's interrogation, rushed to the basket and challenged Dan to a game of Horse.

Chapter 5

Sally shook her head at the unexpected interruption, left the two playing basketball, and walked back inside to fix dinner. Ten minutes later Dan walked in: shirttails hanging outside his pants, his new silk tie wrapped around his neck like a hangman's noose, sweat dripping from his face; God, why did she love this man?

Of course she knew the answer. He was good looking, and she especially loved his cute looking butt. More importantly, however, she had fallen in love with Dan's eyes. Whenever she stared at them, she saw tenderness, compassion, and honesty. It certainly wasn't his athletic body, which had undergone a midlife transformation from a steady diet of fast-food lunches. No, it was definitely his eyes.

"Get upstairs and take a shower. You smell like a pile of shit."

"But do you love me?"

"Maybe just a little bit."

"Then give me a kiss."

"Not till you shower."

"I won't shower until I get a kiss."

Sally gave him a peck on the cheek, contorted her face in mock horror, and ordered him upstairs.

Over dinner Sally sought Dan's advice. "Bobby's got a major problem."

"What is it; that new girlfriend of his?"

"He won't say, but I can tell, it's something really serious. I've been watching him over the last few days and I can tell it's really bothering him. He's on the edge of severe depression."

"But I thought you two were like a brother and sister. Why won't he tell you what's going on?"

"That's the thing; he just won't. I'm really worried."

"So talk to Gloria."

"You know Gloria, she won't do anything. If Bill was here I'd talk to him. I think Bobby needs to see a psychiatrist. I think he'd open up to a friend of mine. He works with a lot of kids Bobby's age."

"You know Honey; one good lie is worth a thousand truths. I think you need to scare the living bejesus out of Gloria. You've got to make this a black and white issue. If you're talking about theoretical problems, she'll make it a grey issue, and she'll never agree to anything."

Sally continued to munch on her tuna sandwich. She had good instincts, and she felt certain Bobby was headed for a dark place, a psychological state where only bad things happen. She guessed a little white lie in order to force Gloria to deal with Bobby's problem was justified. "Detective Dan, once in a great while you offer up great advice, and I do believe this is one of those rare moments."

Dan registered mock-shock on his face. "My God, did I just hear a compliment thrown my way?"

Sally stuck out her tongue, scrunched her nose, and changed the subject. "What's going on at work?"

"Joey's going berserk. We had four new homicides today, and there isn't even a full-moon. The good news is I think we've cracked the Gold Coast burglaries. It looks like all of the victims used the same dog-walking service. Of course the dog-walkers all had access to the homes. Some of these thieves are so stupid. Did they really believe the cops wouldn't see the pattern? We're going to make arrests tomorrow."

After dinner, Sally continued to ponder the problem of talking to Gloria while Dan watched Monday Night Football. She decided to call Gloria from work in the afternoon and meet her at the neighborhood Starbucks after work. She didn't want Bobby to interrupt their discussion.

Chapter 6

The Starbucks on North Avenue was overflowing as usual. Sally ordered a Grande Latte with skimmed, and waited for a table to open up in the corner. Gloria Fowler showed up ten minutes later in a flashy tennis outfit. She waved to Sally, and ordered her own coffee. A dozen eyes followed her as she slowly made her way to Sally's table. Gloria always made a visual statement wherever she went.

"Well, what's up Sally; what's so important that we couldn't just meet at the house?"

"It's about Bobby, Gloria. When Bobby's mother died, I sort of acted as his surrogate mother until you and Bill got married. We're still very close. I've been getting home in the early afternoon the past few months and most days he's been shooting baskets in the backyard. He always challenges me to a game of Horse. It's our little tradition. Anyway, the last two weeks, I've seen a sudden change in Bobby."

"What kind of change?"

"He's exhibiting all of the clinical signs of despair and depression. Have you noticed any changes?"

"Well, actually I've been pretty tied up at the club. Bobby never talks to me very much, but I guess I have seen a change."

"I had a chance to talk to him yesterday afternoon, and he wouldn't tell me what was bothering him, but something happened, probably a couple of weeks ago, something so dramatic it pushed him into this clinical state. Do you have any idea what it could have been?"

Gloria considered Sally's question. She was unable to tie in Bobby's problem with her own actions. "I have no idea what might have caused his change in behavior. Maybe it's a problem with his latest girlfriend. Yea, that's probably it; problems with Susan."

"Her name is Beth, but I asked him about that specifically, and he denied he was having any problems with her."

"Maybe he got her pregnant?"

"No, I asked him about that, and I could tell from his answer that wasn't the problem."

"So what should we do?"

This was going to be the hard part. Sally was certain Gloria would fight bringing Bobby to a psychiatrist. "I've got a friend at the hospital. He specializes in treating children with clinical depression."

Gloria interrupted, "You mean a psychiatrist? No way am I going to let Bobby see a shrink."

Sally looked Gloria in the eyes, moved closer, and then paused for effect. And now for the little white lie. "Let me level with you. It's my clinical opinion that Bobby is close to taking some action, and most of the time in cases like this that means typically a violent act."

"You mean like suicide?"

"That's a strong possibility."

Blood abandoned Gloria's face. She was silent, obviously thinking about Sally's prediction. Suddenly, Gloria's frown turned to a partial smile. She had made a decision. "I'll have to talk to Bill about this."

Gloria was a professional abdicator, and Sally interrupted her. "Gloria, Bill is trying to stay alive. Do you think it's fair to bother him with this problem now? There's no time to wait to talk to Bill. You need to make a decision now."

Gloria searched her mind for a way out. Sally gave her a few seconds and then offered the solution to her dilemma. "If you want, I'll talk to Bobby about this. If you give me permission, I'm sure I can get him to see my friend. You don't need to get involved, but I need your permission."

"Okay, I'll agree to your offer, but I want you to know, Bill is really the person who should be making this decision."

With the meeting over, Gloria left the table, making eye contact with every male above the age of twenty, as she walked out the front door. Sally laughed to herself at Gloria's suggestive behavior and ordered a second latte. Gloria was such a loser, and Sally wondered whether she treated her own daughter with the same lack of parental responsibility.

As Sally walked the three blocks back to the house, she contemplated how to convince Bobby to see her friend. She walked into the driveway, and Bobby was once again throwing the basketball up against the wall, not as part of some game, but with vicious repeated throws. The force of each impact was actually breaking off small pieces of brick from the wall.

"Hi Bobby, can we talk for a few minutes?"

Bobby was too absorbed in his own thoughts to hear her, so she walked up behind him and tapped him on the shoulder. He jumped at the touch and only relaxed when he saw who had invaded his personal space.

"Oh hi Sally, I didn't see you walk up."

"I know Bobby, I called to you, but you were obviously thinking about something else. It's that same problem isn't it?"

Bobby gritted his teeth and decided not to answer her. Sally moved to face him. "Bobby, we need to talk and right now."

Bobby replied, "Do I get some lemonade?"

"No Bobby, not this time. This is going to be the most important thing you and I have ever talked about."

Holding his basketball for security, Bobby followed Sally onto her deck and sat down next to her. A brisk wind blowing in off Lake Michigan threw a chill on the upcoming talk, and the late afternoon sun shining in the clear autumn sky blinded Bobby. He quickly looked down at his feet, not really wanting to become engaged in a two-way conversation.

Sally reached across the table and held Bobby's hand. "We talked yesterday about what's bothering you. Bobby, I'm a good doctor, and I'm really good at diagnosing a patient's problem. I'm going to ask you a few medical questions, and you need to answer my questions truthfully. Okay!"

"Sure, fire away."

"Since this problem started, have you been difficult to live with?"

"I guess, but for good reasons."

"Have you been having mood swings?"

"That's what Beth's been telling me."

"Have you had trouble sleeping?"

"Yes, but that's because I've been thinking about my problem."

"How about lack of appetite or stomach pains? I don't have to ask you about whether you feel things are hopeless, because I have been seeing the despair written all over your face."

"Okay Sally, I've been experiencing all of these things, but what's it mean?"

"Bobby, if I asked any of my colleagues about a person who is exhibiting all of these symptoms, they'd say the person is suffering from clinical depression."

"So I'm depressed, so what?"

"So people who are exhibiting your symptoms eventually go to the dark side, and that usually leads to acts of violence."

"You mean like murder?"

"More likely suicide."

Bobby laughed, "Don't worry, I'm not going to commit suicide."

Sally reached across the table and held Bobby's arm tenderly in both her hands. "Bobby, I want you to do something for me. You're going to want to say no, but you must believe me, it's important, very important, and you need to say yes."

Bobby looked at Sally and saw tears forming in her eyes; he turned away, but had to look back. He loved Sally; next to his father and his Nana, Sally was the next most important person in his life. "Don't cry Sally; I'll do whatever you ask."

"Bobby, I have a friend at the hospital who specializes in treating the symptoms you have. I've talked to your stepmother, and we both want you to see him."

Bobby had not anticipated Sally's request. Seeing a shrink? A shrink wasn't going to help him solve his problem. The solution to his problem involved something else. But what the hell, if Sally asked, he'd do it. "Okay, I'll see him, but not for my stepmother; I'll do it for you."

Sally got to her feet, pulled him up and gave him the type of long hug she usually reserved for Dan. "Thanks Bobby. Let's do this. Stop by the emergency room on Saturday morning. I'll bring you up to see Dr. Simon."

Bobby took his basketball, walked back to his driveway and began shooting baskets. "How about a game of Horse Doc? You know I'll win."

Sally smiled at her friend, grabbed the ball from his hands and said, "I'm going to whip your ass!"

Chapter 7

Sally briefed Dr. Jack Simon the next day, and he agreed to meet with Bobby. Bobby showed up in the ER a little after seven o'clock. Sally passed the patient she was seeing off to one of the Residents and walked Bobby over to Northwestern Hospital's Professional Building. After introducing Bobby to Dr. Simon, and asking Bobby to stop by after the meeting, she left them alone.

It was a Saturday and the office reception area was almost empty. Dr. Simon, dressed in jeans and a sweater, walked Bobby back to his private office and sat down on a chair. Bobby started to lie down on the couch. Simon laughed, "Bobby, you don't strike me as the couch type. I think you've seen too many movies. Come sit over here on the chair."

Bobby had no idea of what to expect, but Simon seemed like a cool guy, someone who might be able to help him. Simon held a notepad in his hand and looked through some notes. "Dr. Lawson briefed me on the conversations she had with you, so I think I've got some of the background. It sounds like Dr. Lawson is a very good friend."

"Sally's my best friend. She helped me deal with my mother's death. I owe her a lot."

"Well she's one very special doctor. We all love her. She's the best. Before we get started, I want to remind you that everything we discuss here is considered confidential. Legally, I can't tell anyone about our conversations unless you want me to. It's considered legally protected like a lawyer and a client."

Bobby gripped the armchair tightly. He was afraid, but he nodded his head yes and waited for Dr. Simon to begin.

"Bobby, Dr. Lawson tells me you're on the football team and involved in the school's Computer Club. What position do you play on the team?"

"Middle linebacker on defense and fullback on offense."

Simon's expression seemed to recall happier times. "I used to play strong safety in high school, but I wasn't good enough to play in college. I really enjoyed football. It was good to be part of a team. What do you guys do at the Computer Club?"

"We write a lot of software programs."

"Do any hacking?"

"Maybe a little."

"Please be careful Bobby. You don't want to get caught. Do you write any viruses?"

"Not me, but some of the guys do some really sophisticated stuff. They can make a computer do almost anything."

Dr. Simon was managing to fill several pages of his notepad. He finally looked up and said, "Bobby, tell me a little bit about your mother. You must have been about twelve when she died."

Bobby smiled at the unexpected question. "She was a loving person Doc. She was always there when I needed her."

"Tell me about something nice she did that you remember."

Bobby thought for a moment and then smiled. "When I was ten, no wait I was eleven, I broke my leg a week before a school dance. I thought I wouldn't be able to go, but she insisted that I go and have fun. She dressed up like a limousine driver and drove me and my date to the dance. She waited at the school and then drove us to Petersen's Ice Cream Parlor. She made me feel special, but she did things like that all the time."

"It sounds like she was a special person. How did you cope with her death?"

"For months I had nightmares. I kept on seeing her fall to the floor and die. It was like the movie Groundhog Day. The same dream every night. It took almost a half year for those dreams to stop."

"Were you upset when your father remarried?"

"You bet. We were both doing okay. I could understand why he wanted to get married again, but I never liked the woman."

Simon looked at his notes. "That would be Gloria. Have your feelings toward her changed in the three years they've been married?"

Bobby squeezed both hands tightly against the armchair and remained silent. Simon observed the body language and waited patiently, just writing some notes in his notebook. Bobby squirmed in his chair, but Simon just waited. "I hate her doctor."

"Hate is a pretty strong word Bobby. What does she do that makes you feel that way?"

"She just married my father for his money. She lives the good life now, but she only cares about her daughter and tennis. I feel just like Cinderella; always shit on by my stepsister and stepmother."

"What about your father. Do you think he doesn't care about you anymore?"

"In the last couple years he's been on three tours of duty over in Afghanistan, but I know he cares about me. We Skype whenever he gets a chance, and when he's back in Chicago we do a lot of things together. Things are good when he's home, but whenever he leaves things go bad again."

"Have you talked to him about your stepmother?"

"No, what good would it do? I don't want to bother him while he's over there."

"But why not talk to him when he gets home?"

"Why bother; he wouldn't believe me; she acts different when he's home."

Simon finally looked up from his notepad. "Bobby, Dr. Lawson tells me something happened to you recently; something that pushed you into this clinical state, and you don't want to talk about it. Why don't you want to talk about it?"

"Because it's my problem. I'm the only one who can solve my problem."

"Doctor Lawson wants to help you. I want to help you."

"I don't want to talk about it."

"It must be really bad if you don't want to talk about it. Is it really that bad?"

"Yes!"

Simon had come to some conclusions, more based on Bobby's body language than anything Bobby had said.

"Bobby, does this problem have something to do with your stepmother?"

Bobby's eyes gave away his true feelings. "I don't want to talk about it!"

"Okay, then I want you to consider this. For you to get better, you're going to have to solve this problem. You want to solve it all by yourself, but for you to solve the problem you're going to have to consider all the alternatives and then decide on the best course of action. Internalizing the problem without making a decision is just going to make you feel more depressed, and despair will eventually lead to a downward spiral and a very bad place."

Bobby sat looking at the floor while Simon delivered his sermon. Simon thought his lecture seemed to sink in, but he couldn't be sure. Simon looked at his watch. They had spent almost an hour together, and he knew they had gone far enough for a first meeting. "Bobby, I'd like to end today's session, but I'd like to meet with you again next Saturday."

"I don't think another visit is going to help Dr. Simon. It's just going to be a waste of your time and mine."

"I hope you'll let me be the judge of that. I'd like to review our meeting with Dr. Lawson. Will you give me permission to do that?"

"Sure, you can talk to Sally."

"Thanks, I feel we've come a long way on your path to getting better."

Dr. Simon stood up, shook hands with Bobby and led him to the lobby. Bobby left the Professional Building and walked over to the ER. He told the receptionist that Dr. Lawson was expecting him. The receptionist called into the back and then told him that Dr. Lawson was busy with a patient and would see him at home after work.

Bobby left the ER thinking about his talk with Dr. Simon. He knew what Simon said was true; he had to decide what to do, but the only real solution to the problem was something he really didn't want to consider. By the time he found his car, he had made up his mind. He now knew exactly what needed to be done. He started his car and headed over to the high school for the football game against New Trier.

How do people decide what to do when faced with a difficult problem? Analyze the alternatives and choose the best course of action? Come on, give me a break; that's not what usually happens. More likely, it's an impulsive decision. Maybe a sudden new course of action comes to mind. Maybe something someone says triggers a respondent cord. Whatever the approach, it's usually not very analytical

Chapter 8

Sally felt bad about not being able to meet with Bobby in the ER after his visit with Simon, but her patient, who had just suffered a heart attack, was definitely a higher priority. She left work in the late afternoon and Dan's car wasn't in the garage. He was probably still at the office working on the new homicides.

Bobby's football game should be over by now, and Sally wanted to talk to him while the talk with Jack Simon was still fresh in his mind. Jack had called her after his meeting with Bobby and had briefed her. Bobby's car was not in the driveway or the garage.

Gloria didn't answer the door, so she would just have to wait for Bobby to show up. While fixing dinner, Sally kept an eye out for Bobby. The screeching of brakes in the driveway announced his arrival. Boys and their cars; they were all the same. She leaned out the backdoor and shouted his name. Bobby walked over to talk to Sally.

"Did you guys win?"

"No, and I had a terrible game. I must have missed a hundred tackles."

"I want to talk to you about your visit with Dr. Simon. Do you have a few minutes?"

Bobby considered the possibility of escape and finally said, "Sure."

Sally held the backdoor open and she led him into the family room. "How did the visit go?"

"Okay I guess, he's sort of a neat guy."

"I thought you'd like him. He briefed me on your visit."

"What did he tell you?"

Sally considered her response carefully. She and Jack had agreed, it was time to use a little shock treatment. "Dr. Simon told me you're definitely suffering from clinical depression, and it has something to do with your stepmother."

Bobby looked shocked as he fumbled for words. "How does he know that? I never told him anything."

Sally smiled, "Because he's an expert Bobby. He understands people. So Bobby, what happened between you and your stepmother?"

"You can't help me Sally. I've got to work this out myself, and I've already decided what needs to be done."

Sally was delighted to hear he had reached closure on whatever was bothering him, and maybe now he could get back to normal. "What made you come to a decision on what to do?"

"It was the visit with Dr. Simon. He made me think through the consequences of not making a decision. It's like what my teachers say about taking multiple choice tests. When you're not sure, your first guess is usually the best answer to the question. The decision's been made, and now I have to make the best of it."

Dan's arrival through the backdoor put an abrupt end to their private conversation. "Hey Bobby, did you guys win today?"

"No, and I played terrible, but there's always next Saturday."

"That there is Bobby, that there is."

After Bobby left through the backdoor Sally said, "I think Bobby worked through whatever is bothering him. Let's hope it all works out."

Chapter 9

Freddie arrived on time for his first scheduled meeting with his parole officer. Betty Jones stood to greet him, and after asking him to sit down, closed the door to her office.

Freddie looked over this new bureaucratic bitch and decided she was an easy mark. He'd have her under his control in a matter of minutes.

"Mr. Moran, we're going to be meeting on a regular basis for the next few years, so let me make a couple of things very clear from the beginning. I'm in control of your future. If you obey the rules, and there are a vast number of rules, then you will find me to be both a friend and a source of help; but if you decide instead to act in a foolish manner and violate the terms of your parole, then you will find me to be a very ruthless adversary. You need to remember; I have the ability to send you back to prison, and if you don't believe me, check around with some of your friends who have been returned to the federal lockup."

Freddie suddenly understood that he had totally misread the person sitting behind the desk.

"First things first, I need to get some information from you. Where are you presently living?"

Freddie gave her the address of his condo.

"Telephone numbers where you can be reached, both land line and mobile?"

Freddie rattled off the condominium's telephone number and indicated he didn't have a mobile phone yet.

"E-mail address."

Freddie provided her with the information.

"Bank where you have an account and the account number?"

Freddie took out a blank check from his wallet and read off the account information.

The request for information went on and on, and Freddie answered each question as best he could. Finally, with the form filled out on the computer, Betty Jones looked up from her keyboard and changed topics. "Have you found a job yet?"

"I'm working for my brother-in-law. He has a construction business."

"And what do you do there?"

"He's training me to be a construction site manager."

"And what will you be doing as a construction site manager?"

"Anything and everything, from checking to make sure everybody is working hard to being sure the port-a-potty is emptied."

"Well that certainly is a change from your previous profession."

Freddie was silent while Jones keyed in the information into her computer. "Freddie, how do you like your new job?"

"Not very much. I'm like a duck out of water. I've never had to supervise others."

Jones grinned as she said, "From the looks of your previous arrests, I imagine you always worked alone. Freddie, you probably have a lot of money stashed away in a number of foreign bank accounts, and from the looks of your rap sheet, you probably wouldn't have to ever work again. But it's very important you keep this job because we've found if you don't stay gainfully employed, there's a strong tendency to revert back to the kind of work you evidently know quite well. Do I make myself perfectly clear?"

"Yes Ms. Jones, I understand completely."

"You're lucky Freddie. Most of the people I work with have a difficult time finding a job. They begin to consort with the same people who got them into trouble in the first place, and I'm sure you can figure out what happens to them."

Jones handed him a pamphlet on the rules of his parole, and the specific consequences of failure to obey the rules. Freddie thumbed through the booklet. There were forty-eight pages of bullshit.

The handing over of the pamphlet seemed to be the last item on the agenda for the day. Jones scheduled another meeting in one month, and handed Freddie her business card. Her last comment was, "The telephone numbers here are being given to you for a reason. If there's anything you need, please give me a call."

Betty Jones stood up and shook Freddie's hand. The meeting was over, and Freddie left her office regretting that he had been assigned to this bitch as his parole officer. It was going to be a difficult couple of years.

Chapter 10

Today was Thanksgiving and the Lawsons were hosting a big dinner with their best friends. Sally stood at the bathroom sink waiting for the results of her early pregnancy test. Sally thought back several months. She and Dan had been trying to have a baby for over a year. After three months of trying, the usual tests implicated Dan's low sperm count as the culprit. The specialist recommended in vitro fertilization, but Dan had other ideas. Sally remembered the conversation.

"Honey I think this is similar to a problem in astronomy."

"What are you talking about?"

"Consider all of the asteroids floating around in space. Why don't they strike the earth? After all, there're billions of them out there. The reason is the concentration of asteroids in outer space is very low; sort of like my sperm count."

"So what are you suggesting to solve our problem?"

"If we increase the number of times per week that we're trying, then we'll increase the chances of an asteroid strike."

"So now you're shooting asteroids from your little gun?"

"Well not quite so big, but you get the point."

"So how many times per week do you think will be needed?"

"I was thinking like twice per day."

"Honey, I don't think your body can survive twice each day."

"Well, let's at least give it a try for a couple of months. Then, if we're not successful, we'll try the in vitro approach."

Dan had sealed the bargain with a kiss and then proceeded to the first of an increased number of attempts.

Now, staring at the test strip, she was shocked to see a blue positive cross show up on the test strip. She couldn't believe the results. After taking a shower, she tried again and waited anxiously until a blue cross again appeared. Shock turned to excitement.

She brought both test strips to the bedroom and shook Dan out of his deep sleep. He opened one eye and found two test strips staring him in the face. It took a few seconds for the visual display to transform into an understanding of the meaning. He almost fell on the floor as he jumped out of bed. Knocking the test strips to the floor, he held Sally in his arms and spun her around the room. "Stop, you're going to hurt the baby."

Dan immediately put her down and kissed her. He was crying, and now Sally began to cry. "What a wonderful Thanksgiving this is going to be. Should we tell everyone?"

"Too soon; let's wait till I get past the third month. Let's make sure everything is okay before we tell our friends."

Six Thanksgiving guests were expected to arrive at five o'clock. The guest list read like a who's who at the FBI. Jimmy Davis, Dan's best friend, was the head of the FBI's Chicago Field Office. His wife Brenda and their three children Josh, Andrew, and Eliza were part of Dan's and Sally's extended family. Benny Cannon, the best techno-geek in the FBI, was in his mid-thirties and still single. Alice Folkman was the final guest. In her early forties, she was also single and felt her mission in life, beyond being the senior FBI agent in Chicago, was to force Benny to get married. She was on his case 24/7.

Dan always felt a special connection with Thanksgiving. His mother, while alive, was a fantastic cook and had passed on her skills to her only child. Sally had to admit his turkeys with a special sausage and mushroom stuffing were something everybody loved and remembered.

After breakfast, Dan began preparing the stuffing and by ten o'clock was filling the turkey and covering the outside of the large bird with melted butter along with large amounts of all the usual herbs and seasoning. He had prepared his special cranberry sauce heavily spiked with a significant amount of cognac a week earlier, and the flavor of the cognac was now fully incorporated into the traditional accompaniment to the turkey. He finished up the morning's work by cooking the giblets in herb-seasoned chicken broth, and then rewarded himself with a cold beer.

The mashed potatoes and green beans were Sally's responsibility. By three o'clock, they both had finished their prep work, showered, dressed, and were now setting the dining room table.

Dan began chilling the white wines and setting out several bottles of an upscale Barbarossa, his favorite red wine. Sally said, "No wine for me for the next nine months."

Dan placed his hand on Sally's belly, trying to feel his child. Sally, feeling the pride of pending motherhood, wrapped both arms around her man and said, "Our lives are going to be changed forever. You know that don't you."

"Dan nodded and said, "I'm ready Honey; I'm definitely ready."

The Davis family, as was their custom, arrived exactly on time, and Benny and Alice each arrived shortly thereafter. While the kids watched TV, the others gathered in the kitchen to help organize the buffet dinner on the center island. Sally, using a sharp knife rather than her normal surgeon's scalpel, expertly carved the twenty-five pound turkey, which had been resting after its ordeal in the oven.

After pulling the kids away from the TV, everyone lined up and began piling their favorite items on their plates. With everyone seated at the table, Dan walked around pouring the wine. He sat down and raised his glass in a toast. "Here's to my late mother who passed on this wonderful sausage and mushroom stuffing recipe, and also a special welcome to our very best friends who Sally and I love so very much."

The glasses clinked together, and then Alice stood up. "I too would like to offer a special toast to our two hosts, and especially to Sally, who I believe has an announcement to make to her extended family."

Everyone looked expectantly toward Sally, who didn't know what Alice was talking about. After an extended moment of silence, Alice said, "Clearly, I'm the best agent in the Bureau. You all have missed a very important clue; our hostess is not drinking wine tonight. Have you ever known our most favorite doctor to ever pass up a good, or even a bad, glass of wine?"

Sally and Dan both blushed, and then Sally laughed. "We just found out this morning; we're going to have a baby."

Their best friends quickly stood up and surrounded them both with hugs and kisses, and then as they finally sat back down at the table, Jimmy, with tears in his eyes, stood and raised his glass in a toast. "I have known my best friend Dan for almost twenty years, and Sally since she helped solve that mutant terrorist case a few years back. Let them both enjoy this special moment, before they have to begin changing diapers; they have both earned it."

The evening seemed to go on forever, but everyone finally left. Dan turned to Sally. "I thought you wanted to wait three months?"

"I wanted to, but Alice is just too observant. What the hell, they're our very best friends. They deserve to share in our enjoyment."

Sally started the dishwasher, and she and Dan walked slowly up the stairs. It had been a long day but the most wonderful day of their lives. "Does this mean I don't have to shoot anymore asteroids?"

"Yes, darling, your job is done, at least for a few nights."

They snuggled together in their king size bed, and as was their custom, only used half the bed's space.

Chapter 11

Freddie threw his briefcase onto the couch. It had been another lousy day at the construction site. Two workers had been missing in action, and he had to help move some heavy equipment through the mud. He hated this job.

After grabbing a beer from the fridge, he sat down at his computer and checked his e-mail. One message screamed out for his attention. It read *A Special Job Offer*, and it was from a source identified as *A Close Friend*.

The message read: A mutual friend gave me your e-mail address. I have a job that needs to be done quickly. It's worth $50,000; $10,000 up front and the rest after the job's complete. If you're interested, I'll meet you in front of the Lion House at Lincoln Park Zoo tonight at six o'clock. I know what you look like, so I'll contact you.

The Raccoon read the e-mail again. He had expected to get requests for his service now that he was out of the slammer, but not so quickly. He didn't like the fact that it was an e-mail rather than a direct contact from one of his intermediaries, but then again, these were modern times. His main concern centered around this being some sort of entrapment by the police. He was smart enough not to reply to the message. Instead, he deleted it once from his message board and then again from the trash.

He looked at the mud on his work clothes. He was not cut out for this second career. He was already missing the thrill of the hunt. He'd go to the meeting; that couldn't hurt. He'd ask the person a series of questions to confirm they weren't working with the police. If it was a set-up, they were legally required to identify themselves as law enforcement types. He could always say he wasn't interested if there was anything suspicious.

He finished his beer, changed clothes, and left the apartment. He hailed a taxi and told the driver to take him to the zoo's main entrance. After walking through the front entrance, he walked up to a large map and found the location of the Lion House. He was an hour early, just the way he liked it. He bought a hot dog and a cup of coffee at an outdoor stand. He quickly finished the stand-up dinner and then began slowly walking toward the meeting place. He wanted to spend some time just walking around getting a lay of the land. He'd also keep an eye out for any surveillance cameras.

He had not dressed properly for the season. A cold wind blew off Lake Michigan, and Freddie's light windbreaker definitely wasn't cutting it. He clutched his hot coffee cup as he moved among the small crowd out for an after-dinner stroll. He found a protected area near the front of the Lion House and scanned the area for anything out of the ordinary.

Five minutes before six o'clock, the Raccoon walked casually to the front of the Lion House and waited. It was dinnertime for the lions, and as they roared in anticipation of their evening meal, the visitors to the zoo, who knew the feeding schedule, began moving into the building to watch the main event.

Freddie paced back and forth trying to keep warm as the minutes passed. Finally, a man dressed in a black hoodie and dark sunglasses walked up the steps of the Lion House eating a hot dog and sat down near Freddie. The Raccoon knew payday had arrived.

Chapter 12

Dan and Sally sat in the kitchen eating a very early dinner. They planned on going to the movies to see the latest James Bond flic after their meal. Suddenly, the backdoor burst open and Janet Bussard screamed at them. "I just came home and found Mom at the bottom of the stairs." She placed both hands over her face. "I think she's dead. My God I think she's dead."

Sally led the way as all three rushed back to the Fowler house. Gloria lay on her stomach on the marble floor halfway between the stairway and the front door. A large pool of clotted blood surrounded her face. Sally rushed to her side and felt for a pulse, but there was no pulse to feel.

Gloria's body felt warm but stiff, a sign that death probably took place between three and eight hours ago. Sally looked up at Dan and shook her head no. Janet started to scream while her body twisted in torment. Dan said, "Take her away. Get her out of here. I'll take over from here.

Sally led Janet out the backdoor while Dan considered the situation. Something seemed out of place, but he just couldn't figure out what. What had happened here? The simple and obvious explanation was that Gloria had fallen down the stairs, and cracked her head open on the marble floor, but something was wrong with this theory. What was it? Dan muttered to himself, "Think Dan, think; what's wrong here? Something's not right."

It came to him in a flash of clarity. If Gloria fell down the stairs, then her body was out of position. If she had fallen from the top of the stairs, she would have tumbled down the staircase and landed near the last step. If she had fallen near the bottom, she once again would have landed near the bottom of the staircase. Her body, however, was almost fifteen feet from the stairs with her head pointed toward the front door. There was only one logical conclusion. If she had indeed met her death from falling down the stairs, then she was pushed; pushed with enough forward momentum to send her flying through the air and to this ultimate position on the floor.

Of course, there were other possible explanations. She could have been walking toward the front door and then collapsed and died right where she fell. That theory, however, was negated by the fact that she had somehow received a major smack to her skull when hitting the floor, and Dan knew you didn't get the kind of blow to the head Gloria received from a five foot fall to the floor.

Another possibility was that she had been hit over the head before she fell to the floor, and that was once again inconsistent with an accident. Of course she could have committed suicide by jumping to her death, but come on, let's get serious. Has anyone ever committed suicide by jumping down a flight of stairs? Everything pointed to a deliberate act of violence.

Suddenly, Bobby walked through the backdoor tossed his backpack onto a kitchen chair and screamed, "I'm home!"

He started to walk toward the foyer but Dan blocked his path. Bobby finally asked, "What's wrong?"

"Janet found Gloria lying on the floor a few minutes ago. I'm sorry but she's dead."

Bobby, standing next to his backpack, looked into the foyer. "Did she fall down the stairs?"

"I don't know what happened."

Dan turned Bobby back toward the backdoor and led him next-door to Sally who was trying to calm Janet at the kitchen table. He told Bobby to sit at the table and motioned to Sally. They stepped out onto the back deck for some privacy. "This wasn't an accident. I'm pretty sure Gloria was the victim of a homicide."

"What! How can you be so sure?"

"I'll tell you later, but right now I'm going to call this in and treat it like a homicide until further notice. You take care of the kids."

Dan grabbed his cellphone from the kitchen counter and walked back to the Fowler's house. He called his precinct, and his boss was still at his desk. "Joey, it's Dan. There's been a death at our neighbor's house, and I'm pretty sure it's no accident. Please send the Medical Examiner and Forensics over to our house. Sally will show them where to go. One more thing Joey, I want this case. There're some strange things going on here. Why don't you give George the Travis case? I'm sure he can handle it."

"Okay, I'll give the Travis case to George. Fill me in on all the details tomorrow."

He ended the call, and decided to look around while waiting for the crime scene experts to arrive. Dan deliberately stayed away from the body. He moved a dining room chair so it faced the body and sat down to review the facts. Gloria was dead, probably murdered. Murder, most of the time was a crime of passion, and that usually implicated a person known to the victim. Gloria was certainly not a candidate for the wife of the year award. She had a reputation on the street of being a flirtatious vixen. He had seen her in action at many parties where she was constantly sending out I'm available signals to anyone wearing pants and shaving every day.

Bill, the usual suspect in these types of things, was over in Afghanistan. Clearly, he had the perfect alibi. Bobby was a different matter. In talks with Sally, Dan knew Bobby was having problems. Sally was trying to keep her talks with Bobby confidential, but now, she was going to have to open up a little and tell Dan what was troubling Bobby. Until further notice, Bobby was definitely a Person of Interest.

Dan took another look at Gloria. Her hair was dangling down over her face, not in her usual ponytail. In fact, it almost appeared that she had met her demise after just having stepped out of the shower. Dan knew Gloria usually played tennis most mornings, and it seemed likely she had just come home from the club, taken a shower, dressed in these blue pants and white blouse, and then it happened. Gloria was wearing only one pink flip-flop. After Forensics finished, he would look on the second-floor hallway to see if the missing flip-flop was there.

Dan then moved onto the personal family issues surrounding this tragedy. What would Bill do now? Who would take care of the kids? Would the army let him stand-down from his tour? It was a real mess.

The sound of police sirens interrupted his thoughts. Forensics arrived ten minutes later followed almost immediately by the Medical Examiner. While the beat cops kept the growing group of onlookers away from the house, Dan met with the crime scene experts. The team discussed the unusual body position and Dan's theory of the lethal shove from the top of the stairs. The team would be doing their thing for the next few hours, so Dan decided it was time to interview Janet and Bobby.

Chapter 13

Looking at the two kids was a study in contrasts. Janet had clearly lost it. She was still lost in personal grief, although the sounds had subsided into a mere whimper. A pile of used Kleenex was growing in front of her. Bobby, on the other hand, was sitting quietly, clearly contemplating what had just occurred, but without much visible emotion.

Dan walked Sally into the living room. I have to talk to both of them now. Sally understood the need. She walked back into the kitchen and asked Janet to talk to Dan in the living room.

Janet brought her box of tissues with her, and Dan directed her to the beige armchair next to the couch. She sat down, and Dan positioned himself in the chair next to hers.

"Janet, I know this is hard for you, but I need to understand what happened. Please tell me everything."

Janet blew her nose again and tried to pull herself together. "I got home from work. I parked my car in the garage and walked in the backdoor. I saw Mom lying on the floor. Then I ran over here."

"Did you go over to her after you saw her lying on the floor?"

"Yes I wanted to see if she was just hurt or unconscious. I shook her, but she felt stiff and didn't move."

Janet lost it again, and the tears started pouring down her cheeks. Three tissues and two nose blows later, she was able to continue. "I could tell she was dead; I just knew it. God, what's going to happen?"

It was more of a statement rather than a question, but Dan answered it anyway. "Janet, we'll get in contact with Bill and I'm guessing the army will fly him home as soon as possible. Do you know what you mother was doing today?"

"She said she was going to play tennis at the club like she usually does. I guess that's what she did."

"Can you think of anything else she might have done today?"

"Why are you asking me these questions? She just fell down the stairs didn't she?"

"That's what I'm trying to figure out; exactly what happened?"

After Janet calmed down, Dan said, "Listen why don't you go back in the kitchen and tell Bobby to come in. I need to talk to him too."

Bobby sat down in Janet's vacated chair looking calm, almost too calm. "Just a couple of questions Bobby. Do you know what your stepmother was doing today?"

"Tennis I guess; she's always playing tennis."

"Do you have any idea what happened to her?"

"When I came in the door you were sort of blocking my view. I could see her lying on the floor with some blood under her head, so maybe she fell down the stairs and hit her head, but I really don't have a clue."

"Tell me about the relationship you had with her."

"It's real simple, she hated me, and I hated her. You're my friend so I can tell you, it's sad she died, but it solves a big problem for me."

"What do you mean?"

"I want to talk to Sally."

"Bobby, I'm asking you. I want to hear it from you."

"Okay, I'll tell you. About three weeks ago, I came home unexpectedly early from football practice. I heard moaning from my dad's bedroom. I thought it was Janet and her boyfriend making out, but it wasn't. It was my stepmother screwing her ex-husband right there in my fathers bed. Can you believe it. Right there in his bed."

"What did you do?"

"I ran away. I should have taken a picture with my iPhone. I would have had proof, but instead I ran away like a coward. Sally and Dr. Simon convinced me I had to take action to solve my problem, letting the problem fester was going to force me into clinical depression."

"So what did you do?"

"I talked to Nana."

"You mean your father's mother?"

"Yes, I talked to her, and she convinced me it was Dad's problem, not mine. She said I should wait until my father's tour of duty ended and then tell him exactly what happened. I should have thought to do that by myself, but I guess I was too involved in the problem to be able to think it through clearly. Nana gave me good advice, and that's what I decided to do."

Dan thought he had just opened the door to a place where he hadn't expected to go. Bobby's story made sense, but it was also clear that he had the motive to see his stepmother gone from his life. Further discussions with Bobby about this subject would definitively have to involve a lawyer from the Children's Services Division. He hoped Bobby wouldn't have to get any criminal lawyers involved.

Bobby returned to the kitchen and Sally sat in the same armchair. Dan reviewed his interview with Bobby. "His story makes sense. I can understand why he didn't want to talk to me about the problem. He was embarrassed. It sounds like Nana Fowler gave him some great advice."

"Speaking of Mildred Fowler, we need to call her. The kids can sleep here tonight, but she needs to help out until Bill gets back. I have no idea of how to get in touch with him. I guess I'll try to contact his National Guard Unit tomorrow. I've got to get back next door. Can you try to reach Mildred?"

"Sure I'll take care of it."

Chapter 14

Dan walked next door, and Amber Carlson, the Medical Examiner, began her debriefing. "I've got a rough time of death; sometime between ten and two o'clock. We'll be able to narrow it when we complete tests back in the lab. I know it's preliminary but I don't think she died from hitting the floor."

"What? You've got to be kidding."

"I think she died from asphyxiation, but I'll need to run some tests to be sure. Stop by tomorrow afternoon. I should have the results by then."

Dan walked over to Julie who was heading up Forensics. "Have anything yet?"

"The front doorknob and doorbell were wiped clean of prints. We've found a mark from her flip-flop where she probably hit the floor. Then she skidded about eleven inches and came to a stop where she is now. I'll know more once we move the body."

"Can I walk upstairs yet?"

"Yep, we've cleared the stairs and upstairs hallway, but not the rooms; wear gloves."

Dan walked slowly up the stairs and stopped after clearing the last step. He turned around and looked down at Gloria. He pictured her walking down the hallway and getting pushed down the stairs. He imagined the trajectory, and the force of the push required to have her land that far from the foot of the staircase. He thought it must have been one hell of a shove.

There were two observations of importance in the upper hallway. First, there were several pieces of delicate furniture and fragile lamps near the steps. The push down the stairs must have taken place at the beginning of the stairway, not further back in the hallway, or these items would definitely have been damaged as part of the struggle. In fact there didn't appear to be a struggle at all, meaning Gloria might have known whoever it was who did the pushing; her ex, another person in for a quick nooner, or perhaps even Bobby. He needed to check on where Bobby was at the time of the murder. He hoped he had an ironclad alibi.

The second point of interest was the missing flip-flop. It was nowhere to be seen. "Hey Julie, has anyone found the missing pink flip-flop?"

"Not yet. Kind of strange, huh?"

Dan walked into the master bedroom and adjoining bathroom. He gloved up and walked into Gloria's closet. It was upscale, one of those California Closet deals or the generic equivalent. A sliding wire basket held a couple days' worth of dirty clothes, including a bath towel. Even through his gloves he could tell it was still damp. As he suspected, she had probably just come out of the shower after tennis at the club. Indeed, beneath the wet towel, a lady's tennis outfit, sports bra, and black panties lay just below the damp towel.

Dan, even at this early stage in the investigation tried to imagine the sequence of events; Gloria returns from tennis, showers, dresses, and then before drying her hair decides to walk downstairs. When she reaches the beginning of the stairs someone comes up from behind and pushes her down with enough force for her to come to rest where she did.

Dan considered the logistics. The person doing the push must have had a running start. He looked back down the hallway toward the master bedroom and entered the bedroom near the top of the stairs. The vast array of sports equipment easily identified it as Bobby's room. So the murderer may have been hiding in Bobby's room, and when Gloria reached the stairs, the killer rushed her and pushed her from behind.

It was hard for Dan not to keep thinking of Bobby's skills as a middle linebacker. It would be just like blitzing the quarterback and hitting him from the blindside. Again, he hoped Bobby had a good alibi.

Gloria's purse sat in an easy-chair in the corner of the bedroom. A quick search revealed nothing of interest except her appointment calendar and cellphone. Dan found today's date. The same note populated the entire week; club 8:00 a.m. through 10:00 a.m. In fact, as Dan thumbed through several pages, it was clear, mornings at the club were the norm.

Dan finished searching the entire second floor, and kept a picture of Gloria and Bill on the nightstand. The missing flip-flop, however, never turned up. Who walks around with only one flip-flop? Two flip-flops yes, no flip-flops yes, one flip-flop no. Would the killer take a flip-flop as a trophy? What the hell for? Why would anyone want just one flip-flop?

"Julie, have you bagged up the flip-flop yet?"

"It's in the evidence bag."

"I'm going to borrow it for a few minutes."

"Okay, just sign it out."

Dan opened the evidence bag, took out the bagged flip-flop, and signed out the evidence. There had been enough cases lost because police officers had been accused of tampering with evidence. Signing evidence in and out helped prevent that from becoming an argument for the defense.

Dan walked back to the Lawson house and found Janet still sitting at the kitchen table with a growing pile of used Kleenex. "Sorry to bother you again, but is this your mother's flip-flop?"

"Yes, she always wore them around the house."

"Did she ever walk around with only one flip-flop?"

"Why would she do that?"

"That's what I thought. One more thing Janet; After your mother showered, did she usually dress and then dry her hair or did she dry her hair first and then get dressed?"

"She always got dressed first. I could never understand it. She said she did it that way ever since she was a little girl."

"And did she always dry her hair before she would leave the bathroom and go downstairs."

"I guess; I don't know for sure; I think she always dries her hair first. Why are you asking me these questions?"

"Your mother's death may not have been an accident."

"What are you saying? That she was murdered!"

"It looks that way."

The floodgates turned back on, and Janet lost it again. Moans built to sobs, sobs to crying, and finally crying to full-blown hysterics. The noise brought Sally into the kitchen. She took one look and gave Dan the get out of here now glare.

Dan found Bobby in the family room watching TV. He turned off the TV and immediately had Bobby's undivided attention. "Bobby, what were you doing today between ten and four o'clock?"

Bobby thought for a moment and answered. "I was in school except for when I went out for lunch."

"Was anybody with you?"

"No, I left school and ate at the Dawg House over on Lake Street."

"Can anyone verify that you were there?"

"Why are you asking me these questions?"

"Bobby, it looks like your stepmother's death wasn't an accident, and I'm trying to find out where everyone was at the time of her death."

"Gee, it sounds like I need a lawyer the way you're talking to me. Maybe the owner remembers me. I gave him a hundred-dollar bill, and he complained about having to make change."

Dan knew any further discussions with Bobby would require the presence of a lawyer. He'd have to work on that tomorrow.

On the way out the backdoor, Sally told him she had talked to Mildred Fowler, and she was going to drive right over to help out with the kids. Back at the Fowler house, Amber Carlson had left with the body in the back of her medical response vehicle. Julie and her team, however, were still hard at work collecting evidence. Dan found her on the second floor. "How's it going?"

"Okay; I'm going to need to collect fingerprints from the two kids. We've got three unique prints from some dirty china in the dishwasher. Can we do that tonight?"

"Let's wait on that. I want to make sure the kids are getting legal advice before we go any further. Still no missing flip-flop?"

"Nope, sure seems strange don't you think?"

"Yep, her daughter says she always wore them around the house."

After gloving up again, Dan began a more detailed search of the house looking for clues. As he carefully explored the main floor, he thought about Bobby. He'd check with the owner of the Dawg House first thing tomorrow. Things were not looking good for Bobby. He had the motive. The only fact that seemed to suggest somebody else might be involved was Julie's observation that the front doorknob and doorbell had been wiped clean of fingerprints. Bobby certainly wouldn't have a need to remove his prints from anyplace in the house.

Death by asphyxiation! What would that mean? Dan thought about the implications. Actually, it wasn't that hard to figure out. The killer pushes Gloria down the stairs. She knocks her head on the floor. She's perhaps unconscious and bleeding, but the killer checks for a pulse and realizes she's not dead. So the murderer finishes the job by pinching off her nose and holding her mouth closed. And there you have it; death by asphyxiation.

It was nine o'clock before Forensics had finished for the day, and Dan was able to walk back to his house. He carried Bobby's backpack. He'd already searched it carefully and found nothing other than the usual school books and a couple of candy bars.

Nana Fowler sat with Sally at the kitchen table looking like death warmed over. She stood up and Dan gave her a hug. "I'm sorry about all this Mildred, but we really need your help right now."

"No problem Dan. Sally tells me it wasn't an accident. I can't believe something like this could happen to our family. Who would think such a thing could happen?"

Sally said, "The kids are in the two upstairs guest rooms. I gave Janet a sedative to calm her down. She's asleep right now and Bobby's watching TV in his bedroom. I made up the hide-a-bed in the family room for Mildred. She says she'll take care of the kids tomorrow."

Dan's half eaten ham and cheese sandwich hadn't moved from where he had left it. He finished the sandwich with a Diet Coke while Mildred and Sally sat in silence.

After dinner, Sally and Dan left Mildred downstairs. Dan brought Bobby's backpack upstairs. He handed it to him and told him he'd see him in the morning.

Dan closed the master bedroom door and found Sally in the master bathroom. "So what's going on?"

"Julie said Gloria didn't die from the fall. It looks like it was asphyxiation. Right now, it looks like murder, and my prime suspect is Bobby. I hope his alibi checks out. Tomorrow's going to be a busy day."

Chapter 15

After Dan and Sally showered and dressed, they checked on the kids, who were still asleep, and then walked downstairs for breakfast. Mildred was already up and had fixed a fresh pot of coffee. She looked terrible. Her walk had become a shuffle as she moved around the kitchen, and without the benefit of makeup, her face looked grey and lifeless. This was certainly not what a woman in her eighties needed to fill in her day. Dan had a full list of things to do on his plate. The highest priority was to get in contact with Bill Fowler. He looked up Chicago National Guard Units on the internet and called the unit he thought Bill belonged to.

"A-Company, 2nd Battalion, 20th Special Forces Group (Airborne); Sergeant MacClosky speaking, how may I help you?"

"Good morning Sergeant. This is Detective Dan Lawson with the Chicago Police Department. Yesterday, the wife of one of your guardsmen died. We need to get in contact with him, and he's presently serving in Afghanistan. How do we make that happen?"

"Detective, if you come down to the Donnally Building, Colonel Kincade can meet with you. He can make it happen. We're located at 1910 S. Calumet Avenue. What's the soldier's name?"

"Bill Fowler. I'm sorry I don't know his rank, but he's a Ranger."

"Thank you. I'll pull his file up and the Colonel can review it before you get here."

Dan walked next door and found a picture of Bobby in his room. He put it in his pocket. He would need it later in the day.

Dan arrived at the Donnally Armory an hour later. Sergeant MacClosky sat just inside the entrance at a makeshift desk. Dan pulled out his badge and credentials and handed them to the sergeant. MacClosky compared his picture to the real Dan, concluded this person was indeed a Detective in the Chicago Police Department, and welcomed him to the armory. "Colonel Kincade is waiting for you."

Sergeant MacClosky led the way down a long hallway. Dan quickly realized the sergeant was walking with a prosthetic leg. The armory looked empty, and the rubber sole on his plastic prosthesis squeaked with each step the sergeant took. "Where is everyone?"

"We're down to a skeleton crew sir. Just me and the Colonel. Everyone else is deployed."

MacClosky stopped at a closed door, knocked twice, opened the door, and introduced Dan to Colonel Kincade. Kincade stood up, clearly suffering with some type of back injury. "Good morning Detective, I have Lieutenant Fowler's file. What happened?"

Bill's wife was the victim of a homicide yesterday. He has two teenagers. My wife and I happen to live next door, so we're helping out. I need your help with two things. First, we need to contact Bill to let him know what happened. I don't know how we do this, but it might be best if I talked to him directly. Second, I'm assuming he would get some type of emergency leave to take care of the funeral arrangements and sort out what to do with the children."

"Let me contact his basecamp. We can make arrangements for you to Skype, but the problem is he may be out in the field on a reconnaissance mission. Give me your cellphone number. I'll contact the base commander, and I'll get back to you as soon as we can set things up. I'll explain to the base commander what happened and make sure the unit's Chaplin is available to talk to Lieutenant Fowler as soon as you're done."

Dan liked working with the military. No nonsense; just get to the point and make it happen. "Thanks Colonel Kincade. I guess you've dealt with this type of stuff before."

"Unfortunately more than you know Detective, more than you know. I'm guessing we can make this happen tomorrow as long as he's on the base."

Dan left the armory dreading having to tell Bill that his wife had been murdered, but knew he was the best person to have the conversation. Next stop was the Dawg House.

The Dawg House was a local institution. Strategically positioned only three blocks from the high school, it offered a pleasant change from institutional food. The founder's son, Mark Goodwin, now managed the fast-food restaurant. The smell of garlic and rancid frying oil permeated the small restaurant as Dan stepped through the front door. It was too early for the lunch crowd. Only one patron was stuffing down a foot-long. Dan looked at his watch. How could anyone eat a foot-long at ten o'clock?"

Dan stepped up to the counter just under the order here sign. Goodwin asked what he wanted and Dan pulled out his badge. "How about a cup of coffee and a few minutes of your time?"

After paying for the coffee, the two sat down at the table furthest from the guy with the foot-long. Dan took out the picture of Bobby Fowler and handed it to Goodwin. Was this person here at lunch yesterday? It would have been around noon to one o'clock. He says you might remember him because he gave you a hundred-dollar bill, and you didn't want to make change."

Mark Goodwin looked at the picture, put on some reading glasses and took another long look. "You know Detective Lawson, there must have been at least a hundred kids here yesterday for lunch. You should see it around noon; it's like organized confusion. I sort of remember having to make change for a hundred, and I always complain loudly; but honestly, I couldn't tell you whether it was this guy or not. He looks familiar, but the thing is most of my high school customers are here a couple times a week. It's like a hangout. After a while, they all sort of look familiar; you know what I mean?"

"So if I understand, your answer is maybe yes, maybe no, you're not sure."

"Yes Detective Lawson, I think that about sums it up."

"One more thing Mr. Goodwin. How frequently do you make change for a hundred-dollar bill?"

"Not too often; maybe a couple times a day; most people pay with a charge card; it's a new world."

Dan left the Dawg House with mixed feelings. Bobby might have been here. The hundred-dollar bill story was only halfway convincing. He'd have to talk to Bobby again. Maybe one of his classmates saw him. In the meantime, Bobby was still a Person of Interest.

Dan returned to his precinct and filled Joey in on the details of the case. "Are you sure you want to stay on the case," Joey asked. "It sounds like you may be too involved to be an impartial investigator."

"Well there is that, but I also have a lot of inside knowledge about the Fowlers. I think that trumps the personal involvement concern. But, I hear what you're saying, and I'll keep you informed about what's going on. You can keep me honest."

Joey looked thoughtful, shrugged his shoulders, and said, "I'm counting on your good judgment; keep me informed."

Chapter 16

After passing the Joey test, Dan headed over to the Coroner's Office. He avoided lunch; a full stomach and a visit to the Coroner's Office were never a good combination. Speaking of lunch, Amber Carlson was eating her lunch at her desk, a brown-bag special. I guess people like Amber were immune to the sight of exposed brains and bowels as luncheon companions.

Dan pulled over a nearby chair, and waited for her to swallow. She took a drink from her thermos to wash down the food. "I've got some interesting information for you."

Dan moved his chair closer and took out his notebook. The notebook thing was definite proof of his profession, just like his badge. It was almost a reflex action. Someone talks about the case, you take out the notebook. Amber cleared her throat. "First, we confirmed the time of death. We're ninety-five percent confident it occurred sometime between 11:45 a.m., and 1:15 p.m. For the sake of argument you could say 12:30 p.m. Also, we confirmed she didn't die from her fall. She could easily have been unconscious from the fall, but she clearly died from asphyxiation."

Dan asked, "Any idea how?"

"She wasn't strangled; there weren't marks of any kind. I'm thinking she was unconscious and someone just held her mouth shut and pinched off her nose. It's probably as simple as that."

"Anything else?"

Amber smiled, "Oh, I think so. It looks like she had moderate levels of cocaine in her blood; she probably took a hit sometime in the morning; and her sinuses show all the damage consistent with a full-time snorter. We'll get some more blood results back in another two days. Maybe we'll find some other drugs."

"Aren't you just full of surprises."

"I've got one more surprise for you. The victim was sexually active sometime in the morning. We've got some DNA evidence from a vaginal swab. It should be good enough for a match if you ever need it."

Dan was busy taking notes while Amber took another bite of her sandwich. "So Gloria got fucked in the morning and maybe took a hit of coke before or after the big event."

"That about sums it up; and a few more things. She seems to have been in pretty good health, although the blood test work-up will hopefully confirm that fact."

"Well, you've certainly been one busy lady."

"We always aim to please."

"And you always do. Give me a call if you find out anything else."

"Will do, and I'll e-mail you my report as soon as the rest of the lab work comes in."

Dan stood up and returned his chair to its original position. Amber, bless her heart, continued munching on her sandwich while only a few feet away a slew of corpses in various stages of disassembly were lined up on stainless steel slabs waiting for her group's professional work-up. There never seemed to be a slow period in this facility.

Although the thought of lunch was depressing, Dan stopped at a nearby Starbucks for a double espresso. He sat down at an open table, pulled out his notes and planned his next steps. Bobby Fowler was still high on the list of possible suspects, but Gloria's apparent penchant for recreational drugs and sexual activity certainly added a new dimension to the case. The front door being wiped clean of fingerprints pointed to someone other than Bobby, but then again, Bobby could have easily done the wiping just to leave a false clue.

A phone call interrupted his thoughts. "Detective Lawson here."

"Detective Lawson, this is Colonel Kincade. I've contacted our unit over in Afghanistan. Lieutenant Fowler is out on a reconnaissance mission and won't return till next week."

"Can he be reached?"

"They're under partial radio silence. It's our policy not to break radio silence unless his team is in imminent danger."

Army procedures; Dan knew it wasn't worth trying to fight policy with the Army. "So when can we reach him?"

"I've talked to their Base Commander. He'll set up an interview with Bill as soon as he returns. We can plan on Monday morning Chicago time."

It was Thursday, so four more days to go. "Okay, but please keep me informed if things change."

"Will do Detective Lawson. Sorry we couldn't reach him sooner. One more thing, The Base Commander will issue an Emergency Leave so Lieutenant Fowler can return for the funeral and make arrangements for his children."

"Thanks for your help Colonel Kincade."

After the call, Dan wrote Monday morning in his pocket calendar and circled the entry. Four more days. Bill having to wait four days to find out his wife had been murdered seemed a shame, but it would probably take five days for the body to be released to the family anyway.

Dan called Family Services, and after ten minutes of being passed from person to person, he finally reached a Child Advocate lawyer. "Miss Mathews I want to question a minor about a homicide. His stepmother was murdered and his father is stationed overseas in Afghanistan, and in all honesty, the boy, Bobby Fowler, is a Person of Interest. I want to make sure he has legal representation. What do you suggest?"

Leslie Mathews proposed meeting with Bobby, and then depending on her findings, she might or might not permit questioning from Dan. Dan figured that would be the procedure; it certainly made sense. Dan provided her with the contact information, and explained the unique situation with Bill Fowler being overseas and Mildred being more or less in charge. Mathews promised to visit with Bobby within the next twenty-four hours, and she would get back to Dan following her meeting.

Dan looked at his watch. He had two choices. He could either visit Gloria's tennis club and interview a few people there, or he could try meeting with the principal of Bobby's high school to get some more information on Bobby. Julie in Forensics wouldn't have her workup ready until tomorrow. He chose to visit the tennis club.

Chapter 17

The Chicago Tennis and Racquet Club was one of those up-scale clubs catering to the upper middle-class wannabes. As Dan walked through the revolving door, a young twenty year old greeted him with dramatically staged enthusiasm. My badge shocked her into a non-rehearsed silence. "I need to speak to the person in charge."

Buffy, can you believe that was actually her name, got on the phone and told whoever was on the other end that the police were here and wanted to speak to the manager. "She'll be right out."

Buffy paced back and forth, wishing her manager would quickly arrive and free her from Dan's presence. Why do people like Buffy behave the way they do in the presence of the police? Dan didn't know the answer but took great delight in just looking at her as she tried her best to avoid eye contact. He found one of the club's brochures on the counter and paged through it. There were pictures of the staff and page after page of programs offered; everything from yoga to a full-service spa.

Finally, Buffy's prayers were answered. A middle-aged physically fit woman arrived and shook Dan's hand. She introduced herself as Mary Ellen Harper, and led him back to her private office.

Dan pulled out his badge and held it in front of Ms. Harper. "What can I help you with today Detective Lawson?"

"Yesterday, one of your members, Gloria Fowler, was the victim of a homicide."

People always react differently to a death announcement. Harper lost a little color in her otherwise rosy-cheeked complexion and stammered, "She was one of our regulars. She was here almost every morning."

It was like Mary Ellen Harper was more concerned with the loss in revenue than the loss of life. Dan waited a few seconds for the initial impact to wear off and then began with some questions. "What did Mrs. Fowler do here at the club?"

Without looking up Gloria Fowler in her computer, Harper said, "She took lessons on Mondays, Wednesdays and Fridays; and on Tuesdays and Thursdays she worked out in the fitness center."

"What kind of a member was she?"

"What do you mean?"

"Well, did she have a lot of friends; did she cause any trouble with other members? You know, those types of things."

"She seemed to have a lot of friends. She was always talking to people. Everyone liked her."

"What was she doing here yesterday?"

Harper logged onto her computer and found a master schedule. "She had a private lesson with Favio Benzinni."

"Did Ms. Fowler have a relationship with anyone at the club, either members or staff?"

"I wouldn't know Detective Lawson. I make it a practice not to get involved in our member's private lives."

It was the way she said it that immediately set off warning bells. Dan looked at Harper's eyes and knew she wasn't telling the truth. She was definitely hiding something. It's always in the eyes you know. Dan had never been able to understand why a person's eyes gave away so much information. Was it a change in the frequency of blinking? The dilating of the pupils? These were questions best left for scientists to answer. The interview had passed the point of diminishing returns, and Dan knew Mary Ellen Harper was not about to provide any more useful information.

"Is Mr. Benzinni in today?"

She looked at her watch. "He's got a clinic now on Court 4; it's over in ten minutes."

Dan thanked Harper for her time and walked out of the office area and into the sport's complex. A jogging track built above the courts circled the outer edge of the building. Dan climbed the stairs leading up to the track and walked around the building. A herd of sweaty stampeding runners avoided him as he made his way above court #4.

Favio was hitting balls to a group of five women, and from the quality of the tennis, they were all obviously beginners. Favio had the kind of looks that attract most women. Those ladies waiting their turn to hit the ball kept their eyes glued to the Italian Stallion, many probably hoping for something more than witnessing a great backhand return. Favio looked to be in his late twenties. At a little over six feet, he was a commanding presence on the court.

At the end of the clinic, the players picked up all the loose balls and spent a little too much time saying goodbye to their instructor. As Favio left the court, Dan hurried back into the center of the complex and found Favio standing near the water cooler. After introducing himself and producing his badge, Dan asked Favio where they could have a private discussion. Mr. Benzinni, looking suddenly ill at ease, led the way to a small private conference room off the main lobby. The two sat across from each other at a small table.

"Mr. Benzinni, yesterday Gloria Fowler was the victim of a homicide. I believe she had a private lesson with you in the morning. Was there anything unusual about her behavior?"

Benzinni looked shocked at the news. "I, I, I can't believe it. What happened?"

Dan repeated himself. "She was the victim of a homicide; she died. Your lesson was over at ten o'clock. Did you see her after the lesson?"

Silence followed. Dan waited almost a minute before continuing. "Mr. Benzinni, the autopsy conducted on Gloria Fowler indicated she had sexual intercourse sometime in the morning. If necessary, I can get a court order to obtain a DNA sample from you. If you saw her after the tennis lesson, it would be best to admit it now."

Benzinni turned beet red and began breathing harder. He looked down at his feet and finally said, "We went to the hotel across the street after the lesson. We spent about thirty minutes there, and then she left."

"Did you have sex?"

"Yes."

"Did she say where she was going afterward?"

"No, and then I went back to the club for my eleven o'clock clinic."

"Did you do any drugs?"

Silence again. "Mr. Benzinni, I really don't care if you were doing drugs. I'm not going to arrest you if you were, but Gloria did take some cocaine yesterday morning, and I'm just trying to find out when."

Benzinni answered, "Yes, she had some coke with her and we both took a hit before having sex."

"I'm assuming people can support your claim that you were at the club for your eleven o'clock lesson?"

"Yes, and I had lessons all day long. You can check with the other pros. I was at the club all day."

Dan left a visibly shaken Favio Benzinni in the conference room and walked out into the parking lot, Dan considered his next move. He looked across the street and decided that a visit to the Midtown Hotel was in order.

The clerk behind the counter looked at Dan's badge and suddenly tensed up. George Hill listened to Dan's explanation for the visit. He looked at the picture of Gloria Fowler that Dan had taken from the Fowler's bedroom. A smile emerged on his face. "Yes, she was here yesterday morning. She's one of our, how should I say this, regular guests."

Dan then opened the club's brochure and handed it to the desk clerk. "Did any of these people check into the hotel with her?"

"Yesterday, or in general?"

"Both."

He pointed to Favio. "He was with her yesterday."

He then pointed to three other tennis pros and also Mary Ellen Harper. "These others have also been here with her on other days, but there were plenty of others she came here with too; other tennis players I guess because they were all wearing tennis outfits."

"How do they pay?"

"The lady always paid in cash, and she always checked in with the name Gloria Mellon."

Dan said, "Well, I guess that beats the name Smith."

The clerk laughed and then offered his defense. "Detective, it's not my job to judge the moral behavior of our guests. I only want to make sure they do not create a disturbance, and they pay their bills."

With that disclaimer for any responsibility from the clerk, Dan left the hotel. Before heading back to his car, he saw a Starbucks and decided to take a break and do some thinking.

While sipping on a Grande Cappuccino, Dan reviewed the case. Gloria was obviously sexually active; both men and women, it seemed to make no difference. With Favio out of the picture as a suspect, that still left four others who might be implicated in Gloria's murder. The list of potential candidates was definitely growing.

Could this be a drug related issue? Dan thought probably not, but he needed to talk to some of Gloria's friends. They might have an idea of who Gloria was buying her drugs from. He wanted to check Gloria's cellphone and computer for names and addresses of friends and maybe even the guy dealing drugs.

Most cases went through phases. In the beginning, as information accumulated, truth was evasive. Then a key clue finally presented itself, and the facts began fitting into a logical pattern. Ultimately, a fundamental understanding of what really happened emerged. Dan was clearly in the very early stages of the investigation.

His analysis was interrupted by a call from Leslie Mathews. She had met with Bobby Fowler, and she would allow a meeting with Bobby as long as she was present. "Good Leslie, can we set it up for tomorrow morning. Forensics should be done today, so the family can move back into the house tonight. Let's meet at my home at nine o'clock tomorrow morning."

Dan returned to his thinking. Tomorrow, after meeting with Bobby, he would talk to Janet and then visit Bobby's school and talk to the principal. Hopefully, he could find some students who had seen Bobby at the Dawg House.

Sally was working late today, and it was his turn to prepare dinner. The choice was an easy one; a rotisserie chicken and Cesar Salad from Costco. Prepared foods were an answer to a busy detective's prayers.

Chapter 18

Leslie Mathews arrived at the Lawson residence on time, and the two walked over to the Fowlers. Mildred had attempted to clean up the bloodstain on the marble foyer floor, the only visible evidence of Gloria's death, but a large dark-red circular stain still marked the point of death. Blood had already seeped deep down into the porous marble tile floor.

Mildred had prepared a fresh pot of coffee. She moved very slowly across the kitchen. Her new and unrequested responsibilities were taking their toll. Dan suggested the meeting with Bobby take place at the kitchen table. After Mildred poured two cups, she left the kitchen and called upstairs to Bobby. He arrived a minute later looking fearful, distrustful, and hesitant. Leslie told him yesterday he was a Person Of Interest, and Dan needed to ask him a few questions.

Dan began the questioning. "Bobby, the reason I asked Ms. Mathews to talk to you yesterday is because you're a minor and since your father isn't here, I wanted to make sure all of your legal rights are protected. Do you know what a Person Of Interest is?"

"Yea, it means you think I murdered my stepmother?"

"No Bobby, if I thought that, you would be considered a suspect. I don't think that yet, and what I really need is for you to answer a few questions as best you can. I'm hoping we can find out exactly where you were at the time of her death."

Dan took out his notebook. "Yesterday you told me you went to lunch at the Dawg House at the time of the murder. You didn't think anyone could verify your story, but you said the manager might remember you paid with a hundred-dollar bill."

"That's right, I gave him a hundred-dollar bill and he was pissed."

"I met with the owner, Mr. Goodwin yesterday, and he remembers making change for a hundred-dollar bill, but can't recall whether it was you or someone else. He says he's asked to change a hundred-dollar bill a couple times a day."

"So, I'm the guy. Why would I claim to have given him the hundred if I didn't?"

"Well yes Bobby, that's certainly in your favor, but you can see, it's not conclusive."

Bobby looked disappointed to say the least.

"Think back to the day of the murder, and tell me in detail what you were doing after ten o'clock."

Bobby considered the question carefully. "I was in my Algebra II class from 10:00 a.m. until 10:55 a.m. Then I had Study Hall until 11:45 a.m.. That's my lunch hour. I walked to the Dawg House, ordered an Italian Beef, fries and a coke."

Dan was busily writing in his notebook. "Just a second Bobby. Do they take attendance in Algebra and Study Hall?"

"Yes."

"Okay continue. Where did you eat the sandwich?"

"Inside at one of the counter chairs. All the tables were full."

"I'm assuming there were a lot of kids from the high school having lunch. This is really important; did you recognize anyone?"

Bobby was silent. "I'm thinking."

Dan waited a full minute before asking, "Can you tell me anything about the people sitting next to you at the counter?"

Silence!

"Did anything unusual happen?"

"Like what?"

"A fight, fire trucks driving by, a person dressed funny; things like that."

Silence again.

"So after lunch what did you do?"

"I went back to school for my next class."

"And what time was that?"

"One o'clock, that's when English starts."

"And did you have classes for the rest of the afternoon?"

"Yes, until 3:30 p.m., and then I went to football practice."

"Bobby, I'm done with the questions for now, but I want you to think real hard about who may have seen you at the Dawg House. I'm going to ask your principal to ask people who were at the Dawg House on that day if any of them remembered seeing you. Let's hope we can find someone."

"Dan, I know it sounds bad, but I swear to God I had lunch there."

"Let's hope we can find someone to verify your story."

Bobby left the kitchen and Leslie looked at me with a contemplative scowl. "I hope his story checks out. Do you think you'll want to talk to him again?"

"Probably, but I'll call you first."

"I'm going to turn this case over to the Public Defender's Office. I think Bobby will need legal counsel if you talk to him again."

Leslie Mathews left through the backdoor and Mildred, hearing the backdoor shut, came into the kitchen. How did things go Dan?"

"I'm sorry Mildred, but I can't talk about the case, but I do have a few questions for you."

Mildred poured herself a cup of coffee, and with a pained expression on her face, sat down at the table.

"Mildred, Bobby told me he talked to you about a problem he was having. What did he tell you?"

Mildred turned one shade lighter than beet-red. "He told me he walked in on his stepmother having sex with her ex-husband."

"When was that?"

"I'm not certain about the date, but it must have been about two weeks ago. I think it was the same day I was at the beauty shop. If the date's important, I can look it up in my calendar. It's at home."

"I'd appreciate it if you could get me the date as soon as possible. Tell me more about that conversation."

"He cried when he told me, and I cried too. We hugged each other, and after a few minutes, we talked about what needed to be done. I told him he should wait until Bill returned from his tour, and then explain what he saw. I stressed this was his father's problem, not his. He seemed to be okay with that, and I believe that was what he decided to do."

"How did you feel after hearing his story?"

"At first I found it hard to believe, but Bobby has never lied to me, and the way he described things in such detail; I knew he believed what he saw. Then, of course, I felt terrible for Bill. His second wife shacking up with her ex while Bill is serving his country. What a violation of their marriage vows! I never did like her. I think she only married him for his money."

"Thanks for the information. I tried to reach Bill yesterday, but he's out on a mission and won't be back on the base until Monday. I hope to be able to talk to him then. They say he'll get an emergency leave for the funeral. Can you help out with the kids until then?"

"I've got nothing better to do. I"ll help out however I can."

"Thanks Mildred, I knew you'd say yes."

Mildred left the kitchen and walked upstairs to get Janet. Swollen-eyed and still clutching a box of Kleenex, she sat down across from Dan. "How's it going?"

"I still can't get over it. Why would anyone kill my mother?"

"That's what I hope to find out. Who were your mother's best friends? I want to talk to them to see if they are aware of any problems your mother was having."

"She spent almost all of her time at the club. She played a lot of doubles with other women. I don't know their names, but the club should know."

"Did she have any friends outside the club?"

Janet thought for a while. "Before Mom married Bill, she was good friends with our neighbor, Harriet Bales."

"When are you going to go back to work?"

"I don't know. I talked to my boss yesterday and he said to take as long as I needed. I guess I'll wait until after the funeral."

"That's probably not going to be for another week. I won't be able to talk to your stepfather until Monday. You know, even though it may be difficult, I think it would be good for you to go back to work sooner rather than later."

"I guess you're right. I'll think about it."

"I'm going to have to talk to your boss about where you were at the time of the murder. I hope you understand."

Janet couldn't say the words, but she nodded her head in agreement.

"One final thing, I need the telephone number of your father."

Janet looked at me with a question on the tip of her tongue, but didn't ask why. Instead, she rattled off her father's office and home phone numbers.

Chapter 19

Ray Bussard sold cars at a BMW dealer on the Near Northside, and Dan called him at his work number. Ray explained Janet had called him yesterday, and he was aware of Gloria's death.

"I'd like to meet with you sometime today if that's at all possible."

"How about noon? That's my lunch hour."

Dan wrote down the address of the dealership and entered the meeting in his day planner. He had plenty of time to stop by the high school to talk to the principal before meeting with Bussard.

Oak Park and River Forest High School was built in the early part of the last century. At that time, the main building sat at the outer edge of the residential area, a mere two blocks from the center of the village. Over the years, the building had been added onto and improved, and the complex now covered over fifty acres.

With heightened security in place, Dan was buzzed through the front door after showing his badge. A student guide then escorted him to the principal's office. The principal's Administrative Assistant checked out Dan's credentials and then talked to her boss on the phone. A moment later a matronly looking lady in her mid-fifties opened the door to her office and introduced herself. Elsie Feingold struck Dan as a no-nonsense woman who had fought many battles with staff, school boards, and students over her many years of service. She was dressed in a grey-woolen business suit. Dan was captivated by her piercing black eyes. They looked like they could easily see through a student's lies and get to the truth.

After leading Dan to a sitting area in the corner of her office, she asked, "What can I do for you today Detective Lawson?"

"Bobby Fowler is a student here at the high school. Two days ago his mother was the victim of a homicide. Unfortunately, Bobby is a Person Of Interest in the case."

"I know Bobby; he's a good student. I can't believe he'd be mixed up in anything like that."

"I'm hoping you're right Dr. Feingold. Bobby claims he had lunch at the Dawg House on the day of the incident, but I can't verify his story. I'm hoping one of the other kids happened to remember seeing him there. How do you suggest finding out whether anyone saw him?"

"We have over three-thousand students here Detective Lawson. I'm assuming you would like the answer to your question as quickly as possible?"

"That's correct Doctor."

Feingold appeared to be running several options through her mind and she nodded her head as if in agreement with herself. "I think the PA system is the answer. That should get you the quickest response."

Elsie Feingold picked up her phone and dialed a special access code. Her voice resonated throughout the entire building. "Good morning; this is Doctor Feingold. One of our students, Bobby Fowler needs your help. This is very important. If anyone remembers seeing him two days ago at the Dawg House during lunch, please immediately ask your teacher for permission to come to the principal's office. I repeat again; this is an urgent matter."

Dan could feel the energy level increase throughout the school. There was almost a detectable buzz as the students were all simultaneously talking among themselves. Dr. Feingold turned to Dan. "This is going to take a few minutes; would you like some coffee?"

It took almost fifteen minutes before a young hesitant girl appeared at Feingold's door. Dr. Feingold stood up and asked the shy girl to enter. "Thank you for coming. Karen Westcott, this is Detective Lawson. Please sit down Karen."

Dan smiled at the slightly terrified student, trying to put her at ease. "Thank you for coming Karen. What can you tell me?"

"I think I saw him, but I can't be absolutely certain. He's a football player right, and I think he was wearing his Letterman jacket. I only saw him from behind, but he's so much bigger than everyone else, it must have been him."

"Karen what time was that?"

"Well, I have lunch period beginning at eleven-forty-five. I guess it took Fran, she's my girlfriend, and me fifteen minutes to walk there. It was crowded, and he was at the front of the ordering line."

"So if I understand you right, you never got a good look at his face, but you're pretty sure it was Bobby."

"That's right."

"Did your girlfriend recognize Bobby?"

"I asked her right after Dr. Feingold's announcement, but she said she didn't notice him."

"Thank you for coming forward; this has been a big help."

After Karen Westcott left the office Dr. Feingold said, "Not the best eyewitness account Detective Lawson."

"No, but it's better than nothing."

The two talked about the educational system for another ten minutes. The Debating Team had just won another state award and had been receiving many accolades for the achievement. Dan looked at his watch. "Dr. Feingold, thank you for your help. If anyone else comes forward, please give me a call. He handed her his business card, shook hands, and left the building.

Dan still had time to check on Janet's alibi before the meeting with Bussard. On the way over to the printing company where she worked, Dan reflected on Karen's words. She wasn't certain; she thought she had seen Bobby. Not much to go on there, but at least it was a slight improvement for Bobby Fowler.

SureQuality Printing was a small facility located just off Printer's Row on the Near Southside. Dan entered through the front door and saw a sign on the counter asking visitors to ring the bell at the reception desk. Dan tapped the button on top of the bell and waited for someone to appear. A door leading to the shop floor opened and a short bald overweight man in his sixties welcomed Dan. Dan's badge produced the usual reaction, a slight but noticeable increase in stress. After the usual introductions the man behind the counter asked, "What can I do for you Detective Lawson?"

"As you know, Janet Lawson lost her mother two days ago."

"Yes, I talked to Janet yesterday. She said her mother was murdered."

"Yes, and I'm trying to confirm where everyone in the family was located at the time of the homicide. Janet told me she was having lunch with some of the people who work here."

"We did have lunch together. We all ordered in sandwiches from the Subway across the street. Janet was here all day."

"What's Janet's job here?"

"She's our receptionist and gets anything else we need done. I'm afraid the bell over here isn't a very good substitute."

Dan thanked the manager for his help and left the building. Back in his car, Dan thought about Janet. She could not have pushed her mother down the stairs. She had the perfect alibi.

Dan drove over to his meeting with Ray Bussard. The dealership where Bussard worked looked like a thousand others throughout the country, too much inventory, and bizarre combinations of colors few customers wanted. Walking through the main entrance produced a chorus of good mornings from the salespeople hovering by the reception desk. "Good morning; Ray Bussard please."

The receptionist picked up her phone and called Ray. Soon Mr. Bussard appeared. Dressed in a dark-blue suit, and red and white striped bowtie, he actually looked nothing like your typical car salesman. A person might actually trust this guy. He led Dan back to his small cubicle in the back of the office area.

"Thanks for meeting with me on such short notice. Let me get right to the point. When was the last time you saw Gloria Fowler?"

"I guess a couple of months ago."

"And what were the circumstances?"

"I bumped into her at the grocery store."

"Do you recall what you were doing on the 5th of this month?"

Bussard looked at his calendar and said, "I was at work all day."

"Mr. Bussard, I have an eyewitness who places your BMW in the Fowler driveway about 4:00 p.m."

"Oh, I forgot, I was there to get her to sign some legal documents."

"Mr. Bussard, I also have a witness who will testify that you were engaged in sexual intercourse with Mrs. Fowler in her bedroom. Would you like to change your story?"

Ray Bussard instantly lost most of his color. His clenched fists squeezed the blood from his hands. He couldn't look at Dan. He looked down at his desk and said, "Yes, I was there just like I said, to have Gloria sign some legal documents. I can show them to you if you want; and yes, we did have sex together. You need to understand, Gloria was a nymphomaniac. When we were married, she was always cheating. That's why we got a divorce. You can check the court records."

"Mr. Bussard, where were you two days ago around lunchtime?"

"I was here at work. My boss and I had lunch together. I made a proposal to him for a new sales incentive program."

"The coroner report indicates Gloria was a frequent user of cocaine. Do you know where she bought the drugs."

"I think off Halsted Street near the University, but she never told me."

"What do you think should happen to your daughter?"

"She's an adult now. If she wants, she can come live with me, or she can stay where she is, but she and I never did get along. Her mother convinced her that the divorce was my fault and had nothing to do with her own weird sexual appetite."

"Do you have any idea who might have wanted to kill her?"

"I have no idea Detective Lawson."

The interview continued for a few more minutes, and then Dan decided to see Bussard's boss to check on his alibi. Dan waited outside Cliff Dillard's office until one of the sales people left with a signed contract and a smile on his face. He showed Dillard his badge and introduced himself.

After sitting down across from Dillard, he asked, "Mr. Bussard says he was having lunch with you two days ago around noon. Is that correct?"

Wilson looked at his calendar. "Yep, 11:30 a.m., and it lasted for about an hour."

"What did you discuss?"

"He came to me with some cockamamie sales incentive plan proposal. It made absolutely no sense. The whole meeting was a waste of time."

"Does Mr. Bussard have lunch with you often?"

"Not really, maybe once a year when I'm doing performance reviews."

"Is Mr. Bussard a good employee?"

"Average, he has good months and bad months, but he's usually here on time, so I guess he's okay."

Dan left with little more information than before he walked in the front door. Clearly, Ray Bussard was not going to win any awards for the father or salesman of the year. One thing for sure, Bussard had a good alibi.

Dan's next stop was going to be Forensics, but his stomach was growling. Every cop knows the best places to stop for a quick lunch. Sammy's Hot Dog Emporium was less than a mile from the BMW dealer. Dan vacillated between the Italian Beef and a Double-Dog and finally settled on the beef sandwich with fries and a Diet Coke. How ironic, the same lunch Bobby said he ordered at the Dawg House.

Nothing made sense from Dan's perspective, except Bobby was still the lead suspect. While munching on his sandwich, he tried to focus on motive. Bobby definitely had a motive, punishing his stepmother. However, it was clear, Gloria was living a risky lifestyle. With so many sexual partners, one may have felt jilted, and pushed her down the stairs in a moment of anger.

Dan wrote down some names in his notepad. He started from scratch. In cases like this one, the list of the primary suspects usually started with the husband, then the immediate family, and finally known acquaintances. He had quickly dismissed Bill Fowler as a suspect because he was serving overseas, but perhaps Bill had found a way to come home; perhaps he knew about Gloria's exploits and decided to do something about it.

Dan took out his cellphone and called into the office. He finally got connected to the office's research assistant. "Hi Shirley, it's Dan. Listen, I'd like you to do me a favor. I'm working on the Fowler case. Please check on whether Bill Fowler entered the country two days ago. You should be able to check his passport number against flights entering the U.S."

Dan gave her Bill Fowler's home address and then asked to be switched over to Joey. After briefing Joey on the case, he finished his lunch and headed over to the Forensics Lab to get Julie's report.

Julie sat at her desk studying some DNA results on her computer when Dan walked into her office. She looked up, smiled, reached over onto the corner of her desk and handed Dan a folder. "What's it say Julie?"

"Not very much I'm afraid. We collected prints and DNA samples from the house. We'll need to get prints and DNA samples from the kids and Bill Fowler when he returns, but the fingerprints seem to be consistent with the rooms where they each lived."

"You can call their house and schedule a visit to collect the kid's prints and DNA samples. Talk to Mildred Fowler, she's taking care of the kids. Anything else?"

"Not much; we verified the skid-mark on the marble-floor came from her flip-flop. We also confirmed the front doorknob and doorbell were wiped clean, and by the way the person used a Kleenex tissue. We checked out the upstairs hallway and foyer for footprints, but couldn't find any. One more thing we found another set of prints throughout the house, but they were also on all of the cleaning supplies and vacuum cleaner. I'm assuming they're from a maid, but you should check to confirm a cleaning person came in periodically. Oh, and one more thing, I sent a flash drive over to your office. I copied all the files and other pertinent information from all the Fowler's computers, their iPhones, and their iPads. There's a root directory that explains how to enter each database."

"Well Julie, I wish you had something more, but thank your team for the quick response."

Dan picked up the folder and headed out to his car. The investigation was going nowhere. He had hoped for something more definitive from Julie's group. He certainly didn't have enough evidence to charge anyone with a crime. Was it revenge by Bobby, a lover getting even, a drug deal gone bad, or something else entirely? He needed more facts, more evidence, something to help break open the case.

Dan looked at his watch and had time for one more stop before the end of the day. He headed back to the Chicago Tennis and Racquet Club. He wanted to confirm that Gloria's part-time lovers were all accounted for at the time of her murder.

Mary Ellen Harper met him in the lobby and led him back once again to her office. "Ms. Harper, do your employees punch time clocks?"

"Most do, but some work under contract. Why do you ask?"

Dan handed her the club's brochures with the pictures circled of people the hotel clerk had seen with Gloria. "The clerk at the hotel across the street confirmed the people he circled were frequent visitors to the hotel with Gloria Fowler."

Mary Ellen Harper's face lost a great deal of color after seeing her circled picture. "I can explain."

Dan interrupted, "Ms. Harper, I don't need to hear an explanation. I don't really care to know anything about your relationship with Gloria Fowler unless it has something to do with her murder. What I do want to know is what each of these people, including yourself, were doing two days ago when Gloria Fowler was murdered."

Harper felt no need to respond. Instead, she entered her computer and began printing out tennis court usage from the day of the murder. Each court being used showed the pro running the clinic or private lesson and the names of the people working with the pro. Harper studied the list. "You can check with the people who took the lessons, but from the looks of it, all the circled people were here between 11:00 a.m. and 1:00 p.m."

"And what about yourself, Ms. Harper?"

"I was here all day. You can check with my staff. I was in and out of meetings all day. In fact, we had sandwiches brought in for a lunch meeting that started at noon."

"I'd like the names of the people who were at your meeting."

"I'll do better than that."

Harper walked out the door and asked six of her staff to enter her office. "Ask them; they were all at the meeting."

Harper then walked out of the office and closed the door behind her. It didn't take Dan long to confirm Harper was at the lunch meeting. All six verified her story.

Harper was waiting outside her office sipping a bottle of water. "Ms. Harper, I'm going to need the names of all of the members Gloria Fowler played tennis with. I need to talk to them."

Harper led Dan back into her office and began a computer search. She wrote down the names of each person Gloria had played tennis with over the past few months. Then she entered another program and printed out the personal information on each of those club members.

After ten minutes, she handed Dan thirteen pages, each one with the names, addresses, phone numbers; and an unexpected bonus, the photos of each of Gloria's tennis partners.

Dan walked back across the street and handed the clerk the thirteen pages. The clerk looked slowly through the stack. He pulled out two from the group. "Both these women were here multiple times. I can't be sure about the others."

Dan left the club without checking on whether the other pros of interest were actually teaching the classes as the computer printout indicated. He'd start on that task tomorrow morning, along with talking to Gloria's tennis partners. Right now, he just wanted to go home and chill out.

Sally was in the kitchen with a smile on her face fixing dinner. "I told my friends at work today."

"What about waiting three months?"

"I know, but I just felt like doing it. I have to start planning for my maternity leave. Someone's got to run the ER while I'm gone."

Dan stood behind Sally and wrapped her in his arms. He rubbed her tummy. "Can I talk to him yet?"

"Well it is just as likely to be a girl, and it's too early."

Nonetheless, Dan knelt down in front of her and spoke to his first child. "Hello in there. Can anyone hear me? I love you, and I can't wait for you to pop out and join us in a few more months."

He then lifted her blouse and kissed her just below her bellybutton. Sally pulled him up and bestowed one of her special kisses on her man. Then, they both laughed.

"What's going on with the case?"

"I'm nowhere, that's for sure. Bobby's still the lead suspect, and everyone else seems to have iron-clad alibis. I'm going onto the second tier of candidates. I'm going to talk to her friends starting Monday; although outside of the tennis club, she only seems to have one that Janet could remember."

"What about the autopsy and the forensic evidence?"

"Amber confirmed she was asphyxiated, and the only thing Julie found that was strange was that the front doorknob and doorbell were deliberately wiped clean of prints. Oh, and of course there's the missing pink flip-flop that makes absolutely no sense."

"So what's next?"

"Monday morning I'm tentatively scheduled to talk to Bill. He should be back on base by then. He may be able to give me some additional hints."

"When's the funeral going to happen?"

"The coroner is going to release the body tomorrow. I'll talk to Bill on Monday. I guess it all depends on when he can get back from Afghanistan."

Dan opened a Stella Artois and sat down outside on the deck. It was one of those rare late fall summer-like days. He looked over at the Fowler house. Janet Bussard was probably still in mourning, but not Bobby Fowler. Dan hoped if Bobby wasn't involved, their relationship could be repaired.

Dan thought again about the facts in the case, and once again gravitated to the front doorknob being wiped clean of prints. Why? The obvious reason was the killer entered through the front door, and wanted to wipe away any evidence. Why the front door? Why not the backdoor? It was out of sight.

Dan took his bottle and walked to the front of the Fowler's house. He stood by the street, and looked at the house. Four concrete stairs led up to a wide veranda stretching across the full width of the home. Wooden columns and an elaborate railing supported an extension of the roof over the veranda, and a collection of white wicker furniture provided an invitation to come sit down and relax.

The murder occurred around noon, not a very busy time of the day on the street. A person could have easily crept up onto the veranda and entered the house without being seen. It was then that reality hit him square in the face. Did the person have a key to the house or was the lock picked, or did the person just ring the bell?

Dan called Julie's office. She had left for the day, so Dan left a message. "Julie, it's Dan. On the Fowler case, I'm wondering whether the person who wiped the front doorknob clean used a key to get in or picked the lock. Can you have one of your people come out to the house and bring the lock back to the lab for analysis. I'll talk to the Fowlers to let them know one of your people will be coming out."

Dan walked up to the Fowler's front door and rang the bell. Mildred answered the door. It was hard to believe, but she actually looked worse. Dan truly felt sorry for the woman. "How are the kids doing Mildred?"

"Janet's better and Bobby, well, he's just being Bobby."

"I've asked the Forensics people to come out tomorrow and bring your front door lock back to the lab for analysis."

"I'll be home all day. What do you want the lock for?"

"Just a routine part of the case."

Mildred correctly interpreted Dan's answer as it wasn't any of her business. "I think the Coroner's Office is going to release Gloria's body tomorrow. Do you have any idea where Bill would want it sent?"

"Well, I guess the same funeral home he used for his first wife. I think he knows the owner pretty well. I'm sure he'd use them. I don't think I'd be acting out of place if I just asked you to have the body sent there. I can call them up and alert them."

"I'd appreciate it Mildred. You've been a great help."

"It's family Dan. You always have to do what you can for family."

Dan walked back to his deck, sat down on a lounge chair, and once again pondered the clean doorknob. If the lock was picked it would implicate a non-family member. If the person used a key, then where did they get the key? Tomorrow was the weekend, but Dan knew he needed to go into the office. He still hadn't analyzed any of the Fowler's computers, iPhones, or iPads. He needed to begin the process of checking with Gloria's friends. Saturday would definitely be a day for planning.

Sally called from the kitchen. Dinner was ready. He walked back inside and brought his half-finished beer to the table.

Chapter 20

Dan dressed in his Saturday business-casual best; torn jeans and a Bears sweatshirt. He was one of the better dressed detectives in the office. There was a message from Shirley in his phone mail. She had checked with Homeland Security and the airlines. Bill Fowler had not entered the country around the time of Gloria Fowler's death.

Dan turned his attention to the Forensics Report and found the flash drive Julie had sent over on his desk. He hooked it up to his computer and quickly found the root directory. Where to start?

He clicked on Gloria Fowler's computer and found a new directory listing over one-hundred files. He started with Gloria's e-mails. Julie's people had already downloaded all the information from Gloria's G-mail account. He started with the most recent messages and worked back in time. Hundreds of messages, mostly a slew of advertisements from retail shops, filled the pages. Dan avoided those and focused on messages from other people. He read a few messages from Bill. They were brief, gave an account of his frequent recon missions without really giving much actual details, and asked about how the kids were doing at school. Gloria's responses were brief and only answered Bill's direct questions, nothing more. It didn't take a psychiatrist to see their marriage was devoid of love, warmth, or caring; at least on Gloria's part.

Dan then moved onto messages from Gloria's friends. Most were in regard to tennis court times. He wrote down the names and e-mail addresses of each person. He opened her Contacts folder and found the telephone numbers and home addresses for most of the people she played tennis with. By the time he had finished his analysis, he had a list of twenty-six people to interview.

He then moved onto Gloria's iPhone. He began by reading saved text messages, but found nothing there. He then scrolled through her contacts and compared the names to the list he'd already compiled from her G-mail account. There were a couple of new names, but one name stood out because it was an unusual nickname to say the least. Toad, the name blinked on and off like a bright neon sign inviting further investigation. Could this be Gloria's drug dealer? One way to find out.

Dan dialed the number. The Toad answered on the second ring. "Yo, what can I get ya?"

"Toad, Gloria Fowler gave me your name. She said you can get some good quality stuff."

"Gloria, Gloria, what's she look like man?"

"Long blond hair, middle forties, five-foot-ten, a good looker."

"Okay man, I know the lady; drives a Lexus right?"

"No Toad, she drives a Mercedes."

"Okay, just checking, you're clean man; you know what I mean. So what do you need?"

"I need a couple dozen lines of coke."

"When?"

"Dan looked at his watch. How about noon?"

"Noon it is man. Meet me in the alley off Wood, between 19th Street and Cullerton."

Dan looked around the office and spotted Amy Green at her desk dressed in workout clothes. He didn't particularly want to make a drug bust alone. "Hey Amy, I need some help on a drug bust. You in?"

"You got it man as long as you get me a Starbucks on the way."

"Don't you know bribing an officer of the law is illegal."

"You're no cop; look at the way you're dressed; you're a slob just like me."

"Okay, coffee it is, but nothing fancy."

"I'm a Grande Latte girl; you're going to have to splurge big boy."

Having lost the argument, Dan and Amy left for coffee and a drug bust. On the way to the meeting with the Toad, Dan briefed Amy on his case, and how the Toad might be able to shed some light on Gloria's demise. They arrived ten minutes early and decided to cruise the neighborhood to get a sense of how the Toad might be operating. The Near Southside neighborhood was in transition; the politically polite way of saying very old abandoned buildings were slowly being replaced with new construction. The change had started near Lake Michigan and the area was very slowly morphing, too slowly for many of the residents, into a Gen X middle-class neighborhood. The owners of the old poorly maintained properties had no incentive to repair their homes, because the value was in the land not the house. In short, it was an ideal area for drug dealers to ply their trade.

The Toad would most likely work the middle of the alley. If he was smart, he'd have hired a number of young kids to deliver orders from his stash, probably hidden within two blocks, where he would exchange the drugs for dollars. He just needed to make sure he never had more than a few ounces on his person. He would be in really deep shit if he was found with substantial quantities, and the young poorly paid runners helped ensure his safety.

Dan pulled into the alley at the appointed time. An upscale Audi sports car had stopped in the middle of the alley to buy something. Dan waited his turn. After the Audi accelerated down the alley, Dan pulled up to the exchange point. The Toad had gotten his nickname for good reason. His face looked like the moon; a series of craters, pockmarks, pimples; and a scar from a knife fight had almost cut short his life. Dan turned off his car and said, "I called earlier; I'm a friend of Gloria Fowler."

The Toad screamed at a narrow gap between two abandoned houses. "Two dozen lines of top quality "C" and make it fast."

Dan pulled out two one-hundred dollar bills and showed them to the Toad. The Toad kept looking down the alley in both directions. He kept hopping from foot to foot. Two minutes later a young kid no more than eight years old appeared at the gap between the two houses and handed the Toad a brown bag. Dan handed the Toad the money and the Toad delivered the drugs.

Dan tried to start the car, but without depressing the brake pedal. Nothing happened. "Shit Honey, it's happening again." He looked at the Toad, "It's something with the ignition system. We've got to push the car forward a few feet and then it will start. Drive Honey; the Toad and I will push the car."

The Toad didn't like the situation. "You're ruining my business man. Get this piece of shit away from here."

"I will. Just help me push the car forward."

Dan and Amy opened their doors. Amy sat down in the driver's seat and Dan moved to the back of the car. "Come on man, help me push the car. The sooner we push it the sooner we get out of your hair."

The Toad, against his better judgment, moved to the back of the car. As soon as the Toad placed his hands on the rear bumper, Dan pulled out his gun and badge. Amy, gun in hand, quickly jumped out of the car and provided cover. Dan cuffed the Toad, removed a gun from his pants pocket, pushed him into the back seat of the car, and then followed him into the back of the car. Amy shut the rear door while Dan continued to cover the Toad. Amy jumped back into the driver's seat and accelerated down the alley. The whole thing had taken less than thirty seconds. Dan looked out the back of the car as the Toad's protection appeared. Three armed men sprinted down the alley, and then quickly gave up the chase.

"Toad, you're in deep shit man. I'm going to read you your Miranda rights now."

Dan read him his rights. The trip to the precinct's lock-up took all of twenty minutes and was executed in total silence. Dan led the Toad, cuffed and smiling, into one of the interrogation rooms. Amy and Dan sat across from the Toad whose cuffs had been removed. "You don't have shit on me man, not shit. I know my rights man; you don't have shit!"

Dan let the Toad ramble on and then said, "When was the last time you saw Gloria Fowler?"

"What you talking bout man; I don't know no Gloria."

"You knew her pretty well when we talked on the phone. You may think we picked you up for selling drugs, but Gloria Fowler was murdered, and I think you had something to do with it."

"I didn't do shit man. I hardly knew the bitch; she was one of my regular customers, that's all, just one of my regulars."

"Did she ever show up with someone else in her car?"

"Sure, lots of times."

Dan showed the Toad pictures of the Fowler family and the staff at the tennis club. The Toad snickered after looking at the tennis club brochure. "What's it worth to you man if I rat on the person?"

Dan answered, "Here's the deal Toad. If you ID the person, we won't file charges of resisting arrest, and possession of an unregistered handgun without a permit."

The Toad mulled the offer over and pointed to the picture of Mary Ellen Harper. Dan followed up. "Did this lady ever buy anything?"

"Sometimes."

Toad, where were you last Thursday at around noon?

"Where do you think I was man? The lunch hour's prime time for me. I was in the same alley where you picked me up, and I got people who'll swear to it."

Amy took the Toad out of the room and booked him for selling drugs. Dan knew the Toad's replacement would be working the alley tomorrow. Life goes on.

Chapter 21

Dan left the station and stopped at a nearby Starbucks for a double espresso. There was something about the smell of coffee in a Starbucks in the afternoon. After brewing coffee all day, you could almost cut the aroma with a knife. He wondered whether you could get a caffeine fix just by inhaling the vapor. He sat at a corner table sipping his double shot. What next, another meeting with Mary Ellen Harper or contacting the twenty-six friends of Gloria Fowler? Obviously, Mary Ellen Harper was into drugs, but she had an ironclad alibi. Dan doubted he would get any additional information from her. No, he needed to start to interview Gloria's friends. They might be able to shed some light on Gloria's death.

Dan scanned his list of twenty-six names. He circled Harriet Bales' name. Janet Fowler had described Harriet as Gloria's best friend from the old neighborhood. She would definitely be first on his list of interviews. He called her at her home number, and she answered on the second ring.

"Mrs. Bales, this is Detective Dan Lawson. I'm with the Chicago Police Department. Last Thursday Gloria Fowler was the victim of a homicide."

"Yes Detective, her ex-husband Ray Bussard, called us. Jack and I can't believe it. Have you arrested anyone yet?"

"No, we haven't Mrs. Bales, and I'd like to talk to you about Mrs. Fowler. Her daughter Janet told me you were her best friend when she lived in your neighborhood. You may be able to shed some light on what happened."

"Do you think I had anything to do with her murder?"

"No, not at all; I'm just trying to get as much background on Mrs. Fowler as possible, and because you were best friends, I thought she might have shared things with you. When's a good time for us to talk?"

"Well Jack and I are going out for dinner with friends in an hour, so today's not going to work. How about Sunday?"

"Tomorrow works for me; what's a good time?"

"We get home from church about ten o'clock; let's say eleven."

"Eleven o'clock tomorrow; what's your address?"

After Harriet Bales gave Dan her address, he continued sipping his espresso and thinking about the case. He knew he was missing something important but just couldn't put his finger on it. Dan looked outside the Starbucks café. It was getting dark. He threw down the last few ounces of killer coffee and headed home.

"How's the mother of my child doing?" Dan asked Sally as he swept into the kitchen.

"Not bad Detective Dan and how about yourself? Any news on the Fowler case?"

"Well, we arrested Gloria's drug dealer today. He didn't know much about Gloria, only that she was one of his regular customers. I doubt he had anything to do with her death. Tomorrow I'm meeting with one of Gloria's girlfriends. Maybe she'll provide some new leads."

"Honey, you need to forget the case for a few hours. It will help you think outside the box and see things from a fresh perspective, and I have just the cure for your stress."

Sally handed Dan two steaks, and sent him out to fire up the barbecue. Dan grabbed a beer on his way out the backdoor. He turned on the Weber, sat down on a deckchair, and waited for the barbecue to heat up.

The weather was definitely changing. The early evenings were getting colder sooner. Dan walked back in the house and put on a warm jacket. Returning to his beer, he looked up into the darkening sky. He could see Venus to the west and a full moon rising in the east.

The case was definitely driving him crazy. Now, he even questioned whether Gloria's death was a homicide. Maybe her fall really was an accident? Maybe she just tried to regain her balance, and in the process, landed so far from the staircase? Maybe the shock from the fall caused the asphyxiation?

He walked back inside and asked Sally. "Could Gloria have fallen down the stairs in such a way that she could have stopped breathing on her own?"

"Why are you asking? Are you thinking she wasn't murdered?"

"That's exactly what I'm thinking. That's why I'm asking."

"Well, it's theoretically possible, but I'm guessing Amber would have done some tests to explore the possibility. But my dear Detective Dan, you're forgetting one critical clue that precludes that possibility."

"What's that?"

"You forgot the missing pink flip-flop! Obviously, a person witnessed Gloria's fall and for some strange reason decided to keep the missing item. If the flip-flop turns up in her closet or there's some other explanation for why it's missing, then I might believe it could have been an accident."

"Thank you Dr. Watson; as usual your deductive reasoning has been extraordinary."

Sally was right; the case was getting to him. Unfortunately, Bobby was looking more and more like a prime suspect, but the evidence supporting his guilt was meager at best. There were plenty of motives to go around, but none really justified murder. Why was Gloria Fowler murdered? Understanding the why would shed light on possible additional suspects. His mind turned to the scheduled interview with Harriet Bales. He hoped she could offer new insights into Gloria's death. He knew when he talked to Bill Fowler on Monday, Bill would certainly ask about whether anybody had been arrested, a question he hoped he could answer with a yes.

Chapter 22

Harriet Bales' neighborhood could best be described as working middleclass. The Bales house, an old well-maintained Victorian, sat on a tree-lined street in the middle of the block. A fall chill filled the air as Dan walked up the concrete stairs to the front porch. Harriet Bales met him at the front door and ushered him into their living room. Her husband Jack was waiting in an easy chair and stood up to greet him.

After the usual introductions, Harriet, who had set up a coffee service in the living room, poured Dan a cup. Dan began the discussion. "I appreciate your taking time from the weekend to meet with me. Just for your information, I live next door to the Fowlers, so I know the family very well. What did Ray Bussard tell you about the homicide?"

Jack Bales said, "I talked to Ray the day before yesterday. He told me Janet had called him to tell him about her death."

"What exactly did he say?"

"Well, I don't recall the exact words, but he basically said someone pushed her down the stairs of her house, and he couldn't understand who would do such a thing."

"Mr. Bales, I'm aware of Gloria Fowler's sexual indiscretions and what led up to her and Ray getting a divorce. I can't believe he would have talked about her death with such detachment."

Jack Bales looked down at his shoes and sat in silence for a few seconds. Finally, he looked up and said, "Okay, he said the bitch deserved exactly what she got. I know it sounds terrible, but you have to understand, their divorce was a messy one; charges and counter-charges, both involved in extramarital affairs. They even tried to drag our family into it."

Dan, who always tried to read people by looking at their eyes, noticed Harriet's eyes. They seemed to be lost in personal thought and were moist. She was clearly revisiting many memories. "Mrs. Bales, Janet told me you were Gloria's best friend when she lived here. Had you seen her recently?"

"We had lunch about three weeks ago. Since Gloria left the neighborhood, we both seemed to have lost touch with one another. I guess that happens when people move on."

"I think you're right about that. Let me tell you what I'm struggling with on the case. I'm looking for a motive. Why would someone want to push Gloria Fowler down the stairs? We have forensics evidence to prove it wasn't an accident. The push was deliberate. Do you have any idea why someone would want to do that?"

Harriet Bales was deep in thought, trying in her own mind to answer that exact question. "I really don't know. Gloria was a strange woman. She was sexually aggressive. We'd go out for lunch, and she would talk to me about wanting to screw our server. One time she even gave a waiter her telephone number."

Jack interrupted, "Come on Honey, get serious, she was a nymphomaniac. She even tried to hit on me. At the neighborhood parties, she was always trying to get in bed with one of the guys. Everyone knew it. Even Ray knew it."

Harriet, looking troubled said, "Okay, so I agree, she was addicted to sex; she couldn't let a day go by without having sex. Maybe one of her flings got jealous and wanted a permanent relationship, and she said no. Maybe that's who killed her, a disgruntled lover."

Dan said, "I know Gloria had sex with a lot of the people at her tennis club, and I'm looking into that, but can either of you think of someone else outside of her club who she might have been seeing on a regular basis?"

Both Jack and Harriet shook their heads no. On a spur of the moment Dan asked, "Do you know if Gloria was seeing a psychiatrist about her problem?"

Harriet answered, "Maybe, she certainly knew she had a problem with the sex thing. I once suggested she see a doctor, and she said she might."

Dan made a note to check for doctor bills, something that might suggest she was seeing a shrink.

"Mrs. Bales, when you saw Gloria from time to time, did she ever talk much about her husband?"

Harriet Bales made a face. "How can I put this delicately. She only married Bill for his money. Gloria, if she was anything, was a status seeker. She would do anything to move up the social ladder. Marrying Bill allowed her to belong to the tennis club crowd and be seen with the rich and famous. That was Gloria."

The three talked for another hour. Dan tried to pick both their brains, but neither could provide any additional insights into who might have a motive for killing Gloria. Dan thanked them both, gave them his business card, and asked them to call him any time if they could think of anything else.

Driving home, Dan couldn't get the case off his mind. No motives other than an angry stepson or a jilted sexual partner. The case was getting nowhere.

Sally handed Dan a beer as he walked through the backdoor. She could recognize the symptoms. Dan was pissed at not being able to crack the case. "Honey, a Colonel Kincade called. Bill is scheduled to return to the base tonight. He wants to schedule the call to Bill at seven o'clock tomorrow morning. He said call back only if you can't make the meeting.

Dan thought about the meeting with Bill and the shock of finding out Gloria was dead. He felt sorry for Bill. It was bad enough to learn your wife was dead, even a cheating wife like Gloria, but to find out she was murdered. This was definitely not going to be easy. How to break the news? Dan focused on that problem for the rest of the night.

Chapter 23

Sergeant MacClosky led Dan to a high-tech conference room near Colonel Kincade's office. After shaking hands with Kincade, Dan asked, "Who's going to be at the meeting, and what does Bill know about what the meeting is going to be about?"

"Colonel Gifford, his commanding officer, will be there, and Chaplain Johnson will be waiting outside the conference room. Lieutenant Fowler, at this point, just believes he will be at a meeting with his CO and me. Detective, unfortunately, I've had to be at these types of meetings too many times, but let me tell you how I think this is going to go down. Bill's a Ranger. That means he's seen all manner of death out on patrol. For these guys to survive mentally, they almost have to become immune to death. Their buddies are dying all the time. I'm guessing he'll respond to the news without much emotion, but don't be fooled. After the meeting, he'll break down. That's why the chaplain is there. He'll talk to Bill after our meeting. He'll work Bill through the grief. Do you want to break the news or should I?"

"I think it would be best if I told him. He knows me and I feel he'd want to hear it from me."

"Okay, fine by me. One more thing, why don't you stay off screen until I give you the signal. It will take us about a minute to adjust the picture and start the meeting. That way, Bill won't be suspicious until he sees you."

"Sounds like a plan Colonel."

At exactly seven o'clock, the eighty inch high definition TV screen came to life and from the side of the room, Dan could see Bill and another soldier, presumably Colonel Gifford, sitting at a conference table adjusting the picture quality. Less than a minute later the meeting began. Colonel Kincaid said, "Good morning Colonel Gifford and Lieutenant Fowler. How's the audio and video at your end?"

Colonel Gifford answered, "A-Okay Colonel."

Kincaid began. Lieutenant Fowler, I'm afraid we have some bad news to relay. Your friend Detective Dan Lawson is here."

Kincaid signaled Dan to enter the picture and take a seat next to the Colonel. Dan looked into the camera, cleared his throat, and began. "Bill, on Thursday of last week Gloria was the victim of a homicide. She unfortunately died the same day. You were out on patrol and couldn't be reached until this morning. I'm truly sorry to have to convey this terrible news. Mildred is taking care of Bobby and Janet. She's been a great help. I understand from Colonel Kincaid that you will immediately be granted an emergency hardship leave to come back to Chicago so you can take care of things."

Dan paused for a few seconds and tried to measure Bill's response to the news. Bill appeared stoic, a slight pursing of his lips, no visible tears. It was much as Kincaid had predicted. So this was the effect of war on soldiers in combat. My God, had humanity stooped so low so as to be insulated from death, even when it was your own wife?

Kincaid took over the discussion. "Lieutenant Fowler, you're scheduled to leave on a flight out of Kabul at zero six-hundred hours tomorrow. Colonel Gifford has all of the details. On behalf of our entire unit, may I convey our deepest sympathy to you and your family."

Dan asked, "Bill, is there anything Sally and I can do right now to help out?"

Bill, his voice cracking, asked, "What the hell happened?"

"The incident occurred in your house. Janet found Gloria dead at the bottom of the stairs. At first it looked like an accident, but the forensic evidence indicated it wasn't an accident; someone pushed her down the stairs. I'll review the entire case with you when you get home."

"Have you caught the person who did it?"

"Not yet, I'll review where we stand on the case when you get here."

The silence dragged on for what seemed like minutes but in reality was only a few seconds. Bill Fowler was still processing the information. Dan knew the questions would come in the next few hours. It was the natural response to these types of situations. "Bill you've got my cellphone number and our home phone number. Give me a call any time, day or night, if there's anything Sally and I can do to help. Please give us a call."

"Thanks Dan, but right now I'm having a tough time dealing with this. I'm sure I'll have more questions, and I'll either call you or e-mail you before I get back to Chicago if I have any questions. Can I contact Mom and the kids?"

"Sure. Bobby's doing okay, but Janet's having a tough time. She still hasn't gone back to work, and I don't think she's stopped crying since she found out. Mildred's been helping out as best she can."

"Thanks for your help on this Dan, and thank Sally too. Do me a favor and catch the son of a bitch who did this as soon as you can."

"I will Bill; I'm personally handling the case."

Colonel Gifford asked, "Is there anything else?"

It was clear everyone wanted to end the meeting, and the satellite connection with Afghanistan was terminated.

Kincaid said, "Thanks for your help Detective. These meetings are never easy. I think Bill took it about as well as could be expected."

As Dan left the armory he thought, "About as well as could be expected. What bullshit; how do you tell your friend that his wife just died and then measure the response with about as well as could be expected."

With the thoughts of the meeting still fresh in his mind, Dan headed over to the precinct. After briefing Joey on the case, He grabbed a cup of coffee from the communal urn and sat down at his desk. He took one sip and almost spit it out. He was convinced the Starbucks' Manager near the precinct snuck in each night and pissed in the coffee urn just to drum up business.

Where to go on the case? It was a reasonable question considering how little had been accomplished. What was he missing? There must be something. Out of frustration, he picked up the Forensics Report and began thumbing through the eighty-six page analysis. As usual, Julie had done a professional job of organizing the pertinent facts. He found the fingerprint section. He wanted to look at the housekeeper's prints. He made a note to talk to her. Perhaps she had some useful information, or perhaps she too was involved with Gloria.

He immediately thought of the game Clue. It wasn't the butler with the candlestick in the library, but maybe it was the maid with a push down the stairs into the foyer.

The fingerprint section was organized by location within the house. Dan flipped to the master bedroom tab and scanned the photographs of the locations of lifted prints. Hundreds of good-quality prints had been found. The vast majority were identified as Gloria's with a fair number of prints probably belonging to Bill. Dan made a note to have Sergeant MacClosky forward Bill's prints to Julie. Other prints had been identified as those of Janet, a few of Bobby, and the remainder from what Julie felt was the housekeeper. Dan flipped to the broom closet tab and saw the hundreds of prints presumably from the cleaning lady.

The front door tab showed close-up pictures of the doorknob and bell. Julie's pictures indicated that both had been wiped clean. Once again, Dan gravitated to the conclusion that someone, perhaps the killer, had entered through the front door and had wiped away the evidence. That of course pointed to premeditation not a momentary outburst of anger. But why wipe the doorbell, and then when Gloria answered the door, walk her upstairs? Just to then push her back down into the foyer? Hard to believe it would have happened that way, unless of course, she knew the killer and thought nothing of letting the person inside.

The backdoor section included prints from the entire family. Given the nature of the doorknob, the partial prints were not of the best quality, but Julie's crew had been able to make some reasonable conclusions, given the other prints in the house.

Dan looked at the picture of the back doorknob. It was remarkable that Julie's team had been able to pull any partials at all. Then it hit him. How could Bill's print be found on the doorknob. He had been overseas for over four months. The backdoor was used every day by the entire family. How could his prints have survived this long without being obliterated by newer prints? Maybe the print lifted from the hardware had been misidentified?

Dan called Julie. She answered the phone on the fourth ring, clearly out of breath. "Julie, this is Dan. Listen, I've got a question on the Fowler case. Can you pull up your copy of the report."

A minute later Julie was back on the phone. "Go to the backdoor tab in the fingerprint section."

"Okay, got it."

"If Bill Fowler has been away in Afghanistan for over four months, how could he still have a print on the back doorknob?"

Silence followed; prolonged silence. Then Julie said, "I'm pulling up the raw pictures on my computer right now. It does seem strange doesn't it? Okay, I've got the picture of the dustings on the screen, and I'm comparing the partial prints to the prints we have of the family."

Dan waited for Julie to do her thing. She finally cleared her throat and said, "I see your point Dan. The print's not the greatest. Not conclusive, but I think it is Bill Fowler's print, and looking at the shape of the doorknob, it's hard to see how the print could have survived four months of repeated use."

Wow, what were the implications? Bill Fowler recently used the backdoor, but Bill Fowler was overseas and had not recently entered the country. So how could his fingerprint appear on the doorknob? The question was clear but the answer was not forthcoming.

Dan usually did his best thinking at the scene of the crime. Being there created a degree of focus not possible at his desk. He called Mildred. "Hi, it's Dan. Listen I talked to Bill this morning. He just returned from patrol. Is it okay if I stop by the house? I want to check out a few things, and we can talk about the conversation."

Mildred readily agreed. Dan took the Forensics Report with him as he left Headquarters.

Chapter 24

Dan parked in his own driveway and walked next-door. He stopped at the Fowler's backdoor and studied the doorknob. He tried to imagine the various ways a person could grip the hardware and quickly concluded Bill's print must have been placed on the doorknob within the last few weeks. Dan rang the doorbell, and Mildred soon appeared at the backdoor.

They sat down at the kitchen table, and Dan described his conversation with Bill in great detail. Mildred, with tears in her eyes, listened quietly and finally started to cry. This had evidently been the tipping point for her. Excusing herself, she hobbled from the kitchen. She returned five minutes later and apologized for her outburst. Dan held her in his arms and comforted her. "Dan, I'm sorry. I guess all the stress finally got to me. There's so much to do and I don't know if I'm making the right decisions without Bill's help."

"Mildred, you're doing fine. I know Bill will agree with all the decisions you've made, and he'll be here in a few days." Dan changed the subject. If you don't mind, I'd like to spend a few minutes looking around the house."

"Sure, I've got some errands to run, but you're welcome to look around all you want. Just lock up when you leave."

Dan walked into the foyer and looked down once again at the marble tiles still stained with Gloria's blood. The deep crimson colored liquid had penetrated deeply into the porous stone. Mister Clean wasn't going to remove this constant reminder of Gloria's death. The tiles would all need to be replaced, and Dan was certain this would be high on Bill's list of things to do in order to get back to a normal life.

Mildred yelled from the kitchen that she was leaving, and her departure meant he would be undisturbed for several hours, enough time for him to really focus on the case without interruption. He slid a dining room chair into the foyer and sat down.

In his mind, he tried to recreate the crime scene on the day of the murder. Gloria was upstairs in the shower. The killer, assuming it wasn't Bobby, enters the front door, either with a key or by picking the lock, or with Gloria letting him in. Dan stood up and walked to the entrance, mimicking what the killer must have done. He first considered the more likely scenario where the person snuck into the house. The killer hears Gloria upstairs and silently walks up the stairs to the second floor. Dan walked up the stairs and stood in the upstairs hallway. The killer's close enough to the master bathroom so he can hear the water running. He moves into Bobby's room and waits for Gloria to start walking down the stairs. Then he bursts into the hallway and pushes her from behind. Gloria, caught unaware, plunges to her death. The killer then walks down the stairs and checks her out. She's still alive so he holds her mouth shut and pinches off her nose. After confirming she's dead, he takes one pink flip-flop and leaves by the front door, taking the time to wipe off any fingerprints left on the front doorknob and bell.

The scenario was certainly possible, but Dan questioned the implications. There were too many unanswered questions. How did the killer know Gloria would be upstairs taking a shower? If he used a key, where did he get the key? Did he really wait for Gloria to walk downstairs? If this was the plan, he might have been waiting for hours before she decided to leave her bedroom. And, where was the missing flip-flop? And what about motive; what was the motive? Could Gloria's craving for sex have gotten her into trouble with one of her lovers; enough trouble to have resulted in her death?

Too many questions and not enough answers. Dan walked into the master bedroom and sat down on the edge of the Jacuzzi. He tried to picture Gloria showering after tennis. She would have thrown her tennis outfit into the clothes hamper and walked into the shower stall. After shampooing her hair, she toweled off and dressed in the blue pants and white blouse. Then for some reason, and before she dried her hair, she decided to walk downstairs. Why? Why walk downstairs before blow-drying her hair? There could have been a thousand reasons, but sometimes the simplest answer is the most likely. Someone rang the front doorbell. That would certainly get her to break her routine and go downstairs to see who was there. Someone at the front door, however, would surely implicate a person she knew, inless of course it was the Avon Lady.

Dan stood up and walked into the master bedroom. His eyes scanned the room, moving from left to right. A nightstand with a lamp and pictures of Janet, Gloria and some of her female friends. Clearly, Gloria slept on this side of the king size bed. To the right of the bed was another nightstand with a large white fluted lamp and three pictures; one of Bobby and Bill, a second of Mildred with Bobby and Bill at the beach, and a third of Bill with another soldier, both in full battledress, standing in front of a wooden Kabul Hilton sign above a camouflaged tent.

Dan walked over to the picture of the two comrades in arms and held it up close. An inscription at the bottom of the picture read, Best friends forever and it was signed Don." But there was something of greater interest to Dan. Bill's friend Don almost looked like Bill's twin brother. They both had the same chiseled nose, high cheekbones, brown hair, and deeply tanned skin.

Staring at the picture, Dan began to think outside the box. What if Bill posed as his best friend and returned to the states to murder his wife. It sounded ridiculous at first, but the more he thought about it, the more he considered it plausible. The army had said Bill was out on patrol and couldn't be reached the day of Gloria's murder. If this was the partner Bill went out on patrols with, and if it was only a two-man recon mission, then perhaps Bill somehow made his way back into Kabul and took a plane to Chicago using Don's passport.

Dan called Sergeant MacClosky. "Sergeant, this is Detective Dan Lawson. I'm hoping you can answer a question for me."

"Shoot Detective."

"I've found a picture of Bill Fowler with his best friend whose first name is Don. They're both dressed in full combat gear. I'm assuming they work together as a team. You told me before that your Ranger unit specializes in two-man reconnaissance patrols. Can you tell me Don's last name?"

"I should be able to get you the answer to that question. Let me pull Lieutenant Fowler's profile up on my computer."

Dan could hear MacClosky punching his computer's keyboard. Finally he returned to his phone. "It looks like Lieutenant Fowler teamed up with Sergeant Don Burke four years ago. They've been partners ever since. We encourage that. The more two soldiers work together, the better the team."

"Can you tell me Don Burke's passport number?"

"Just a second."

Again the computer keyboard sounds came through the phone line. "Okay, here it is."

Sergeant MacClosky read off the number and asked if there was anything else he could do. "Well there is one more thing; do you know when Bill is scheduled to arrive in Chicago?"

"I have his itinerary right in front of me. He's going to be on a flight from Hawaii to Chicago tomorrow. He's scheduled to arrive at 12:40 p.m., on American Airlines flight # 3017."

"Thanks Sergeant; you've been a big help."

"Anytime Detective."

Dan immediately phoned Shirley at the precinct and asked her to run a check on Don Burke's passport number to see if he arrived from Afghanistan around the day of Gloria's murder.

Dan considered it at best a longshot that Bill had arrived in Chicago posing as his best friend, but what the hell, at this point nothing else made sense. Then again, even the arrival of Bill Fowler wouldn't explain the missing flip-flop or the cleaning of the front doorknob. Maybe the housekeeper had for some reason cleaned the doorknob. But why use a Kleenex tissue and not a dust rag to clean the door?

Dan left the Fowler house after locking the backdoor, and decided to have lunch at home. He found some leftovers in the fridge, and made a chicken sandwich. A Diet Coke and some potato chips rounded out the meal. Dan sat at the kitchen table thinking about his friend Bill. Could Bill have done it? He certainly had a motive, and he was familiar with killing people, albeit our country's enemies and not a cheating wife.

Shirley called while Dan was opening his second Diet Coke. "Dan, Don Burke cleared Customs in Hawaii the day of the murder. I checked with the airlines and he arrived in Chicago at 12:46 p.m."

"Thanks Shirley. This might be the big break in the case. Great job!"

Dan sat back in his chair and felt a sharp pain in the pit of his stomach. He whistled to himself and considered the timeline. If he was traveling without any checked baggage, then he could have caught a taxi and arrived at his house no earlier than 1:30p.m., right on the edge of the estimated time of death. Time to call Amber.

"Amber, hi, it's Dan Lawson. Listen, I've got an important question for you on the Fowler case. You gave me an estimated time of death between 11:00 a.m. and 1:15 p.m. I've got a suspect who could have been at their house at 1:30 p.m. What's the probability of the death occurring at 1:30 p.m.?"

"Let me look at the statistical tables."

Dan could hear her opening a book and thumbing through the pages. "Okay, here it is; wait a second; okay the statistical table says there's a one in one-hundred chance that the death occurred at 1:30 or later. But, I'm warning you, if I was to get on the witness stand, a good defense lawyer would have the jury thinking it was more like one in a million."

"I read you Amber, and thanks for your help."

"Anytime Dan."

Dan threw the rest of the sandwich in the garbage can. He had suddenly lost his appetite. A serious one-on-one discussion with Bill as soon as he arrived was definitely in order. God, he hoped for the sake of the family that Bill wasn't the killer, and the thought of Bobby as the other possible suspect didn't help much.

A quick call to American Airlines confirmed Bill's flight had arrived twenty minutes late. That would push the odds of death later than 1:50 p.m. to something far greater than one-hundred to one.

Chapter 25

O'Hare Field looked like Times Square on a Saturday night. Dan pushed his way through the crowd and flashed his badge as he quickly passed through security. Rank does have its privileges or something like that. He waited patiently at Gate K3 watching CNN on the monitor until Bill's plane finally pulled up to the gate and began disembarking. Hundreds of exhausted passengers left the gate before Bill, dressed in civilian clothes, walked down the jetway. Dan caught his attention and met him just outside the gate area. They hugged and then Dan said, "I wanted to talk to you before you got home."

"Thanks for coming Dan, I certainly didn't expect anyone to be here."

"I want to bring you up to speed on the case and let you know what's been happening at your house. I think it's best if we talk about it at the precinct."

"Sure whatever you say, but just to let you know, I'm exhausted. I've been traveling for over twenty-seven hours, and I feel like shit."

"I'll let you sleep on the ride over to Headquarters."

After picking up Bill's luggage, they headed to the parking garage. Bill was asleep in the front seat even before Dan merged onto the highway leading into the city. Just as well. Dan really didn't want to get into the discussion until Bill was sitting at a table in front of him.

Traffic was unusually light and they pulled into the precinct parking lot after a twenty-five minute ride. Dan woke Bill, and they walked into headquarters and over to Dan's desk. Dan picked up his case folder and after stopping to get some coffee, they entered a small conference room and sat down at the table.

"I'm going to bring you up to speed on the case, and much of what I have to say, you're not going to like. I could have had another detective with us to serve as a witness, but we're good friends and even though I'm breaking regulations, I wanted to have a less formal discussion with you. If at any time you feel like you want a lawyer, just tell me and we'll stop."

Bill hadn't been expecting Dan's opening remarks. Ready for a long rest in his own bed, he became instantly alert and cautious. "What are you saying?"

"I have a lot of questions that need answering and I know you have some of the answers. I want to share all the facts on the case with you, and I'm not going to do it in perfect chronological order, but I think it will make more sense that way."

Bill was now fully alert from the adrenalin pumping through his veins.

"Let me begin with an event that occurred a couple weeks ago. Bobby came home unexpectedly early from football practice. When he entered your house, he found Gloria having sex with her ex, Ray Bussard."

Bill held his head in his hands and said, "How could she? In my own fucking bed and with her ex. What did Bobby do?"

"Well according to Bobby, they didn't see him, and he left the house, got back in his car, and drove up to North Avenue where he sat on a curb for several hours. Sally, who sees him almost every afternoon after work for a game of Horse, immediately noticed something was seriously wrong, but Bobby wouldn't talk to her about it. His behavior became progressively worse over the next few days, and finally Sally convinced Gloria to have Bobby see a psychiatrist friend of hers."

"My God, a shrink?"

"After seeing her friend, Bobby told Sally he now knew what he had to do, and in fact, his outlook seemed to improve dramatically."

"What did he do about it?"

"I'll get to that in a minute. Then last Wednesday, while Sally and I were having dinner, Janet came running into the house telling us that Gloria was lying on the foyer floor and appeared dead. The three of us immediately ran to your house. Sally confirmed Gloria was dead and had been for several hours. I immediately called in Forensics and the Medical Examiner. I'm not going to share all of our facts with you, but suffice it to say the evidence pointed to someone pushing her down the stairs where she hit her head on the marble floor."

"You mean someone deliberately killed her?"

"It seems that way. I was assigned to the case and began questioning everyone. Unfortunately, Bobby does not have a perfect alibi. At the estimated time of death, he says he was having lunch at the Dawg House, but at this point nobody can absolutely say they saw him there."

"You think Bobby did this?"

"Well, after witnessing his stepmother having sex with another man, he certainly had the motive. I asked him about what he meant when he told Sally he had decided what to do, and he said he told Mildred; and she convinced him to wait until you returned from active duty, and then for him to tell you about it. By the way, I talked to Mildred and she confirms Bobby did talk to her about the incident, and she did convince him to talk to you when you returned."

"So Bobby didn't do it!"

"Well, I'm hoping he didn't, but as I said, he doesn't have an ironclad alibi. But there's an additional piece of information that I have and it's of great concern to me."

Dan reached into his folder and pulled out the picture of Bill and his friend Don. He placed it on the table in front of Bill and watched Bill's reaction. Bill's eyes twitched, and his face became slightly flushed.

"As you can imagine, this is not the first homicide case I've worked on, and any detective's first reaction is to consider the husband as the prime suspect. The data shows that in most instances the spouse is the guilty party. But of course you were away overseas and seemed to have the perfect alibi, but as I learned more about what you were doing at that time, I thought you might have been able to secretly return home and commit the act. Passport control, however, didn't have a record of your arrival in the country at that time, but it turns out they did have a record of your best friend's entry into the country on the day of the murder. But of course he was with you out on patrol, right. So, who entered the country on that day? I think you did, posing as your friend Don. You did, didn't you?"

Bill placed his elbows on the table, clutched his hands together over his face, and began to sob. A long period of silence followed, but Dan refused to say anything. The ball was in Bill's court and it was important to wait until Bill could gather his thoughts and respond to his question.

Bill finally looked up; his eyes had become resolute and sharply focused on Dan. "You have to understand, she was dead when I got there. I thought she fell down the stairs, but I knew if I called the police, I'd have some explaining to do. I immediately left the house and walked up to North Avenue where I caught a taxi back to the airport."

"Bill, I think you need to start from the beginning, and I would advise you to hire a lawyer before you get into any more details."

"I don't need a lawyer. I didn't do it, and when I tell you the details, I know you'll believe me."

Dan started to take out his notebook and then, seeing the look on his friend's face put it back in his pocket.

"I was still feeling the loss of Sarah when I met Gloria, and she made me feel like a real person again when I needed it most. After we got married, things changed. It soon became clear; she married me for my money. Now she could live the good life;

tennis, the opera, sporting events, company parties, expensive vacations; everything she always wanted and Ray Bussard could never give her.

"Then the stories started. Acquaintances of mine told me they saw her with other men at hotels in the city. It soon became clear she was fucking everyone. When I left on my first tour in Afghanistan, things really fell apart. She was really into sex; the more men the better. I talked to her about getting a divorce, but she said she would take me to the cleaners. You must have seen her behavior yourself. You know what I'm talking about, right?"

Dan answered, "I knew she was that way, but I didn't really know she was obsessed with sex. Sally didn't know either."

"Well anyway, Don Burke is my best friend. We've been doing recon missions together for three years, just the two of us. You know when you're out there on patrol, you have a lot of time to talk. We both knew more about each other than either of our wives. That's just the way it is. When they say Band of Brothers, they know what they're talking about.

"So there we were sitting out there on patrol and we concocted this scheme. I would pose as Don and enter the country using his passport. I have a gun in my upstairs closet, and I was going to use it. I made arrangements with one of the locals to pick me up when we were out on patrol. He drove me to the airport. But by the time I had arrived in Chicago, I knew I couldn't kill her; I just couldn't. Instead, I decided to tell her I was going to file papers for a divorce.

"When I got to the house, she was lying on the floor, and I panicked. So I got the hell out of there as fast as I could and caught the next flight back to Kabul and rejoined Don out on patrol.

"Nothing else. I swear that's the truth, and I'm willing to take a lie detector test to prove it."

"Did you go in the front door?

"No, the backdoor."

"Did you touch anything?"

"Yea, I felt for a pulse, but she was dead."

"Then what did you do?"

"I left by the backdoor."

"Bill, you're in big trouble. In addition to your having the motive and admitting to being at the scene of the crime near the time of death, you were AWOL and God only knows what that means. You need to get yourself a good criminal lawyer. As I'm sure you know, lie detector tests aren't definitive, but your willingness to take one is certainly a step in the right direction. Talk to your lawyer about it. As for the AWOL thing, I won't be the person who brings it to the Army's attention, but if asked, I'll tell them the truth."

"Thanks Dan, I appreciate that."

"Right now let's get you home. Mildred and the kids are waiting. I think there's been enough shit in your life for one day."

Chapter 26

The Fowlers spent almost a week arranging the funeral. During that time, Bill Fowler hired a lawyer, and after countless hours of discussion, the legal eagle convinced Bill not to take the polygraph test. The lawyer also advised Bobby against taking one. So, as Sally and Dan entered the funeral home, Dan was no further along on the case, and others might have correctly argued, he was even further from establishing the truth.

The casket containing Gloria's body lay in the front of the room, and the extended family waited in a receiving line near the entrance. Bill, Bobby, Janet and Mildred were there. In addition, Sally and Dan were introduced to Gloria's mother and older sister. Enough time had elapsed between the death and this event to create a somber but not hysterical scene. Even Janet had dispensed with her Kleenex and had worked her way through the early stages of grief.

The Lawsons, after expressing their condolences, viewed the body and then sat down near the back of the room. A parade of many of Bill's and Gloria's friends lined up to pay their respects. Dan was particularly interested in Gloria's friends. Of course, the attendees didn't have a sign on their backs identifying them as a friend of Gloria, but Dan made some pretty good guesses. The past suspects, all with perfect alibis, were there; Mary

Ellen Harper, Favio Benzinni, several of the other tennis pros, and Gloria's tennis friends.

Strangely, Ray Bussard was missing from the ceremony. Maybe he realized his presence might create a scene, and he wisely decided to avoid the potential for any disruption.

Dan wondered what the priest could possibly say. Did the guy get briefed by Bill on her inappropriate behavior? Did he know she was murdered? Did he realize the murderer might actually be sitting in this room right now?

Right on schedule the priest entered the room, and the extended family took their seats in the front row. Father Matthews began the ceremony with a reading from scriptures, a passage usually read at funerals. He then read a few prayers and finally began his prepared remarks. He avoided the usual comments about how wonderful the person had been in life and instead focused on the sadness of a person being removed from the living during the prime of her life.

His eulogy lasted all of five minutes, and then the speech was over. He ended the ceremony by extending his best wishes to the family and telling the audience that the Fowlers would be accepting visitors at their house later in the day.

Bill and Janet had agreed to have Gloria cremated, so there would not be a graveside ceremony. After leaving the funeral home, Sally left for the hospital and Dan called into the office. Shirley answered the call and explained that Joey needed to talk to him right away. She forwarded the call into Dan's boss.

"Dan, thanks for calling in; you're not going to believe this. Last night Ray Bussard was shot dead in his condominium's garage. I got a call just an hour ago from Captain Jones over in the fourteenth precinct. It took that long for them to make the connection to the Fowler case. It's your case now, so get your ass over there right away."

Joey rattled off Bussard's address, and Dan headed over to the crime scene. He had a hard time focusing on driving. What were the implications of Ray Bussard's death? It was impossible to believe there was no connection between the two murders. Traffic was relatively light, but it still took him almost twenty minutes to reach the mid-rise condominium on the Near Northside. The ten-story building's garage was located below ground. The garage door was open, and two police cars were parked just inside.

Dan added his unmarked car to the assembly and began walking down the concrete incline leading to the garage's lower levels. At the bottom of the ramp, he could hear the sounds of people talking and as he rounded the corner, he could see familiar faces near the back corner of the lower level. Julie from Forensics was there with one of her people along with two beat cops.

Dan introduced himself to the two cops and then walked over to Julie. She looked up at Dan. "Well, it took you long enough to get here. Where were you?"

"My, what a pleasant welcome, and I was attending Gloria Fowler's funeral."

"So I heard this guy is related to the Fowler case."

"Yep, the victim was Gloria Fowler's ex-husband. What have you got so far?"

"Amber left with the body. She estimates about ten o'clock last night as the time of death. I'm guessing this was a professional hit; a single shot in the center of his forehead. Looks like a nine millimeter, at least what's left of it. It hit the wall behind the victim. It was pretty much smashed. I'm not sure if we'll be able to tie it to a gun, but I'll know more when I get it under a microscope. I'm guessing the shot came from behind that car over there."

Dan looked at the white Toyota. "That's a fifty-foot shot."

"I know; that's why I think it was a professional hit."

"Who's the Detective on the scene?"

"One of the cops answered, "Charley Baker; he's upstairs in the guy's apartment, Unit #8D."

Julie said, "As soon as we pull prints off the outside of the Toyota, we'll be done here."

Dan said he'd give her a call tomorrow to see if she could ID the bullet. He then took the elevator up to the eighth floor and found Unit #8D. Charlie Baker stood in the center of the apartment looking out the living room window. He turned, recognized Dan, smiled, and walked over to shake his hand. "Captain Jones called to tell me we were handing the case over to you."

Dan, who had worked with Baker in the past asked, "What have you got so far?"

"I checked with the Manager. There're no security cameras in the garage. Anyone could have walked into the garage when the door was up. A Mr. Tom Schiller found the body this morning at about seven o'clock. He's in Unit #4C. I talked to him and he says he found the body when he left for work. He called it in at 7:04 a.m. He doesn't know shit, and he doesn't know the victim."

"Well Charlie, that's quite a workup. I guess I'll be starting from scratch."

As Charlie exited the apartment he said, "Oh, the Manager's name is Steve and his office is located on the first floor, just off the lobby."

Dan looked around the two-bedroom condo. It looked tired and was furnished in early bachelor; that is to say, old, cheap, second-hand furniture. He sat down on the living room couch and pulled out his notepad. It was more of a natural reaction rather than as if he had something important to write down. My God, what a turn of events. Ray Bussard is taken down by a professional hit-man. Dan's first reaction was obviously Bill Fowler. He definitely had a motive, and probably was a good shot. He had a gun in his house. However, there were other facts. Dan had seen people going in and out of the Fowler's house all night, and most would be there to talk to Bill. It would be easy to confirm whether Bill was home all night. For Bill's sake, he hoped there were several people who saw him.

Where to start? Why would someone want to kill both Gloria Fowler and Ray Bussard? Of course the simple answer would be because Ray Bussard was fucking Gloria Fowler. Simple was always better, but if all the Fowlers were accounted for at the time of death, then what conclusion could be derived from that? Could Gloria and Ray have been involved in something; some deal that went bad, and they paid the price with their lives? Gloria's non-accident could have been staged by a professional killer, and clearly Ray's death had all the signs of a professional hit.

Dan got up from the couch and started to look around the apartment. He took out his cellphone and called Julie. "Have you left yet?" Her answer was no. "Good, can you come up to Unit #8D after you're done in the garage?"

Out of habit, Dan gloved up while he waited for Julie. The condo was a two bedroom unit with the second bedroom set up as an office. Dan sat down at Bussard's desk and began looking through the drawers. There were the usual files containing important receipts and bills; utilities, payroll stubs, automobile expenses, monthly bank statements, but also one unusual folder titled Gloria.

Dan pulled out the thick grey sliding folder and placed it on the desk. The file contained mostly legal documents. The first was a copy of the divorce decree. Dan skimmed through the early legalize and found the section headed distribution of assets. Dan read the section in detail. Ray Bussard evidently had a terrible lawyer, because Gloria had received just about everything. The proceeds from the sale of the house wound up in her column as well as most of the cash in the bank. Ray was left with his 401k, his car, the stocks and bonds in the broker's account, and all his underwear.

Dan continued looking at the legal documents in the folder. The last document was titled Revision to Divorce Agreement. Dan read the four-page document. It essentially stated that as a final settlement, Gloria Fowler would pay $100,000 to Ray Bussard for past pain and suffering. However, the document was not signed. Could this be the legal document Ray was referring to when he visited Gloria the afternoon they had sex? If she refused to sign the paper, could that have been the reason she died, and Ray didn't do it himself, he hired a professional killer. That way, he could have the perfect alibi; he was at a meeting with his boss.

Then for some reason, the killer has a falling out with Ray and kills him. That would certainly explain a lot of things.

Just then, Julie interrupted his train of thought. "What you got big boy?"

"I think we need to get inside Mr. Bussard's computer. I'm going to need the total dump including any e-mails that may have been deleted, and while you're at it, see what you can pull off his cellphone, and fax machine."

While Julie started to collect information on Ray's computer, Dan continued to look at Ray's legal file. The latest unexecuted document provoked a reread of the original divorce agreement. This time Dan read every page in detail, and he was glad he did, because hidden in one of the clauses in the agreement was a key statement. "The two parties agree that in the event of Ray Bussard's death, Gloria Fowler will receive all remaining funds derived from the sale of those stocks, bonds, and other assets listed in Addendum III, attached; said funds to be retained in a brokers account in the name of Ray Bussard. The two parties also agree that Gloria Fowler agrees to pay premiums on a life insurance policy listed in her name, see Addendum IV, attached, and in the event of Gloria Fowler's death, Ray Bussard will receive all funds derived from the payout on said policy ."

That little paragraph might explain a lot. Dan opened Bussard's desk drawer again and pulled out a file labeled Morgan Stanley. In the file were several years of broker statements, and the most recent showed an account balance of $2,536.55. Apparently, Ray had gone through most of the assets listed in the divorce settlement.

Next, Dan pulled out Ray's bank file and Ray's most recent monthly statement. He had a balance of $14,657.88 in his checking account. Recent credit card company statements indicated Ray was paying the bare minimum on his credit card, and had an unpaid balance of over $18,000 dollars. So, it looked like Ray Bussard had a serious cash flow problem; ergo the attempt to negotiate a one-time payout from Gloria. There was motive here, definitely motive.

Dan left Julie. His highest priority now was to ascertain where the Fowlers were at the time of death. The drive back to the neighborhood took another thirty minutes. It was too early for the friends of the family to pay their respects, but a van from the local deli was in their driveway along with two other cars. Dan knocked on the backdoor and Mildred let him in. "How's everybody doing Mildred?"

"Gloria's mother and sister are up in the guestroom. I think they're pretty much out of it. They really broke up when they first saw the body in the casket. Janet's not too bad. I think there're no more tears left in her. She's all cried out. Bobby and Bill are about as well as can be expected, and I'm just too old to get overly worked up with all this. I did all my crying when my husband Barry died ten years ago."

"I need to talk to Bill. Ray Bussard was murdered last night."

Mildred's eyes grew large and wet as she added this latest news to her plate of woes.

"He's upstairs. I don't have the strength to walk up the stairs again. Just go upstairs."

Dan left Mildred in the kitchen and passed through the dining room. The caterers from the deli were setting up an incredible spread on the dining room table. Dan noticed that a new oriental carpet had been placed over the blood-stained marble. Dan walked up the stairs and found Bill in the master bedroom. He was sitting on his bed going through a picture album. He looked up, surprised to see Dan.

"Hi, what's up?"

"Bill, last night someone murdered Ray Bussard."

Within the span of only a few seconds, a sequence of emotions crossed Bill's face; first surprise, then shock, followed by a smile, and finally concern. "Janet's going to go over the edge. She wasn't really close to Ray, but still he was her father after all. And, before you even ask, I was here all last night. Bobby, Janet, and I had friends over till almost midnight, and then we all went to bed."

Bill looked thoughtful, thinking about Ray's death. "Ray's and Gloria's deaths, they must be related, right?"

"That's what I'm thinking."

"I guess I need to find Janet and tell her what happened."

"Do you want me there or do you want to wait until Sally gets home?"

Bill thought for a second and said, "No, let's get this over with now. I'll tell her and then I'll tell the rest of the family."

"Mildred already knows. She's in the kitchen. She took it pretty hard. Listen, I have to get back to Ray's condo, but Sally and I will come over tonight. Just let me know if you need any help with anything."

Bill left to find Janet, and Dan walked back into the kitchen where Mildred was still sitting at the kitchen table. She had poured herself a cup of hot tea, but was just staring out the kitchen window. She had been crying. Even Mildred, the pillar of the family, had finally succumbed.

"Mildred, Bill's going to talk to Janet now, and then the rest of the family. Sally and I will see you later tonight. You have my number. Please call if you need anything."

Dan squeezed Mildred's hand in a comforting way and then left the Fowler house.

Chapter 27

After finishing at Ray Bussard's unit, Julie had placed yellow crime scene tape across the entrance. Dan rode the elevator down to the first floor and found the Management Office. Steve Fuller, the building's manager, sat at a desk in the small office with glass walls overlooking the building's main entrance. He stood up to greet Dan, and after Dan showed him his badge, he asked Dan to please sit down.

"I can't believe anything like this could happen in my building. Have you caught the person yet?"

"Not yet Mr. Fuller; at least give us a few days. Actually, I'm here to collect the key to Mr. Bussard's unit and to ask you a few questions."

Fuller unlocked a wall cabinet and found the key to Unit #8D. He asked Dan to sign a form and then handed him the key.

"Mr. Fuller, tell me about the security here in the building. I understand there aren't any security cameras on site."

"That's right. Every year I put a security system in the budget, and every year it's turned down. You're looking at the security system right now.

During the day, I can see people coming into the building, and if I don't recognize them or they need to be buzzed in, then I check them out before I let them in the building. After I leave, a resident has to buzz in a visitor unless they have a key."

"Tell me a little bit about Mr. Bussard."

"What do you mean?"

"Did Mr. Bussard pay his assessments on time?"

"Most of the time; I guess he was no worse than any of the other residents."

"I'm going to need to question other residents in the building. Do you have a list of residents?"

Fuller entered his computer and printed out a list of all the residents along with their telephone numbers. As he handed over the sheet, Dan asked, "Were there any stories or complaints about Mr. Bussard?"

"No, as far as I know, there were never any complaints. We have a very quiet building here."

Dan thanked Fuller for his time and gave him his business card with the usual request to call if he thought of anything. Handing out the card was almost always a waste of time. Dan smiled; of course there was the time he had handed his card to a beautiful doctor by the name of Sally Graff, and that had turned out very well. There were always exceptions.

Dan found his way to the building's garage and walked over to the crime scene tape. The white Toyota Prius was still parked in the same spot. Dan walked behind the hybrid and looked at

Bussard's car. Julie was right; this would have been the perfect shot for a professional killer. Hidden behind the car, he could have waited until Bussard left his car and then killed him with a single shot.

Dan looked down at the trunk and could see all of the places where Julie's team had collected fingerprints. Hopefully, the killer left a few prints, although a professional would probably have worn gloves. Dan wrote down the Toyota's license plate number and returned to the management office. Fuller provided him with the owners name, a Lisa Abraham, Unit #5C.

Lisa Abraham looked a little shy of eighty years old. It turned out she lived alone and hadn't used her car in the last week. She hadn't heard about Bussard's death. Dan briefed her quickly and asked her to provide a set of fingerprints for comparison purposes. She readily agreed and Dan explained that he would arrange to have a Forensics Lab person stop by.

Dan looked at his list of residents and mentally circled the names of Bussard's two neighbors. Ray's unit was situated on the northwest corner of the building. The Goldmans were the next-door neighbor to the south of Bussard. Mrs. Goldman answered the door. She had already heard about the murder. She invited Dan into her unit. She seemed like a nice lady and offered him some coffee which he accepted. The two sat at the kitchen table. Dan looked at Mrs. Goldman. She looked to be in her early fifties, and was talking nonstop. Dan finally interrupted her and asked, "Mrs. Goldman. Did you know Ray Bussard?"

"Well we certainly said hello on occasion, but he was never around that much. I think he was a car salesman."

"Did you notice anything strange going on next door?"

She leaned forward and whispered, "Well he did have a girlfriend and she was a howler."

"I don't understand."

"Our bedroom and Ray's bedroom share a common wall. The sound insulation in the building isn't very good, and at night when he was having fun in bed, his girlfriend would always howl. My husband Ralph called her Lassie."

Dan laughed at the imagery and asked, "Did you ever hear anything that might tie in with Mr. Bussard's death?"

Ruth Goldman thought for a few moments and finally said, "No, I really can't think of anything I ever heard that might tie in with his death. I'll ask Ralph if he ever heard anything when he comes home from work."

"Was Mr. Bussard friends with anyone in the building?"

"I never saw him with anyone, or at any of the building's meetings either."

Dan left Mrs. Goldman not knowing anything new other than Ray Bussard seemed to have a girlfriend. Her name and telephone number were probably on Ray's cellphone and he would check that out with Julie tomorrow.

Dan tried the other corner unit, Mr. Glen Hathaway's apartment, but there was no answer. Dan looked at his watch and decided to head home and prepare for the Fowler visitation.

One question kept on begging to be answered. Where had Ray Bussard been last night? The killer probably knew Bussard's plans for the evening.

Chapter 28

Sally was changing out of her surgical scrubs when Dan walked into their master bedroom. After a quick peck on her cheek, Dan filled her in on the demise of Ray Bussard and his event-filled day. "They're related aren't they; the two killings I mean?"

"It's hard to imagine they're not related, but so far I haven't found the connection. Ray was running out of money, and you know what the first law of criminal investigation is? Follow the money. Before Gloria's death, he asked her to sign a document and after checking in his legal file, I found an unexecuted document that would have generated enough money to pay off all his debts. It also looks like Ray had a girlfriend. I'm going to ask Janet if she knows who it might have been."

Sally zipped up her dress and began walking toward the medicine cabinet. "Speaking of Janet, I'm guessing she's pretty depressed right now. I'll bring her something to make her feel better."

One thing Dan had learned about living with a doctor; there was always an ample supply of free drug samples for every occasion. Drug addicts should have been stealing from doctor's medicine cabinets, not pharmacies.

Dozens of cars crowded the street outside the Fowler's house. Mildred stood watch in the kitchen, helping the caterers clean dishes. Dan and Sally, as was their usual custom, entered through the backdoor and gave Mildred a hug. Her eyes were swollen and red, a sure sign of visible grieving. Sally looked into her eyes, but before she could say anything, Mildred held up both hands in defense and said, "I'm all right. Janet's the one you need to take care of. She's up in her room now and totally out of it."

Sally, the Florence Nightingale of the neighborhood, immediately disappeared, obviously heading up the stairs to see Janet. Sally worked her way through the crowd and after knocking, found Janet in her room, sitting in front of her bathroom vanity staring in the mirror. Sally asked, "What do you see in there?"

"Death, unhappiness, a cruel world, and a deep painful hurt."

Sally forced Janet to stand up and then engulfed her upper body in a heartfelt embrace. Janet began to sob and then suddenly stopped. "I can't cry anymore, I'm out of tears. I must have lost ten pounds of tears in the last week. The funny part about this is, I hated my father. My mother was certainly no saint, but my father made her look like Mother Teresa."

Sally pulled out a packet of pills and asked Janet to take two. "They'll make you feel better, and right now, you definitely need to feel a lot better."

"What are they?"

"A mild sedative. They aren't addictive."

Janet threw down the pills with a glass of water. She turned to Sally for answers. "Why has all this happened?"

Sally thought for a moment, "That's what Dan's trying to figure out. He needs to ask you a couple of questions. Do you feel up to it?"

Janet never answered, but she headed downstairs to face her friends and relatives and to fulfill her obligations as the grieving daughter. Luckily, Janet found her boss and other co-workers huddled in a corner and began what was destined to be a long difficult healing process.

Dan cruised the house, looking at the array of guests, wondering whether the killer of Gloria or Ray was here. The more he thought about the two cases, the more he thought the killer, might very well be in the house pretending to grieve with the rest of the family. The professional style of Ray Bussard's death, however, pointed to a new possibility, a hired killer who provided the contractor with the perfect alibi.

Dan spotted Janet with her co-workers. He needed to talk to her and didn't feel like waiting an hour until she was free. He walked up to the group and touched Janet on the shoulder. She turned quickly. "Janet, have you had anything to eat? You really need to have some food. Come with me; I want to make sure you eat something.

Janet excused herself from her friends and Dan led her to the dining room. They found a stack of clean china plates and moved slowly past the array of cold cuts and salads. With their plates full, Dan led Janet into the empty library, where they both sat down on a plush leather couch.

"Janet, I hate to bother you at a time like this but I need the answer to a single question. I found out your father had a girlfriend, and I need to talk to her. Do you know her name?"

"Her name is Betty, but I don't know her last name. I think she works with dad at the BMW dealer. What really happened Dan?"

"I don't know yet, but I promise you, we'll find out who did this, and whoever did it will pay the price."

Gloria's mother opened the door to the library and peeked in. "I hope I'm not interrupting, but I wanted to check on you Honey."

"Grandma, please come in. I'm just talking to Detective Lawson, but I think we're done."

Dan introduced himself to Gloria's mother. He doubted whether she would have remembered his name from the funeral home. "I understand you're the detective assigned to my daughter's case. Please do everything you can to find out who did this."

"I can assure you, I will not stop until I find the person who did this."

It was just like a "B" movie script, but what else could he say? Your daughter was a nymphomaniac and got just what she deserved.

Dan left the library after asking Janet to call if she could remember the last name of Ray Bussard's girlfriend. Carrying his still full china plate, he found Sally talking to some people in the living room. He joined her and together they finished their visit talking to a variety of people who were close friends of Bill or Gloria.

Back in the privacy of their bedroom, Sally tossed Dan a paperback book, 1001 names for your newest member of the family. Dan laughed. "If it's a boy, I vote for Brutus, and if it's a girl, I'm fond of Chardonnay."

"Honey, we're not naming dogs; get serious."

They lay in bed, methodically going through each page, circling possible names along the way. Dan stared at his wife; she was aglow with the miracle of what was growing inside her. He kissed her on the cheek. "I love you Honey. I've never seen you this happy before."

"Well Detective Dan, I've never been pregnant before."

Chapter 29

Dan's cellphone erupted with its ear-piercing announcement of an incoming call. Dan jumped out of bed and got to the phone just in time. Not yet fully awake, he asked who was calling.

"Dan, sorry to wake you. It's Julie; you need to get down here right away. We just found some important stuff on Ray Bussard's computer. It looks like he hired a professional hit man."

Dan looked at his watch. It was a little after six o'clock. "I'll be down there in half an hour."

Dan skipped his morning shave and shower, and instead dressed quickly and left for the Forensics Lab. He should have asked Julie some questions regarding exactly what she had found, but he'd know soon enough.

He found Julie at her desk. She had poured two cups of coffee and the second cup was getting cold. "I poured your coffee ten minutes ago. You said thirty minutes."

"Traffic was heavy. So what have you got for me? It better be good. I lost a good hour of sleep because of your call."

"Oh, I think you'll agree it was worth losing a few minutes of sleep. First, let me give you the bad news. The killer used a nine-millimeter gun, but when the bullet left his body and hit the concrete wall, we lost the ability to run any ID test. Also the killer picked up the spent casing, so we can't get any ID on the gun used."

So, what's the good news?"

"We got into Bussard's e-mail account. We found some messages he thought he deleted, but in fact we were able to pull the messages up from the provider's server. I've printed the messages in chronological order."

Julie, trying unsuccessfully to suppress a grin, handed him a stack of papers. The first message was sent to f.moran@gmail.com. It read, "A mutual friend gave me your e-mail address. I have a job that needs to be done quickly. It's worth $50,000; $10,000 up front and the rest after the job's complete. If you're interested, I'll meet you in front of the Lion House at Lincoln Park Zoo tonight at six o'clock. I know what you look like, so I'll contact you."

Dan's jaw dropped. Julie laughed and said, "Wait, read on, it gets better."

The next e-mail message was from f.moran@gmail.com to r.bussard@aol.com. It said, "I'll consider your offer, but I don't want to meet with you until I find out the details about the job."

Bussard's next response was the clincher. "My ex-wife needs to be taken out, but it must look like an accident. The timing is critical because I need to make sure I have an ironclad alibi. She plays tennis almost every day in the morning, and then comes home to shower before leaving for the rest of the day. We can talk about the specifics when we meet, but it needs to happen in the next two weeks."

Dan smiled after reading the e-mail. "God, I don't believe it's actually in writing. So now I need to find out who f.moran is."

Julie smiled, "I know that's your job, but I couldn't resist finding out the answer to that question, and here's the best part, f.moran@gmail.com is the e-mail address of one Freddie Moran, a known felon who was recently released from prison. The Raccoon, that's his nickname, has definitely been associated with a number of professional contract killings in the last fifteen years. He's apparently very clever. He was never found guilty of the killings, but the DA got him on illegal possession of a firearm."

"The Raccoon; I remember reading about him. The way they wrote him up in the papers, you'd think he was Captain America, only taking out gangsters and other bad guys."

Dan left Julie with a sense of pending success. This was the break he had been looking for. If Ray Bussard did indeed hire the Raccoon to kill Gloria, then according to the e-mails, he would have paid an upfront fee of $10,000. Bussard had just enough money in his bank account to cover that transaction, but not enough to pay the Raccoon after the job was complete; probably a good enough reason for the Raccoon to take Ray out. Bussard was probably counting on the payout from Gloria Fowler's insurance policy, and maybe the Raccoon decided he couldn't wait that long.

Sitting at his office desk, Dan considered the need for a court order, and called Julie instead.

"Julie, it's Dan. Do you know whether Bussard was doing any online banking?"

"He was, and he kept his password and user name on his desktop."

"Go into his checking account and tell me whether he pulled out $10,000 in the last couple of weeks."

Dan waited impatiently as Julie tried to pull up the information on her computer. "This is indeed your lucky day my friend. Mr. Ray Bussard made a wire transfer of $10,000 a week before the murder."

Julie gave Dan the bank routing number and account number. Things were looking good, very good, but things were not looking so good for the Raccoon. He now had probable cause, and the transfer of money, more than enough evidence for an arrest. He located the Raccoon's residence in his file and looked around the office for some help. "Hey Amy how about helping me bring in a possible killer for questioning?"

"Buy me another Grande Latte and I'm yours for the rest of the day."

Dan briefed Amy on the way over to the Raccoon's apartment. Dan parked his car out in front of the condo. After showing his badge to the doorman, they were buzzed past security. During the elevator ride up to the second floor, they both checked their guns just in case the Raccoon resisted arrest. Amy stood in front of the door and Dan off to the side, out of sight. Knowing a woman's voice was always less confrontational, Amy knocked on the door and after Freddie Moran asked who was there, she said, "Mr. Moran, this is

Amy from the Management Office. I have some questions about your last assessment bill."

The Raccoon opened the door, and Dan and Amy both quickly surrounded him. Dan showed Freddie his badge while Amy cuffed the Raccoon.

"What's this all about man? I ain't done nothing wrong; I'm clean."

"Mr. Moran, we're bringing you in for questioning about the murders of Gloria Fowler and Ray Bussard."

Dan Mirandized the Raccoon, and after cuffing him, he and Amy escorted Freddie Moran out to Dan's car. With the Raccoon locked up in the backseat, they returned to the precinct. Moran insisted on his right to an attorney, and after allowing the Raccoon to make the call, he was placed in a small lockup just off the office area.

Sheldon Murphy arrived on the scene in less than thirty minutes and after checking in with the Desk Sergeant, was brought to Dan's desk. "Detective, what's going on here? My client said he was being questioned about two murders."

"That's correct Mr. Murphy, and I wanted to make sure Mr. Moran had legal counsel present before we talked to him. I've already Mirandized him."

"I'd like to speak to my client before you begin questioning him."

Dan led Murphy to the lockup and unlocked the door to the secure room holding the Raccoon. Knock when you're done talking to him, and then we'll begin questioning.

Chapter 30

Sheldon Murphy, attorney at law had seen it all in his defense of the most unsavory characters in the city. He had represented Freddie Moran on several occasions and personally questioned whether the Raccoon should not have been sentenced to life in prison long before this day.

He sat down at a small conference table across from Moran. "What the hell have you gotten yourself into this time? Less than two months out on parole and you're back at it again. Why the hell do I bother representing you?"

"Shelly, I didn't do shit. I've been clean. They say I killed two people, but I don't know anything about it. I swear to God, I had nothing to do with it."

"Well, let's hear what they have to say. And you my friend; you keep your big mouth shut. Let me do the talking unless I direct you to speak. Do you understand?"

The Raccoon was fuming but shook his head yes. Murphy knocked on the door and an officer unlocked the conference room. "We're ready to talk to Detective Lawson."

Amy Green accompanied Dan and the four participants sat down around the small conference table. Dan set a small recorder down on the table and looked at the Raccoon, wondering what his response would be to the questions he would soon be asked. "Mr. Moran, two weeks ago Thursday, Gloria Fowler was murdered in her home. One of the suspects in the case, Ray Bussard was also murdered two nights ago. Our forensics lab determined Mr. Bussard had exchanged a number of e-mails with you."

Moran said, "I don't know any Ray Bussard."

Sheldon Murphy grabbed hold of the Raccoon's arm. "Stop talking Freddie!"

"Here are copies of the messages exchanged between Mr. Bussard's e-mail account and yours."

Dan pushed the copies of the e-mails across the table. Murphy and Moran looked at the e-mails and Murphy said, "What else do you have Detective?"

"On the third of this month, $10,000 was wired from Mr. Bussard's checking account into Mr. Moran's checking account."

Murphy looked at a copy of the bank transaction faxed to Dan from Julie. Murphy said, "Would you please excuse us for a few minutes. I need to talk to my client about these charges."

Dan and Amy knocked on the conference room door and the door was quickly opened. After the door was once again closed, Murphy said, "Explain!"

"Shelly, I don't know anything about this. Here's what happened. I received this first e-mail, but I never saw any of these other messages. I did go to the zoo and waited for this person to show up, but the guy never showed, and that's the total story. Look Shelly, I've never lied to you. Even during the other trials, I told you exactly what I had done, and those things were a lot worse than this. I swear to God, I didn't kill anyone, and I never saw or wrote any of those e-mails. Listen, I'm even willing to take a lie detector test to prove my innocence."

"Don't be so quick to take the test. A lot of people fail those tests who are really innocent. They just get nervous and fail the test."

Sheldon Murphy represented clients who never leveled with him, but Freddie Moran had always admitted to what he had done, regardless of how unsavory the act, and there were many, many acts. Murphy, therefore thought seriously about letting Freddie take the lie detector test. Of course, he had a series of questions for Detective Lawson, just the type to get Lawson to think about alternate explanations. He went through the questions in his mind while Dan and Amy reentered the conference room.

"Detective Lawson, I'm sure you've read the file on my client and have formed certain, shall we say, strong opinions regarding his potential for doing the types of acts you're accusing him of committing. However, I want you to think about some hypothetical situations. Would a professional killer ever communicate using e-mails? Wouldn't that be the most stupid thing to do? Would a hypothetical killer ever accept a down payment for a contract using a wire transfer? Why would a professional killer ever leave a traceable trail for the transfer of money? Of course, I'm not saying Mr. Moran is a professional killer, but you must think he is, and that's not how a professional hit man would act.

Dan answered, "That's all well and good Mr. Murphy, but the string of e-mails is quite convincing, don't you think?"

"Detective, anyone who knew Mr. Moran's e-mail address and password could have written those messages from any computer in the world. You know that, and I know that."

"Mr. Murphy, that's why Mr. Moran hasn't been arrested yet. We're here today to try to understand what Mr. Moran knew, and what he did. Did he in fact receive these e-mails?"

"Mr. Moran did receive the first e-mail that you showed me, but he has assured me he did not respond to the message and never received any of the other e-mails you have submitted to us."

"And what did Mr. Moran do after receiving that first e-mail? Did he in fact go to the zoo to meet with the person who wrote the e-mail?"

Here was the slippery slope Murphy feared. "Mr. Moran did go to the zoo that night, not to consummate any contract, but rather to find out what the job was all about. He was intrigued by the message. For all he knew the offer could have been made for some very legitimate proposal."

"And what happened at the zoo?"

"Nothing, Mr. Moran never met with anyone at the zoo. The person never showed up." Murphy didn't like the way the discussion was going. Moran actually going to the zoo presented a real problem. He decided it was time to put an end to Freddie's detention, and he hoped Freddie was telling the truth. "Look Detective Lawson, Mr. Moran has done nothing wrong, and he is willing to take a polygraph test to confirm that fact. He does this willingly because he knows the test will prove he is innocent."

Dan was shocked but showed no visible emotion. He now actually believed the Raccoon's explanation of the e-mails. "Mr. Murphy, we both know anyone can fool a lie detector test, that's why the test is never allowed as admissible evidence."

"That may be detective, but nonetheless, Mr. Moran, who has no experience with lie detector tests, is willing, as an act of good faith, to submit to this test."

Dan thought about the offer and said, "We'll be happy to schedule the test. I'll have the session set up for tomorrow morning."

"Until then, I would like Mr. Moran to be released."

"No Mr. Murphy; as is our right, we will hold Mr. Moran until the completion of the lie detector test, and we will make a decision to charge or release on the basis of the results of that test."

The meeting ended. The Raccoon was placed in a lockup inside the precinct, and Sheldon Murphy left the precinct hoping Freddie was telling him the truth.

Chapter 31

Chicago Polygraph Services, an independent group licensed in the state with an excellent reputation, administered the polygraph test. The professional examiner, Jacob Merriman, introduced himself to everyone and set up his equipment in one of the conference rooms at the precinct. Murphy insisted the questions asked only pertain to the Bussard case, and Dan agreed.

The Raccoon was brought from the lockup. Sheldon Murphy stepped to the corner of the office area and talked to Freddie Moran. "You wanted to do this, so here's the deal; remain calm and answer all questions truthfully, and good luck."

Dan led Moran into the room where the polygraph test was going to be administered, and introduced him to Mr. Merriman. Dan then left the room and Merriman asked the Raccoon to sit down at the table. After attaching a variety of electronic sensors and a blood pressure cuff, Jacob Merriman began the pre-test by explaining the process that he was going to use. "Mr. Moran, the whole test should take less than five minutes. Here's how it works. I'm going to ask you a few questions that I will use as controls. For some, I will ask you to tell the truth, and for others, I will ask you to deliberately lie. Do you understand?"

"Yes, Then what happens?"

"After establishing the positive and negative controls, I will ask you a number of relevant questions. These have been supplied by Detective Lawson, and relate to the case he is working on. The test will be over after these questions, and I will then analyze the results of the test and write a report."

"When will we have the results of the test?"

"I will give a verbal opinion within a few minutes of the test and my written report will be sent to Detective Lawson, with a copy to Mr. Murphy, tomorrow. Shall we begin?"

"Yes, I'm ready."

Merriman sat down across from the Raccoon and made some final adjustments to his equipment. "Please state your full name."

"Fredrick Paul Moran."

"Please state your present legal address."

"1436 N. Clark, Unit 2C, Chicago, Illinois."

"Please state your age."

"I am forty-eight years old."

"Okay Mr. Moran, I'm now going to ask you some questions and I want you to give incorrect answers. What is your mother's first name?"

"Mary."

"How many children do you have?"

"Eight."

"Have you ever been married?"

"Yes."

"Okay Mr. Moran, I'm now going to ask you the relevant questions. Did you murder Gloria Fowler?"

"No."

Did you murder Ray Bussard?"

"No"

"Did you receive an e-mail from a person asking you to meet them at the Lincoln Park Zoo?"

"Yes."

"Did you meet with anyone at the zoo on that day?"

"No."

"Did you open any other e-mails from the person who sent the first e-mail?"

"No."

"Do you know anything about the $10,000 wire transfer into your checking account?"

"Only what Detective Lawson told me. Other than that I don't know why the money showed up in my checking account."

"Do you know anything about the murders of Gloria Fowler or Ray Bussard?"

"No."

"Mr. Moran, the test is now concluded. Thank you for your cooperation."

Jacob Merriman opened the door to the conference room and signaled Dan and Sheldon that the test was completed. Since the Police Department had paid for the polygraph test, Merriman told Dan that he was prepared to immediately meet with him in the conference room.

As soon as they sat down at the table Merriman said, "Detective, Mr. Moran is definitely telling the truth. I'm sure of that. He admitted to having received the first e-mail, but said he didn't receive any others, and he knows nothing about why the $10,000 showed up in his bank account.

Dan met with Murphy and Moran out in the office area. "Mr. Moran, you passed the test and you're free to go. Obviously, someone has tried to frame you. I would like to have an expert look at your computer. We need to find the person who did this. I can get a court order, but it will be a lot easier if you grant your permission."

"Yes Detective Lawson, I'll give you permission. I want you to find out who did this to me."

Sheldon Murphy and Freddie Moran left the precinct with smiles on their faces. Dan, on the other hand, sat back at his desk contemplating this latest setback.

Chapter 32

As if things weren't bizarre enough, the case now took a new twist with the results of the polygraph test. The implications were clear. First, someone was trying to frame the Raccoon for the murders of Gloria and Ray. Second, whoever that person was, they had a great deal of knowledge of computer viruses or had hired someone who had that knowledge. The one person who came to mind was Bobby Fowler, and his association with the Computer Club at school. Dan guessed that a bunch of computer geeks just might have the skills necessary to get the job done.

Dan called Julie at the Forensics Lab. "Hey, I've got some bad news. The Raccoon just passed a lie detector test. He admits to receiving the first e-mail, but knows nothing about the others or the transfer of $10,000 into his checking account."

A few moments of silence followed as Julie processed the news. "I guess that means a cybercrime. So, my good friend, the plot thickens. We're not very good at checking out cybercrimes. You've got a good friend over in the FBI who's an expert on this stuff, don't you?"

"Benny Cannon, he's definitely in the super-geek category."

"Why don't you work with him? Since the virus probably had to cross state lines as it moved from the computers to the provider's server, it's most likely a federal crime."

"I was thinking the same thing, but I just wanted to check with you before I got the FBI involved."

"Go for it; you've got my permission, that's for sure."

Dan walked over to the communal coffee urn and filled his cup with the rancid brew. Even cream and sugar couldn't camouflage the acid taste. And to think, he actually had to put ten dollars a month into the kitty to pay for this crap. It was definitely time to call his best friend, Jimmy Davis.

"Jimmy, it's Dan, how's it going."

"Great, how's my future godson or goddaughter doing?"

"Everything's great. Sally hasn't even had morning sickness yet. Listen, I've got a problem I think Benny can help me with."

Dan briefed Jimmy on the details of the case. "Cybercrime; well I think Benny is definitely the man for the job. I"ll talk to him right away and have him call you to get all the details."

"Great, tell him to call me at the precinct."

Dan sipped his coffee waiting for Benny's call, and he didn't have long to wait. The phone interrupted his brief moment of peace. "I understand you have a need for the BennyMeister's services. How can I help?"

Dan did the entire data dump; everything he could think of about the two murders, all the suspects and their alibis, and finally the e-mails arriving in the Raccoon's computer without his knowledge. He ended with the $10,000 transfer from Bussard's account to Moran's checking account.

"Wow Dan, it sounds like a real murder mystery, and now you're counting on the BennyMeister to get you a break in the case. I'll tell you what; your case is a lot more exciting than the stuff I'm working on, so I'm ready to accept your challenge. Where's Bussard's computer?"

"Julie downloaded everything and those files are in the Forensics Lab."

"I need the computer, not the downloads."

"His computer is still at his condo. I can meet you there to let you in. When can you start?"

Benny looked at his watch. I've got a lunch meeting with my staff, but I can leave here at one o'clock. Let's say I'll be there at one-thirty."

Dan gave him the address of Bussard's condo and after hanging up reflected on his conversation with Benny. Benny was indeed the best, and if anyone could figure out what happened, it was certainly his good friend. Dan reviewed the case file for the umpteenth time. He eventually slammed the file closed and left for Bussard's condo, hoping that Benny would be able to shed some light on the growing mystery.

Benny, as if trying to make a grand on-stage entrance, waltzed through the open door to Bussard's condo on time, and after giving Dan the full manly two-arm embrace, sat down at Ray Bussard's desk.

Benny laid out the e-mail messages in chronological order, focusing on the dates and times. "The time date stamps on these messages shows they were sent only minutes apart. For this to have been done from this condo, someone would have to have broken in here and at Freddie Moran's at the same time. A person can't be at two places at the same time. Now there could have been two simultaneous break-ins, however that would implicate a second person, an accomplice. Pretty unlikely, don't you think?"

"You're right, that's possible but not probable."

"So, we're left with the only other explanation, a computer virus was inserted into both computers, and that's exactly what the BennyMeister is going to look for."

As they waited for the computer to boot up, Dan sat next to the super-geek as Benny held up a printout of one of the messages and explained the facts. "Okay, look down here at the bottom of each page; that's the address bar. The string of characters indicates where this e-mail was sent from, in other words, an account at google.com. The character string after the forward slash indicates where in Google-land this originated from, and these kinds of characters indicate it was from another server and someone else's e-mail account. Now I'm assuming the other account is Freddie Moran's, and we can check that later. Are you with me so far?"

"Yes, but you're at about my limit of understanding."

"The other important thing you told me is these messages weren't found in Bussard's deleted files, that they were deliberately removed. But, deleted doesn't always mean deleted, and so Julie was able to restore them by working on Bussard's e-mailbox. Now comes the interesting part. The Raccoon proved he only knew about the first e-mail message. He'll allow us to look at his computer, so we can analyze it. Anyway, we think there's hanky-panky going on here, and we think an unknown third party, maybe the killer, has been playing with these computers."

"So does that mean they snuck in here and found his e-mail account?"

"Well, that's the simplest explanation, but that doesn't explain what happened at the Raccoon's end, unless of course the person also entered the Raccoon's condo. The problem with that approach is the person would have to do this stuff multiple times and at the times indicated on these different e-mails. Impossible, don't you think?"

"You're right, that would be very difficult."

"No, I'm thinking the approach used was a virus introduced into these computers, a very sophisticated virus. Once introduced, it controlled everything, and without the knowledge of either Ray Bussard or Freddie Moran."

"So, how do we find the virus?"

"Well, that's why the BennyMeister is here, because I have just the tool to help us."

Benny reached into his briefcase and pulled out a portable hard drive. He plugged it into Bussard's computer while he explained what he was doing. "Bussard's computer uses the Widows 7 operating system. This external hard drive also has the Windows 7 program plus some additional very sophisticated software designed to compare the two programs. It's just being developed by the FBI, and I've been selected to act as a beta-site evaluator. It's so new, very few people even know it's around. If Bussard's operating system differs at all from my perfect program, the software will tell us the exact difference, thus allowing us to identify the virus."

Benny started up the program. "The virus may not be hidden in the operating system software, but that's where I'd hide it. This is going to take at least one hour to run, so let's go across the street to that MacDonald's"

"I thought you had a lunch meeting with your staff?"

"I did, but I was doing all the talking, so I didn't have a chance to eat, and a Big Mac and Super-Sized fries sounds great."

They left the program running, and after Dan locked the door, they walked across the street to the local eatery.

Both Dan and Benny were well into their 2000-plus calorie fat-man's specials when Dan asked, "So are you still dating that girl at the CIA?"

"Yep, but long distance romances are hard to keep going. I think one of us is going to have to agree to move, and we both love our jobs. Sounds like an impossible problem to resolve, don't you think?"

"You're a smart guy and so I know you'll figure it out. If she's the right person for you, you'll both work it out."

"How did you know Sally was the one for you?"

Dan thought about the question. He'd never really given it much thought. He and Sally just fell in love. "I really don't know Benny. The first time I saw her walking down the hallway in the hospital, I knew I wanted to get to know her. Then, as we began working together, I realized what a wonderful person she was. She was all about helping people, and she was a lot smarter than me. Somehow, she had this uncanny ability to see patterns and connect the dots. I guess that's what makes her such a great doctor. The more time we spent together, the more I wanted to see her, and then I guess we both just fell in love. After one week, I knew she was the one."

Benny processed Dan's comments. "You know, I'm not very good at the romance game, but I think she may be the one. When we're together, I can feel the electricity in the air. It just feels right. You know what I mean?"

"Actually, I do Benny, but I can't put it into words."

The two finished their Big Macs in silence; Dan thinking about his future son or daughter, and Benny contemplating whether his Washington based girlfriend was the one.

After lunch, they walked back to Bussard's condo where the results of the computer analysis were ready to be printed out. Benny printed the report and began analyzing the information.

Benny finally whistled and said, "Holy shit, you're not going to believe this!"

"Try me."

"Here's what we've got. A virus was loaded into the computer's operating system. It was hidden in the software program controlling access to the internet. The virus was hidden in an e-mail from Bussard's daughter. When Ray opened the e-mail, the virus was transferred into his operating system, and the virus software package contained all the software code needed to send the e-mails and record the responses at the proper times."

"You mean Janet Bussard did this?"

"Not necessarily; I'm just saying the message was signed with her name. The message tells Ray about her new job, and the virus prevents his reply from ever reaching her. Let me check out the IP address of the computer that sent the message."

Benny copied the IP address to the clipboard and then, after typing in the correct username and password, entered an FBI website. He pasted the IP address they were looking for into a blank box and hit the enter key.

After a few seconds, the response came back. "Well I'll be; it looks like the message was sent from a computer located at the Chicago Public Library."

"So let me summarize to make sure I understand the sequence of events. Someone, maybe Janet Bussard, maybe not, went to the Chicago Public Library and sent an e-mail to Ray Bussard. Hidden in the e-mail was a virus that sent a message to Freddie Moran from Bussard's computer, but without Bussard knowing it."

"Yes that's all correct, and in addition, hidden in that message was another virus that when Moran opened up the first e-mail, infected his computer and without his knowledge began replying to the first message from Bussard's computer."

"Okay, I understand all of that, but there's a bigger question; how did money get transferred from Bussard's bank account into Moran's bank account?"

"Well, whoever did all of this would have to have gained access to Bussard's checking account, and would have to have known Moran's checking account number and his bank. So how could that have been done?"

"Well Dan, there are two possibilities. First, whoever developed these viruses hacked into the two banks and did it without the bank's knowledge. Second possibility is that the person found out all this information in some other way."

"Like how?"

"That's your question to answer Dan. I can only help with the first possibility."

"So, I guess it's time to take a trip to Bussard's bank and check out the first possibility."

Chapter 33

First Liberty Mutual Bank's headquarters was located in the downtown banking district just off LaSalle Street. Benny pulled out his FBI ID and explained to the main receptionist that they needed to speak to the president of the bank. The receptionist made a phone call and then asked them to wait until the president's administrative assistant came down to meet them.

It didn't take long before they were being escorted up to the forty-third floor and the corner office of Maxwell Montgomery. Mr. Montgomery was waiting to meet his unexpected guests with a somber face. A visit from the FBI was not an everyday occurrence for Montgomery. He directed Dan and Benny to a sitting area in the corner of his spacious office and asked if they would like some coffee. Dan and Benny declined but thanked him for his offer.

Dan began the discussion. "Thank you for meeting with us without any notice. I'm working on two murder cases that appear to involve a cybercrime. Our evidence suggests that $10,000 was transferred from one of your client's checking accounts to another individual at another bank. We have reason to believe someone may have hacked into your bank's computer system and executed the wire transfer without anyone's knowledge."

"Detective Lawson, I can assure you our bank has the most advanced security protection against that sort of thing."

Benny replied, "Mr. Montgomery, I can assure you that the person who may have done this has already developed a number of computer viruses that are probably more sophisticated than your bank's security firewall."

"So what do you want from us?"

Benny answered, "I would like to talk to your head of Information Services and determine whether a breach in your security actually took place."

"Mr. Cannon, I think you'll need a Search Warrant to do that."

Dan had met this kind of resistance before. "We can do it one of two ways Mr. Montgomery. The easiest way would be for you to just go ahead and allow Agent Cannon to conduct his analysis. Of course, it is your right to demand a Search Warrant. However, I can assure you, we'll have no problem getting one; and while doing that, it is possible that the local newspapers might find out about the FBI examining your bank for security issues. It's your call."

Montgomery could already picture the headlines in the Chicago Tribune and the immediate run on the bank that might ensue. He quickly made up his mind and reached for the phone. He summoned a person named Isidore, who showed up in less than a minute. Isidore Hopkins was the Chief Information Officer of the bank. In his sixties, he looked like he had never seen a computer let alone set up sophisticated security systems; but he did look like the kind of person who had made numerous PowerPoint presentations to the global financial community.

Montgomery explained the situation to Hopkins who looked like his world was beginning to fall apart. Montgomery ordered Hopkins to give Dan and Benny access to the bank's security system and any other assistance they required.

Hopkins led them down to the twenty-sixth floor and another corner office. He introduced them to Debbie Chen, the head of the bank's Security Department. He asked her to provide all the assistance the FBI needed and then quickly fled the room.

As Benny and Dan reviewed the facts with Ms. Chen, it quickly became apparent that unlike her boss, she really knew her stuff. Benny and Debbie Chen began conferring in a technical language Dan couldn't comprehend. Rather than interrupt he just let them continue undisturbed.

As soon as Chen understood the problem, she went into her computer and pulled up the wire transfer. She confirmed what Benny had already discovered. Benny asked, "How would a person gain access to Bussard's account without knowing his password or account number?"

"First, they would have to hack their way past two firewalls. The first is set up for all bank employees. It allows them access to non-confidential files. From there, they would have to hack past a second firewall. Once inside the confidential file area, they would need to use an assigned password. There are only about two-hundred people who have access to these files, and we keep a log of each time one of them enters that database."

"Can we look at your log to see the number of people who entered the confidential database?"

Debbie Chen entered her computer database again and soon a listing of passwords, dates and times appeared on her screen. Dan and Benny looked at the list. They started on the date of Ray Bussard's murder and looked backward in time. Luckily, there were not many users accessing the confidential area in the three months prior to Bussard's death. Debbie explained, "There's really no reason for this database to be visited frequently."

A quick scan of the passwords showed about forty employees had visited the database during that time. Benny said, "Can we find out the names of the employees who have these passwords, and can we call them to confirm they were on the site on the dates indicated?"

Chen answered, "I doubt whether many people will be able to remember if they visited the site three months ago."

Benny answered, "You're probably right, but we might get lucky and one of these people might say they haven't been on the site for a very long time."

Satisfied with Benny's answer, Chen again worked her computer's keyboard, and a screen correlating employee names and passwords came up on the monitor. Debbie Chen printed the screen and began looking up telephone extensions in the bank's telephone directory. She stopped at the last name on the list. Her eyes moved back and forth between the list and the telephone book. "Oh shit, this last name on the list, Roger Blake, his name doesn't show up in the phonebook. Maybe he's only been here a few months and that's why his name isn't in the book?"

It was a hope more than a likely explanation. She entered the Human Resource database and looked up the name Roger Blake. Chen looked at Benny with embarrassment and disgust. "Roger Blake doesn't work here. I don't know what to say. It looks like someone hacked into our system and then issued themselves a valid password to access the confidential database. How could they have done this?"

Benny said, "I can help you figure out how this was done and then make some recommendations on how to prevent it in the future."

Dan said, "So now we know how the person got into Bussard's bank account and wired the money, but what we don't know is how they got hold of Moran's bank information. I think we're going to have to talk to Moran. Maybe he can tell us who might have that information."

"So let's do it. We've still got time today."

"Okay, but I want to call his attorney first."

Dan and Benny left a shaken Debbie Chen after Benny again offered to help her correct her security problems. Walking outside the bank building, they decided to stop at a nearby Starbucks.

"Benny, you seemed very eager to assist Ms. Chen with her security problem. Might there be something brewing between the two of you?"

Benny's face turned a noticeable shade of red. "Well, she's definitely one hot-looking babe. I think the BennyMeister may have discovered a new opportunity in the dating game."

"But what about your CIA girlfriend back in Washington; I thought she was the one?"

"Perhaps the BennyMeister is rethinking his romantic commitments."

After getting their coffees, Dan called the Raccoon's lawyer. "Sheldon, this is Dan Lawson. We've identified that the money transferred to Moran was accomplished by someone who hacked into Bussard's bank account. Now we're trying to find out how that person could have gotten your client's bank account information. I want to talk to Mr. Moran and we may need to have access to his computer to help find out how it happened."

Sheldon Murphy thought about Dan's request. He could sense that Lawson had already reached the conclusion that Freddie was framed, so gathering more supporting information could hardly hurt his client. "Detective Lawson, I'll call Mr. Moran immediately and explain the situation to him. I'm sure he'll agree to your request. After all, he too would like to find out who did this. I'll call you back after I talk to him."

Dan and Benny continued to talk about Benny's latest potential girlfriend. Five minutes later, Murphy called Dan back. "I talked to Mr. Moran and he would be happy to work with you to determine who did this. He's expecting to hear from you shortly."

Murphy gave Dan the Raccoon's phone number and Dan called him. Freddie Moran wanted to meet with Dan and Benny immediately. He wanted his name cleared, and he wanted to do anything necessary to make that happen.

Chapter 34

Freddie Moran buzzed Dan and Benny into his condo. Dan introduced Benny, and after Dan explained the facts to the Raccoon, Benny sat down at his computer. Benny quickly found the first e-mail from Bussard's computer. He transformed the message into computer software code and analyzed the mysterious language. He copied six mysterious symbols onto the clipboard and then entered the computer's operating system. He executed a search for the six symbols and waited.

Two minutes later, the screen lit up with more software code. Benny analyzed the string of symbols and finally spoke. "Okay, here's how it was done. The first e-mail message contained an unusual string of six symbols written in Assembly Language. Those symbols moved the software code over to the operating system where the code then immediately modified the message to what you now see, and that code, now in the operating system then controlled all of the subsequent messages sent between the two computers."

The Raccoon shouted, "Who did this? Who tried to fuck with my life?"

Dan answered, "That's what we're trying to find out Mr. Moran. Whoever did this found out your e-mail address, the place where you do your banking, and your bank account number. Who would have that kind of information?"

"Are you accusing me?"

"No, I'm only saying we need your help in trying to figure out how whoever did this got your confidential information."

"I have no fucking clue, no clue at all! No wait, I think I know who has that information. When I had my first meeting with my Parole Officer, she asked me for my e-mail address and the bank where I did my banking. Maybe she did this?"

"What's your Parole Officer's name?"

"Betty Jones."

"Mr. Moran, I'll talk to her, and we'll be able to determine whether she was involved. Does anyone else know where you bank?"

"My sister knows. She paid my bills for me when I was in prison."

"How about where you work. Is your paycheck automatically deposited?

"Yes, they have my bank account information, but they don't have my e-mail address."

"Could your sister have given the information to another person?"

"Are you accusing her?"

"Absolutely not, but maybe her computer was also compromised, just like yours; and whoever did this found the information on her computer. That's what we need to find out."

Dan called into the office and talked to Shirley. She looked up Betty Jones in the police department directory, gave Dan the number, and transferred the call to her extension.

"Ms. Jones, this is Detective Dan Lawson. I work out of the twelfth precinct. I'm working on a case involving Freddie Moran. Someone has tried to implicate Mr. Moran in two murders and has tampered with his computer. Mr. Moran says he provided you with his e-mail and his bank account number when he met with you for the first time."

"Yes Detective Lawson, that's standard information we get from every parolee."

"Is it on a computer database?"

"Yes, I loaded it into his file which is on the computer."

"We think someone may have hacked into your database to steal that information. I'm working with the FBI on this matter. One of their experts on cybercrime is with me now. Is it possible for us to meet with you this afternoon? He needs to analyze the database to see whether it's been compromised."

"Sure, I'm free this afternoon. Let's meet in an hour, and I'll have our Information Technology expert join us."

Benny and Dan left the Raccoon, and Dan promised to keep him updated on what they learned.

Chapter 35

Betty Jones and a person she introduced as Jeff Carter met them in a conference room at their Monroe Street Office. Dan reviewed once again the details of the case, and Benny brought them up to date on the possible hacking of the Parole Office's computer system. Jeff Carter looked intently at Benny through thick coke-bottle glasses and listened carefully. He seemed like the type of person who wasn't overly defensive but rather concerned about the possibility of their security being breeched.

"Agent Cannon, let me assure you, we will cooperate with the FBI in understanding whether our system has been compromised, and if there is a problem, then I hope you can recommend some measures to prevent this type of cyber-attack from happening again."

Jeff Carter reviewed the security system deployed by the Parole Office, and then he and Benny went online and reviewed the file on Mr. Freddie Moran. Betty Jones confirmed she hadn't looked at the file since the first meeting with the Raccoon. Yet as the file log indicated, the file had been entered a little over two weeks ago. Carter tried to determine the IP address of the computer that entered the file. He knew from the address that it wasn't a computer from the Parole Office. Benny, however, did recognize the IP address. It was from the same computer involved in Bussard's cyber-attack, the one located at the Chicago Public Library.

Carter asked, "What should we do?"

Benny answered, "I can recommend some very good computer security firms. They'll analyze your entire system, and make suggestions on what steps to take to prevent the kind of hacking that took place."

Carter appreciated the offer, and Benny promised to e-mail the names of the security firms the next day. Dan drove Benny back to Bussard's condo to pick up his car. They talked on the way. "Benny, I guess we understand what happened, but we don't understand who did this. The impression I'm getting is that whoever did all of this really understands computer systems."

"That's an understatement. These computer systems at the bank and Parole Office were hacked into by a very sophisticated person. The virus on Bussard's computer used a state of the art technique. I've never seen anything so sophisticated"

"So who could have done this is the question? The only person involved in the case who knows anything about computers is Bobby Fowler. He's in the Computer Club at school. So the question for you Benny is could high school kids know how to do this stuff, either Bobby or one of his friends?"

"That's a tough question to answer. They might have the skills, but probably not. You never can tell. There might be a future BennyMeister in their group."

"So how do we assess the club's capability?"

Benny thought about the problem. He finally laughed and said, "I think it's time for the Benny-Meister to become a guest lecturer at the next meeting of the Computer Club. I'm sure you can arrange it."

"Let me see what I can do. I'll talk to the Principal."

Benny seemed eager to visit the club

"But one more thing my good friend. You offered Ms. Chen the opportunity to have her security problems resolved with your personal involvement, but you never made the same offer to Mr. Carter. Why not?"

Benny laughed, "Because Mr. Carter wasn't wearing a size 36D bra."

"And you can ascertain Ms. Chen's bra size without inspecting the label?"

"Yes I can. The BennyMeister is a man of many talents."

Dan left Benny at the entrance to Bussard's condo and thanked him for his help.

"No need my friend; the BennyMeister is here to serve."

Chapter 36

The Oak Park and River Forest High School Computer Club was located in the bowels of the main building, just next to the boiler room that generated the heat for the entire school. Benny, trying hard to act the part of a hip teenager, was dressed in torn jeans, a Bears sweatshirt, and an old pair of Van gym shoes; that is to say his normal working attire. Mr. Donald Webster, the Advanced Placement Computer Science teacher who mentored the club, introduced Benny to the group of fifteen club members, almost all of whom were boys.

"Club members, we are fortunate today to have the head of the FBI Cybercrime Unit from the Chicago Office here with us. He wants to talk to you about cybercrime, something that I think many of you are aware of."

There were several snickers from the group who were all seated around a large conference table. Two upscale computer workstations, positioned off to the side of the room, were turned on and running some crazy combat type screen savers. One of the boys with thick glasses and a ponytail asked, "You mean like hacking?"

Benny decided to interrupt the kid and said, "Yes, hacking would be the common name for the act. Let me tell you a little bit about why I'm here today. As you might guess, the FBI is very interested in cybercrime. It can take many forms: identity theft, entering and tampering with private databases, illegal transfer of money, even government against government acts of sabotage. The definition is very simple; the committing of an illegal act using computers or the internet."

A girl raised her hand and asked a question. "What's an example of government against government acts of sabotage?"

Benny asked her name and then answered the question. "Jennifer, you may have heard that recently the Iranian uranium enrichment centrifuges were attacked by a computer virus. All of their centrifuges spun out of control and destroyed themselves. It is thought that the Israelis or our own CIA may have been involved."

"So are you saying if our Government did it, it's okay?"

"No Jennifer, in the example I gave, the act was illegal. If the CIA did it, and if they were caught doing it, they could be prosecuted in the World Court."

A student named James asked, "Have you ever caught people doing any serious hacking?"

"As a matter of fact James, we just arrested a group of hackers who were trying to steal personal identity information from a major credit card company."

"Well, how did you catch them?"

Benny smiled and waited until he had everyone's undivided attention, about two seconds. With a straightforward expression on his face he said, "It happened around Christmas time, so we worked very closely with Santa, and he had Rudolph lead us to the bad guys."

Everyone groaned at Benny's bad humor, but they also understood that Benny was not about to divulge secret FBI methods.

Benny then moved on to his real agenda. I'm here today to ask for your help. The FBI is trying to ascertain at what age people become sophisticated enough to write software programs for various types of malware; viruses like: worms, Trojan horses, ransomware, keyloggers, rootkits, or spyware. Are you guys familiar with these terms?"

The entire group nodded in agreement. They were now following Benny closely, because he was obviously respecting their knowledge of the subject.

"Now I'm not saying any of you write computer viruses, but if you were going to write a virus program, what code would you write it in?"

The group now felt uneasy, thinking that to answer the question would implicate the person in hacking. Benny watched their body language carefully. He noticed that they all seemed to be looking at the boy with the thick glasses and ponytail. He looked at the others and then said, "If I was going to do such a thing, I'd use Assembly Language and I'd write it for a 32- bit microprocessor."

Benny asked the boy's name. "Why is that Jason?"

"Well, Assemble Language is a low level programing language. It would take me longer to program than C++, but it would be more efficient, and I'd write it for the 32- bit microprocessor so it would work on the Windows operating systems. That way it would affect the most people."

Benny asked, "How many of you know Assembly Language?"

To his surprise, all but one person raised their hand. "I'm really impressed. Do you think most kids your age interested in computer science would understand Assembly Language?"

Again, Jason answered the question. "I have some friends, who go to other high schools, and none of them program in Assemble Language; it's just too difficult to learn."

Mr. Webster interjected, "I like to teach my students Assembly Language. It helps them understand how computers really work. It prepares them for top-paying jobs in the computer science field."

"You're right Mr. Webster. software companies are always searching for people who can write software code in Assembly Language."

Mr. Webster beamed with pride. A real expert had confirmed his approach to teaching. Benny then turned back to the kids. You guys have been really helpful. I'm going to have to rethink the FBI's strategy for dealing with cybercrime. We're going to have to reach out to kids your age and convince them not to get into the hacking game. If caught they could find themselves in prison, and screw up their lives. Do you guys have any questions that I can answer?"

What followed was a lively discussion of Benny telling stories of how criminals engaged in cyber-crimes were eventually caught. The teenagers listened to every word. For them, it was the equivalent of Michael Jordan talking to the high school basketball team.

At the end of the meeting Mr. Webster thanked Benny for his presentation. After the kids left the conference room, Benny stayed and talked to Webster. "Don, I'd like to get on your two computers to see if there are any virus programs."

Webster said, "I thought there may have been an ulterior motive for your request to speak to my kids."

"We think it's possible that one of the kids here today might have written a very sophisticated virus that's involved in a case we're working on."

"Well as you might have guessed Jason Harken is the whiz-kid in the group. I can't teach him anything anymore. I hope he's not involved because he's the smartest kid I've ever taught and I'd hate to see his life destroyed."

Benny, with Don Webster's help, checked out both computer stations. Nothing could be found to indicate any virus software programs had been developed on either of the two computers. Of course, the programs could have been written on another computer or stored on an external flash drive. A smart programmer would never store their programs within a computer.

Benny thanked Webster for his help and congratulated him on his skills as a teacher. He then left and called Dan from his car.

"Well Dan, here's the story. I couldn't believe how much these kids know about cybercrime. One of the kids in particular knew enough to be able to write the kind of software embedded on Moran's and Bussard's computers. The FBI is going to have to rethink the age at which hackers begin to do their thing."

"Was Bobby Fowler there?"

"No, I didn't see him."

"He was probably at football practice. There're a couple of more weeks until the end of their season. Thanks for your help Benny. I'm going to go home and think about this. We're not getting anywhere. I'm almost ready to go on to other cases."

"Give it some time Dan. You'll think of something; you always do. Let me know if I can help with anything else."

"Will do my friend."

Dan left work and headed home. He needed to talk to Sally. She had this ability to cut through the fog, and create clarity, and talking through the case with her would force him to rethink things.

Chapter 37

Indian Summer had definitely departed for warmer climates and the first Alaskan Clipper of the season had brought winter to the city of Chicago with a sudden vengeance. Dan decided to turn on their gas fireplace while waiting for Sally to return from work. He sat on his favorite easy-chair, the one he had purchased when he was still a bachelor, and sipped a cold beer. He heard Sally's car pull up the driveway, and he handed her a Diet Coke as she walked in the backdoor.

She kissed her favorite detective and asked, "What's up?"

"Change out of your scrubs. I'm taking my favorite mommy out for dinner."

"Great, I have a taste for barbeque; Let's go to the Rib Shack."

Sally changed clothes and fifteen minutes later they were sitting at a corner table at the Rib Shack. Sally felt hungry; she was now eating for two. She ordered a full slab, and Dan decided on the half slab and half brisket combo-plate. "So, where are you on the Fowler case?"

"I thought you'd never ask."

"I knew there must be a reason for an evening out on the town."

Dan summarized where they were on the case, and added, "Today, Benny visited the Oak Park and River Forest High School Computer Club. It seems some of the people in the group have enough knowledge to be able to write the sophisticated software virus we've seen on Bussard's and Moran's computers. So right now the best scenario I can muster is Bobby Fowler either wrote the virus or had one of his friends in the club help him write it. It seems like all of the computer hacking was done from the Chicago Library. I contacted the library, and it turns out anyone can access their computers, and there's no need to log in. So the bottom line is we have no idea who used the library's computer."

Sally thought for a moment and then spoke, "I think the key question is who wrote the virus. There're two possibilities. First, the killer actually wrote the program; or second, the killer got someone to write it for him. Let's consider the two possibilities. It would be pretty risky for the killer to get someone to help write the software. I remember the messages. The helper would know he was assisting in a murder. That would take one pretty good friend, don't you think?"

"I see your point. So you're thinking the killer is also an expert software programmer?"

"Yep, that's exactly what I'm thinking."

"But all the usual suspects have alibis."

"So maybe one of the suspects hired a contract killer to do both jobs, and went through the whole virus thing to pin the killing on the Raccoon. I know that's getting pretty complex, but it's a possibility, right?"

"It's possible. If I follow your theory, then what I really need to do is look at all the suspects again and see if any have the computer programming skills necessary to write these virus programs. If that fails to turn up any leads, then I need to search contract killers who have programing skills, but I have no clue how to do that."

Dan began to think through the process. He decided to check out the Fowler house first thing in the morning. One thing was clear, if you're an expert software programmer, then you would have a lot of computer science books around, and certainly a book on Assembly Language. Even if the killer was smart enough to hide all the computer science books, there would still be some evidence to suggest the person was an expert.

Dan called Benny and reviewed his latest line of thinking. Benny agreed with Dan's approach, and he agreed to accompany Dan in the search of the Fowler house first thing in the morning.

The arrival of the dinners put a quick end to the phone call. Dan watched Sally devour her ribs, sucking the meat off each rib, leaving nothing but bare bone as she worked her way down the full slab. Between ribs, Dan asked, "So we still don't have a name for Baby Lawson. How soon before we know if it's a boy or girl?"

"We'll have a pretty good idea in another five weeks. I'm kind of liking Debbie for a girl and William for a boy. What do you think?"

"I like Debbie, but I had a cousin named Bill, and he was a real dork. William won't work for me; I'll always be thinking about my relative."

"Then how about Jeffrey?"

"I like that; Jeff Lawson, that sounds good."

As he lay in bed that night, Dan couldn't clear his mind of the Fowler case. There just weren't enough leads, and for some reason, he kept coming back to Bobby Fowler. He wished their lawyer would have allowed Bobby to take the lie detector test, but he understood the risk. Innocent people could easily fail the test.

Chapter 38

Benny arrived with a dozen Dunkin Donuts. Of course, two were missing. Benny said it was the price of delivery. Sally grabbed two of the chocolate with sprinkles before the others could choose. She was eating for two after all. It was Sally's day off. She said she was going to solve the Fowler case all by herself. That was her job for the day.

"Solve the case and I'll take you to Gibson's for dinner."

"Since when can you afford Gibson's?"

"Believe me, you solve the case, you've earned the biggest steak they've got."

"What should I do once I've figured it out?"

"Come down to the precinct and I'll make the reservation."

Benny and Dan left to check out the computer science capabilities of the Fowler household. Mildred was manning the fort, and she still looked terrible. She said Bill was at the armory, Bobby was at school, and Janet was at work. Dan said, "Mildred, is it all right if we look around the house. I left the Search Warrant back at the office. I'll go get it if you insist."

"No, go ahead; I've already seen the Search Warrant, so I know you have the right to search the house. I'm fixing some coffee. Do you guys want any?"

After receiving two yes votes, she left for the kitchen. Dan and Benny decided to check out the library first. Benny studied the bookshelf. One computer science book, Windows for Dummies; not the kind of books you would expect to see on a software programmer's bookshelf. Benny sat down at Bill's desk and turned on his computer. He spent time searching his programs and files, and quickly concluded that Bill might have been many things, but an expert in computer science was certainly not one of them.

Mildred called from the kitchen, "The coffee's ready whenever you want some."

Dan called back, "Thanks Mildred, we'll be right there."

Mildred filled three coffee mugs, and the three sat down at the kitchen table. Mildred had a box of Kleenex on the table and was blowing her nose and filling up a wastebasket next to her chair. "I've got some kind of bug. It started yesterday and it's getting worse.

Dan said, "Sally's home all day today. Stop by and let her check you out. She's got a large supply of prescription drugs in her closet. I'm sure she's got something to make you feel better."

"Thanks for the offer Dan; I just might do that if it doesn't get any better."

Dan asked, "Does Bill know when he's going to have to go back to Afghanistan?"

"That's why he's at the armory today. He's meeting with Colonel Kincade. Are you getting any closer to finding out who did this?"

"I really can't talk about it Mildred."

"I understand Dan, but you need to find the person who did this. A terrible cloud of guilt is hanging over our family, and it's not going to go away until you catch the person."

"We're doing everything we can Mildred. We'll find the guilty person; I promise."

Mildred began to cry. She stood up embarrassed by her outburst and walked over to the stove. Dan walked over to where she was standing and held her in his arms until she recovered.

"Come on Benny, we've got some other things to check out."

Dan and Benny left Mildred in the kitchen and headed up to the second floor. Janet's computer revealed nothing of great interest; in fact, it appeared she didn't use the computer for anything other than checking her Facebook account.

On the other hand, Bobby's room offered up several tidbits of information. His bookshelf contained two books on software programming; one for Basic, another for C++; but nothing on Assembly Language software. His computer contained many games. Benny reviewed Bobby's history file and found nothing of interest except a number of porn sites that Benny identified as first-class.

Benny reflected on everything he had seen. "Bobby knows a lot about software programming, but there's nothing to indicate he knows anything about Assembly Language. It's a big jump to go from Basic and C++ to Assembly Language."

"And I'm assuming Bill and Janet are far behind Bobby?"

"That's putting it mildly. I think none of them could have come even close to the level of sophistication of these viruses."

After thanking Mildred for the coffee, Benny and Dan left the Fowler house. They both stopped for bathroom breaks at Dan's house. Sally questioned whether they had found anything. Dan said, "Nothing, it seems none of them were capable of writing that software code."

Sally smiled and said, "I'm going to solve your case today Detective Dan. Just you wait and see, I'll have it all figured out in a couple of hours."

Dan wished her luck as he and Benny left. Benny headed back to FBI Headquarters and Dan, after thinking about the case, decided to try to find Ray Bussard's girlfriend.

Chapter 39

Sally sat back in the library and reflected on the case. What could she add to the analysis of the case that hadn't already been covered by Dan. She walked to the kitchen and poured herself a fresh cup of coffee. Back by the computer, she began thinking about the case from 30,000 feet. That was Dan's problem; he couldn't see the forest for the trees. First she made a list of all the possible suspects, and she left nobody off the list.

The list was exhaustive: Bill Fowler, Bobby Fowler, Janet Bussard, Mildred Fowler, Ray Bussard, the Raccoon, Mary Ellen Harper, Favio Benzinni, Harriet Bales, and even the Fowler's housekeeper. She had forgotten the names of the other tennis pros, so she just added Pro #1, Pro #2, and Pro #3 to the long list. She even added Gloria Fowler to the list; maybe she had tried to commit suicide. Sally tried to recall all of the names that had come up over the course of the investigation. By the time the long list was complete, there were thirteen possible suspects.

She drew up a matrix, the names down the left side of a page and the key requirements along the top. The requirements were few: ability to write sophisticated viruses or very close friends with someone who could write the software code, a questionable alibi, a plausible motive for killing Gloria Fowler, and a plausible motive for killing Ray Bussard. Then of course, the person would have to be very accurate with a gun or have hired a contract killer to shoot Bussard.

She sat back in her chair, sipped her coffee, and contemplated the list of suspects and requirements. She felt certain the killer probably wrote the virus software code.

She began putting checkmarks beneath the requirements. If the person had a motive, they got a yes in their box. If they had an alibi, they got another yes; the same for the ability to write software code, and the skills needed to shoot a person right between the eyes with a single shot.

After she had completed her analysis, several things became apparent. First Gloria Fowler couldn't have killed Ray Bussard. Brilliant deductive reasoning, don't you think? Second, there was no evidence concerning the housekeeper who cleaned the Fowler house once each week. Third, Mildred Fowler was apparently the forgotten person.

Sally thought long and hard about Bobby's Nana. Okay, she was over eighty years old, but certainly had the motive. Dan had never questioned her whereabouts at the time of the two murders. She just seemed like everybody's perfect grandmother, such a nice thoughtful caring person. She couldn't possibly have done it, but then again she might have done it; who could say for sure. She would have to be skilled in writing computer code and an expert shot. Was that even possible for Mildred Fowler?

Sally didn't really know anything about Mildred. Playing a hunch, she turned on the computer and

Googled Mildred Fowler. Surprisingly, the search came back with a number of hits. As Sally anticipated, there were several Mildred Fowlers, but several of the hits were for a Mildred Fowler who lived in Chicago and had an interesting history. This person had been the Chief Technology Officer of a company called AntiVirus, a Chicago based company that sold anti-virus software for computers.

Sally Googled AntiVirus. It was no longer in existence, having been bought out by Norton ten years earlier. Sally, however, was able to find biographical resumes of the officers of the company before it had been sold. Mildred Fowler's biography was very interesting. The woman had received over forty U.S. patents for antivirus software, and most importantly, the year she graduated college indicated she was probably in her eighties, just the right age.

Sally whistled through her teeth. Mildred had the perfect motive. Bobby had talked to Mildred about his encounter with Gloria Fowler and Ray Bussard. After hearing that story, she must have despised the woman and her ex-husband. She had access to the Fowler house and probably knew Gloria Fowler's schedule. She could have been waiting in Bobby's room, and when Gloria walked down the hall, Mildred could have given her the fatal push down the stairs.

She circled Mildred's name on her matrix, and the more she thought about Mildred, the more she became convinced Mildred was indeed the person who had killed Gloria. She made it look like an accident, then killed Ray Bussard for having been involved in the sexual act, and also framed the Raccoon with the elaborate computer virus scheme.

Sally decided to drive down to Dan's precinct with the matrix and prove to him that Mildred was the killer. She decided to take a quick shower before leaving for Dan's office.

Chapter 40

Mildred Fowler felt miserable. She had a temperature of 102 degrees, and every muscle in her body ached. She decided to take Dan up on his offer and have Sally check her out.

Mildred knocked on the backdoor and after nobody answered, she opened the door and peeked inside. She called out Sally's name but there was no answer. Her car was still in the driveway, so she must be home. Mildred walked throughout the first floor calling her name. When she entered the library, she noticed the matrix with her name circled and the computer's screensaver showing birds flying through the air.

She hit the computer's escape key and a website with her name and personal history appeared on the screen. Mildred immediately knew Sally had discovered the truth. She quietly backed away from the study and left through the backdoor.

She thought of the various options and quickly concluded she would have to immediately go into hiding, but first she had to find out whether Dan knew what Sally had found out. She walked into her son's closet and found his loaded gun. The pistol had a full clip. She liked Sally, but survivability trumps likeability everytime. Otherwise, it would only be a matter of time before Dan arrested her.

With renewed resolve and a fully loaded pistol, she walked back into the Lawson's house and once again began searching for Sally. As she approached the front stairs, she could hear the faint sound of water running through the drainpipes. Sally must be taking a shower. Mildred walked slowly up the stairs and stood in the upstairs hallway listening to the sound of the shower.

Sally finally turned off the water, dried off with a large bath towel, and wrapped it around her body while she blow-dried her hair. She dressed in a pair of black slacks and a white top, and as she turned to leave her bedroom, she encountered Mildred Fowler and a nine-millimeter Glock pointed directly at the center of her body. The look of determination on Mildred Fowler's face convinced Sally that Mildred meant business. "Mildred, what's this all about?"

"Oh, I think you know exactly what this is all about. I was looking for you because I'm sick with a fever, and Dan said you would be home all day. I knocked on the backdoor, but you didn't answer, so I went looking for you. I couldn't find you, and you didn't answer my calls, but I did notice something in your library. You know what I did, don't you?"

"Yes Mildred, I thought you did it, and now I'm sure of it. I was going to drive down to the precinct and show Dan my analysis. Why Mildred, why?"

"Are you kidding me; you know why. After Bobby told me what he saw, I began following her. She was screwing anyone with two legs, and it didn't matter if they were men or women. She was doing drugs, cocaine, and even crack. What an example for her daughter and stepson. She caught my son at a weak time in his life. I told him she was no-good when he said he was going to marry her, but he wouldn't listen to me. I did it for them, Bill and Bobby. They'll live a much better life with her out of the way."

"But why kill Ray and try to frame Freddie Moran?"

"Ray Bussard was a good for nothing. And as for Freddie Moran, he murdered my friend's husband. Then he murdered a key witness, and the D.A. had to drop the case. I wanted him to pay for his crimes. He got off too easy; only a few years for illegal possession of a firearm. What a joke that was."

"So what now Mildred? What are you going to do?"

"From the very beginning, I knew I might be caught, but I have a plan. Your finding out about me alters it a bit, but only slightly."

Mildred handed Sally two plastic Cable Ties and told her to tie one around her wrist, and then use the other to make plastic handcuffs. With the gun pointed at her chest, Sally had no option but to do as Mildred asked. Mildred then tightened both ties and followed Sally down the stairs. They stopped in the library and Mildred pulled Sally's analysis sheet from the pad, stuffed it in her pocket, and turned off the computer.

With the gun pressed into Sally's back, the two left the house and headed for Mildred's car parked in the driveway. Mildred opened the trunk, and after looking around for any witnesses, ordered Sally to climb in. Sally could barely squeeze into the confined space. She lay in the fetal position as Mildred closed the trunk.

Mildred lay the gun next to her in the front seat, started the car, and left the Fowler house for what would be the last time. She looked at the home of her son and grandson in the rearview mirror and began to cry. She had done all of this for them, and she hoped they would understand.

Mildred had a plan, one she had been preparing for weeks. With Sally, having figured out what had happened, the plan needed only a minor modification. There was no need to hurt Sally; she liked Sally. She only needed to keep Sally from contacting Dan for a day. That would give her the time she needed to escape.

Mildred lived on the Near Westside in a small house on a quiet residential street. She pulled into the alley behind her home and used her remote to open the garage door. After pulling into the garage, she closed the garage door and opened the trunk.

Sally, stiff from the cramped ride, stretched her muscles after climbing out of the trunk. "Welcome to my house Sally. I wish you could have seen it under more favorable conditions."

"What are you going to do with me?"

"Nothing other than make sure you can't talk to Dan in the next twenty-four hours."

Mildred led Sally at gunpoint from the attached garage into her house. The single story ranch, a product of the mid-fifties building boom, was small, but very tastefully decorated. "Barry and I loved this house, and when he died, I couldn't bear to move; just too many memories."

After passing through the kitchen, they turned into a hallway and entered the master bedroom. Mildred ordered Sally to lie down on the four-poster bed, and Sally, with her hands still tied together, followed her instructions. Mildred used two more large Cable Ties to secure Sally's ankles to the two posts at the foot of the bed. With Sally's feet now immobilized, Mildred cut Sally's plastic handcuffs with a scissor and then retied her arms to the posts at the head of the bed with new cable ties. Sally was now secured to the bed, spread-eagled and unable to move.

Sally watched in silence as Mildred prepared her escape. She rolled a suitcase, apparently already packed, from the closet into the bedroom. She then pulled some things from the bathroom and added them to a side pocket of the luggage. "Dan's going to find you. I guarantee it."

Mildred ignored Sally's taunt, and when she had finished packing, she handed Sally an envelope. "I was going to mail this to Bill, but you might as well give it to him."

Mildred looked terrible. She had been crying and her tears had caused her mascara to run down both cheeks. "I have a maid who comes in once a week. She'll be here tomorrow. She starts at seven o'clock. She'll be able to cut you free, and by then, I'll be long-gone."

Mildred opened the top drawer of her dresser and pulled out a thick wad of money. She had obviously been planning her escape for a long time. "I know you think I'm a bad woman, but I had to do it for Bill and Bobby."

"Bullshit Mildred; you killed two people and tried to pin it on a third person. There were other ways. You didn't have to kill them."

"It was the only way I could be sure, and they all got what they deserved."

With that, Mildred left Sally, and after several minutes of her puttering around the rest of the house, Sally heard the door to the garage open and then shut with a loud sense of finality.

Sally tested the plastic ties, but they would not give an inch. She lay back, resigned to the fact that she would have to wait in bed for the maid's arrival.

Chapter 41

Finding Ray Bussard's girlfriend proved easier than Dan expected. It turned out she was the receptionist at the BMW dealer. Betty Wolinski, a.k.a. Lassie the howler, asked someone to staff the phones and led Dan to a small private conference room. She had already heard about Ray's death. "Ms. Wolinski, I'm sorry to bother you, but as the investigating officer, I need to ask you a few questions about the night Mr. Bussard was killed."

Betty Wolinski, whose eyes were swollen and red from countless hours of grief, nodded in understanding. "When was the last time you saw Mr. Bussard?"

"The day he was killed. He was at work, and we said goodbye to each other."

"Do you know what he was doing that evening?"

"He had gotten a call from someone who wanted to hire him for a sales manager position at a new dealership. He was all excited and was going to meet the person at nine o'clock that night."

"Do you know the name of the person he was going to meet?"

"No, he never said, but he told me they were going to meet at a restaurant over on Clark Street."

"Was that the last time you talked to him?"

"He called me around ten o'clock. He said the person was a no-show, and he was on the way home."

"Did Ray ever talk to you about his ex-wife?"

"No, I guess it was our little understanding; we never talked about her."

"Do you know if Ray knew anyone with computer programing skills?"

Betty Wolinski thought for a moment and then answered no. Dan sensed he wasn't going to get any more useful information from Ray's girlfriend. He thanked her for her time, handed her his business card with the usual request, and headed back to the precinct.

Sitting at his desk, he thought about Betty Wolinski's words. The killer almost certainly had set up the meeting with Ray in order to get him to return to his garage at around ten.

He looked at his watch and decided to call it a day. He headed home realizing he was getting nowhere on the weirdest case he had ever worked on.

Chapter 42

Dan called out to Sally after walking in the backdoor, but there was no answer. He searched the house and still no Sally. He found her purse in the kitchen and inside the purse were Sally's pager and cellphone. She would never go anywhere without her pager. She always said it was her responsibility as the head of the department to always be on call. So where was she? Her car was still in the driveway; she had to be nearby.

Dan walked next-door, and found Bobby eating a snack in the kitchen. "Bobby, have you seen Sally anywhere?"

"Nope, and I haven't seen Nana either. Nana's car's gone, so maybe they went someplace together."

Dan walked back to his house and decided to check the basement, but still no Sally. Where could she be? He found her day-planner in her purse and looked at her schedule for the day. It was completely empty because it was her day off. Surprised, but not yet worried, Dan opened the fridge and pulled out a beer. He turned on the kitchen TV and sat down at the table. He became more concerned the longer he waited; it was just so unlike Sally to do something like this. An hour later, Dan was really getting worried. He called the Emergency Room and spoke with the second shift crew. Nobody had seen her or knew where she might have gone.

He looked at his watch. It was now eight o'clock. This was not good. He called Jimmy. His best friend answered the phone and listened to Dan. He never questioned Dan's concern. He knew Sally very well, and once Dan said her pager was still in her purse, he knew Sally was in trouble. "I'll be right over, and I'll get Alice to come over too."

Dan hung up and began searching the house again. There must be some clue, something to provide a hint as to what happened. A damp towel lay on the back of Sally's make-up chair in front of her vanity. Sally had a habit of putting her towel there after a shower, but she always hung it on the towel rack after she dressed. He finally noticed something in the upstairs hallway, a small black button. Not the kind of thing you would pay much attention to, but nonetheless a clue. He found a second button at the bottom of the stairs and a third by the backdoor. Sally was leaving a trail; he was sure of it. After ten minutes of searching, he found another button on the Fowler's driveway just as Jimmy pulled up to the house. Alice screeched to a stop one minute later.

Dan explained the trail of black buttons. Jimmy said, "So you think someone took her against her will, and she left a trail to help guide us."

"That's exactly what I think."

Alice asked, "What was Sally doing today?"

"She had a day off, and she said she was going to solve the Fowler case. I laughed, but knowing Sally, she probably spent some time thinking about the two murders. Alice asked, "If she was going to work on the case, where would she have worked?"

"I'm not sure; probably the library."

Jimmy said, "Let's look there."

The three friends headed for the library. Dan saw the pad of paper sitting next to the computer. He picked it up and noticed the slight depressions from what had been written on the page above it. Taking a pencil from the desk drawer, he began shading in the writing to make it more legible. Every word wasn't visible, but it looked like a list of all of the people who could possibly be suspects. Dan could see that one name had been circled. After examining it closely, he finally recognized Mildred's name.

Meanwhile, Alice had turned the computer back on and had pulled up the internet history file. She clicked on the most recent URL address and Mildred Fowler's biography came up as part of the company's website where she had worked. Dan looked at the website and screamed, "What a dumb shit I've been. Mildred Fowler, of course Mildred Fowler, I never even suspected a loving grandmother could possibly have killed two people, but it's clear, she had the computer skills to write the software programs and definitely a motive. My God, she was the Chief Technical Officer of a software company."

Jimmy said, "So Mildred discovers Sally figured out she killed Gloria Fowler and Ray Bussard. What would she do?"

Dan didn't like thinking about the consequences. She could have killed Sally, but there wasn't a body in the house and that would be the logical place to kill her if that's what Mildred had in mind. Dan said, "She probably panics. She might have come to see Sally. She said she had a cold, and I suggested she have Sally check her out. So maybe she sees this paper with her name on it and suddenly goes berserk. Then she takes Sally away in her car. That's why Sally left the trail of buttons going out to the driveway, and Bobby said Mildred's car was missing."

Dan suddenly thought of the gun in Bill Fowler's closet. Leaving his friends, he ran next door, and rang the back doorbell. As soon as Bobby opened the door, Dan sprinted past him and up the stairs to Bill's closet. He reached up onto the top shelf searching for the gun but found nothing. He asked Bobby, who had been following him, "Where's the gun?"

Bobby answered, "I don't know; Dad always keeps it there. He must have taken it down."

"Where's Mildred? I've got to find Mildred."

"I already told you, I don't know. She wasn't here when I got home from school."

Jimmy and Alice finally caught up with Dan. Dan turned to them and said, "Bill Fowler keeps a gun up here, but it's missing. Jimmy and Alice didn't need to ask the significance of the missing gun. Mildred had taken it and had taken Sally at gunpoint.

Dan thought about where Mildred might have taken his wife. The encounter with Sally would have been unexpected. After initial confusion, she would probably want to escape, but she would need to get some things before she left town. "Bobby, where does Mildred live?"

"On the Near Westside just off Damen and Division."

"I need the address Bobby. What's the street address?"

"It should be in our address book."

He led the way down to the library and found the Fowler's address book in the top drawer of the desk. He thumbed through the pages until he found Nana's name. "Here it is. It's 1136 N. Hoyne Avenue."

Dan said, "Bobby, this is very important. Sally's life is in danger. If Mildred calls you, please find out where she is and call me on my cellphone."

Dan, Jimmy, and Alice left in Jimmy's car, hoping they would find Sally alive and safe in Mildred's house.

Chapter 43

Sally had to pee. She had been lying spread-eagled on the bed for over four hours. Dan would be home by now, and with any luck would have found her trail of buttons. She hoped he would conclude that Mildred had taken her in her car. He probably wouldn't know why, but would have found her purse and pager, and he knew she would never go anywhere without her pager. At least she hoped that was the case.

The thing is, once you know you have to pee, you can't stop thinking about it. She had two choices; either figure out how to free herself from the bed, or pee in her pants. The later didn't seem overly attractive, and the thought of lying in her own urine for another ten hours forced her to concentrate on an escape plan.

She looked at the bedposts again hoping to find a solution to her dilemma. Each post was made from a four-inch square piece of oak. The upper section of each had been carefully turned on a lathe with intricate details cut into each spindle. Sally clearly wasn't strong enough to break the base of the post, but if she could somehow gain some mechanical advantage, she might just be able to fracture the solid oak post at a weak spot.

She studied the upper shape of the posts. If she could somehow raise her hands or feet to a point four feet above the bed, then she just might be able to get enough leverage to break the post near where the ball shapes of the tapered post began. She tried moving her feet up the bedpost, but the plastic ties were just too tight. The same was true for her left hand. She tried her right hand with slightly better results.

By moving her right hand back and forth, she was able to raise the plastic tie about two inches. Exhausted, she rested and groaned as the plastic tie slipped back down the post. She needed to move the plastic tie all the way up to the first carved ball before she could rest, a total of almost twelve inches.

After resting a few minutes, she tried again. This time the plastic tie moved more easily up the post. She had figured out just how to move her hand in order to move the tie. Slowly, she advanced the tie up the post until she reached the first carved ball. The tie easily slipped into the first groove, and Sally rested, trying to regain her strength. Her brain, sending work faster signals from her full bladder, quickly forced an end to the brief rest period.

Once again she attacked the plastic tie, moving it steadily up the carved section of the bedpost. It took another ten minutes of hard work before she had advanced the tie up to the tenth carved ball. She rested again and then, with all her might, began pulling her right hand toward her. With the increased mechanical advantage, the bedpost began to bend toward her, but not enough to fracture the wood. She moved the plastic tie further up the bedpost until she couldn't lift her hand any higher. If the wooden post wouldn't break now, then she would have to try something else.

She rested a moment and then pulled her hand toward her with all the effort she could muster. A cracking sound sprang from the wood as the post began to break, and with a final pull of her hand toward her body, the bedpost broke free and fell to the bed.

Sally laughed. She had done it. Exhausted, she rested on the bed and tried to figure out her next move. She still couldn't move her feet or left hand; the plastic ties were just too tight. She looked at the plastic tie on her right hand. The plastic teeth of the tie passed through the tip and could only be moved in one direction. If she could just find something to wedge into the lock mechanism, she just might be able to free the plastic teeth from the tie. Reaching into her hair, and pulled out a bobby pin. She examined the tip. If the plastic end could be removed, the metal tip might just be small enough to fit inside the plastic tie. She placed the bobby pin in her mouth and bit into the plastic tip. It suddenly broke free from the bobby pin. Sally spit out the small piece of plastic and looked again at the plastic tie on her left hand.

Rolling over onto her left side, she dragged the broken bedpost close to her left hand and then forced the end of the bobby pin into the plastic lock mechanism on her left hand. Holding the bobby pin in place, she tried to open the plastic tie. She could hear an audible clicking sound as the ratchet teeth began to slide past the plastic lock. With a final pull the plastic tie broke free. Using the same technique, she removed the plastic tie and broken bedpost from her right hand. With both hands free, she sat up quickly and freed both legs with the same bobby pin.

Free at last, Sally ran to the master bathroom, pulled down her pants, plopped down on the toilet, and suddenly lost control of her bladder. Freedom felt good, but not as good as being able to empty her bladder.

Suddenly, Sally heard the front doorbell ring. She screamed at the top of her voice, but the bedroom door was closed and there was no response from outside. The doorbell rang again, and Sally screamed again with even more urgency. If she got up to answer the door, she'd leave a trail of urine on the way to the door. The doorbell rang a third time and then Sally saw a familiar face staring at her through the bedroom window.

Alice broke the bedroom window using the butt end of her gun, and slipped through the broken windowpane. "Well Dr. Lawson, fancy meeting you in a place like this. I guess I've caught you at an inopportune time."

"Cut out the theatrics; I've got to pee so bad, I think my bladder's going to burst. Please close the door. I'll be out in a few minutes."

Sally finally emerged from the bathroom with a smile on her face amidst the laughs of her best friends. Dan hugged her but couldn't stop laughing at Alice's explanation of how she had found Sally. Even Sally had to laugh.

Sally finally said, "Mildred killed them. She was the CTO of a computer software company."

Dan answered, "We know, we found the information on our computer. See what happens when you get involved. You're just too smart for your own good."

"If I hadn't discovered the truth, you'd still be trying to find the killer."

"Well that's true, but you could have gotten killed. If she killed two people, she might just as well have killed a third."

"She wasn't going to kill me. She just panicked and wanted to keep me from talking to you until she left town. By the way, she left this letter for Bill."

Sally took the letter from the bed and handed it to Dan. He opened the letter and read it aloud.

"Dearest Billy: By now you know what I have done. I couldn't allow Gloria's sexual indiscretions to continue any longer. Having sex with her ex-husband in my son's bed was the last straw, and the fact that Bobby witnessed it was just too much to bear.

"I will not see you again, and I regret not being able to say a final goodbye to you and Bobby. My estate is in order and you should contact my attorney, Lester Montrose, who handles all my legal matters. I have given you Power of Attorney.

"Please do not search for me. I have gone someplace where you will never find me. Please forgive me for what I have done. Now I must make peace with God. I will be praying for both of you."

Love,

Nana.

The letter had a sobering effect on them all. Her rational for the murders was flawed, but in Mildred's mind, it was done out of love.

Dan asked Sally, "Do you have any idea where she went?"

"No, but she was already prepared. Her bags were packed, and I saw her with a full wad of money. She had already written the letter to Bill."

Jimmy said, "Well, we can add kidnapping to charges of murder and cybercrime. She's one hell of a Nana, don't you think?"

Dan Called Joey and after explaining what happened, had Joey issue an All-Points Bulletin. Dan put his arms around Jimmy and Alice and thanked them for their help. I'll call you in the morning if I need any help."

While Dan escorted Alice and Jimmy to their cars, Sally walked around Mildred's house. She entered the small library and stared at the walnut paneled wall. It was filled with patent certificates from the United States Patent Office. Sally read some of the certificates: Method for Elimination of Trojan Horse Viruses, Method for Malware Cleansing, and Unique Software for the Prevention of Virus Attacks. In all, there were thirty-six patents. Hanging on another wall was a series of awards for marksmanship issued by several gun clubs, including the NRA.

Sally shouted to Dan as he entered the front door. "I'm in the library. Come here, you've got to see this."

"Well this explains a lot," Dan said after studying the awards. "How could I have been so stupid?"

"Don't blame yourself. Who would have thought Mildred could have done this?"

"How's the baby?"

"Fine, but I think I want to go home now."

"As soon as I drop you off at the house, I need to talk to Bill and give him this letter."

The ride back to their house was made in silence. Sally was thinking of her close encounter with Mildred's gun, and Dan was already thinking about where Mildred would have gone.

Chapter 44

Janet answered the door. Dan asked if Bill was home and Janet's call brought him into the kitchen. "Bill, we need to talk in private."

Bill led the way into his library and closed the door. The two sat face to face across Bill's desk. "I'm not sure where to start Bill. A couple of hours ago, Mildred confronted Sally at gunpoint and tied her hands together with plastic handcuffs. She then made her get into the trunk of her car and drove to her house, where she tied Sally down to her bed."

Bill interrupted, "What, are you crazy? Why would Mildred ever do something like that?"

"Let me continue. Sally discovered Mildred was involved in the deaths of Gloria and Ray, and out of fear, she probably panicked and decided to abduct Sally in order to give her time to escape. We found Sally at Mildred's house. Mildred left this letter for you. Sally says it had already been written, and Mildred asked her to give it to you."

Dan handed over the letter and waited for Bill to read the short message. Bill held his head in his hands and began to sob. "My God Mom, what have you done? It's my fault Dan; she warned me not to marry Gloria. She was right, and I should have divorced her long ago. If I had only done what needed to be done, then she wouldn't have done this. It's all my fault."

Tears dripped down Bill's face staining the leather inlaid desktop. Dan couldn't imagine what Bill was going through. This was worse than finding out your mother had just died. In Bill's mind, this was all about failing as a son, a crime far worse than murder. "Why didn't she just talk to me? Why did she have to do this?"

"I don't know Bill, but the only way to answer those questions is to find Mildred. Do you have any idea where she might have gone? Sally said she had already packed her bags, so it seems she had been planning to leave for some time."

Bill thought about Dan's question. Why should he help capture his own mother? If she wanted to escape, shouldn't he help her? Then he considered his mother's mental state. For her to have murdered Gloria and Ray, she must be mentally ill. Surely, a jury would never convict her of murder. She obviously was not in control of her actions. Most importantly, he wanted to see his mother again and beg her for forgiveness. He owed her that much. "She has a few friends in the city from when Dad was still alive. If she left town, I have no idea where she might have gone. She never went on vacations or anything like that since Dad died. Her sister is dead, she has no other relatives. Dan, you've got to find her. I need to ask her to forgive me for all of this."

"I can understand how you feel, but Mildred did this Bill, not you. You can't blame yourself for all of this."

"Easy for you to say, but she's not your mother. You just don't understand."

Dan thought Bill was probably right. He seemed to be telling him the truth when he said he had no idea of where she might have gone. It was time for him to leave and begin the search for Mildred Fowler. "Bill, I'm going back to Mildred's house now to look for clues as to where she might have gone. Do you have a key to her house?"

Bill opened up one of the desk drawers and removed a key chain with Nana written on a small white label. Dan took the keys and said, "Bill, nobody will be allowed in her house until Forensics have finished their work. I'll let you know when they're done."

Dan left the Fowler's house and found Sally sitting down at the kitchen table eating a deli-sandwich. "How you doing?"

"Pretty good. You know for some reason I knew Mildred would never shoot me. I think she just panicked, and she couldn't decide what to do with me. She just wanted to buy herself some extra time in order to escape."

"Well if you're okay, I'm going to go back to Mildred's house and try to figure out where she went."

As Dan drove cross-town, he called Joey at his home. "Joey, sorry to bother you, but I'm going to need a Search Warrant so we can look at Mildred Fowler's bank account, phone records, and her credit cards."

"I'll have it for you first thing in the morning. I got her license plate number and the car's description from the Motor Vehicle Department and the APB went out about an hour ago."

"Great, if you need to reach me in the next few hours, I'll be at her house."

A light misty rain had changed into snow, and the white flakes were melting as soon as they hit the car's windshield. It was definitely a prelude to the season's first major snowfall.

Chapter 45

Where to start? Dan thought about where Mildred might have gone. He knew the rules for this type of search. First check with friends and relatives. People who want to hide usually go someplace they are familiar with. They need to know the lay of the land, or they need a friend, a very good friend, someone who is willing to help them remain hidden. Bill had already said Mildred's relatives were all dead, so he needed to focus on her friends, or places she had visited in the past, or other cities where she had lived.

Dan sat down in Mildred's library. Looking up at all of the patents, Dan added old business colleagues to his list of her potential friends. He turned his attention to the contents of Mildred's desk. One by one, he examined each file. Mildred, unlike Dan, didn't save any bills from previous years, so it didn't take very long to go through all of her records. Nothing, just the usual bills from a variety of vendors and other suppliers. Dan entered Mildred's telephone menu and punched in history. He copied the phone numbers into his notebook, a little over fifty numbers before the history ran out. The FAX machine history revealed another eleven numbers in memory. Dan turned on Mildred's computer but was stopped when the computer asked for a password. He'd have to wait for Forensics to gain access to her computer.

Dan now began a search of Mildred's bookshelf. There were numerous computer science textbooks, including a few books on Assembly Language. Mildred was an avid reader, but almost everything was of a technical nature. On one of the shelves, he found a diploma from MIT. She had received a PhD Degree in Computer Science. It was dated 1959. Dan was surprised Computer Science even existed as a major back then.

Things were definitely missing from Mildred's bookshelf. Dan could see the dusty outline of pictures and other objects recently removed. Mildred had evidently been planning her departure for a very long time and wanted to ensure no clues to her whereabouts were left lying around.

The thing about trying to remain hidden for a long time is everyone is hooked on paying by check, credit card, or online. Each of those payment methods can be traced, and that eventually leads to the person. You just can't pay all your bills with cash. How do you pay for car insurance with cash? It just can't be done. So, given enough time, Dan knew Mildred Fowler would surface somewhere. It was only a matter of time.

Dan looked at his watch. Enough for today. He wanted to get home and check on Sally. She said she was okay, but a person couldn't go through that ordeal and not be affected. He'd pick up on the case again tomorrow morning after the Search Warrant had been approved.

On the way home, he thought about Mildred Fowler. What gets into a person's head that results in a logical conclusion to kill another person? Is it a person's sick mind just not understanding the gravity of the action, or is the decision grounded in the belief that it is the best, or perhaps only, solution to a complex problem?

Sally was lying down on a couch in the family room watching the Discovery Channel. She had a smile on her face and reached up to him as he approached. "I think I could feel the baby move. It wasn't a lot of movement, but it moved; I just know it."

Dan knelt down on the carpet and put his ear to Sally's tummy. "Can he talk yet? I can't hear him."

"How do you know it's a boy?"

"I don't, it's my default sex. Otherwise, it gets too complicated. If I'd just say baby, it sounds too vague. If you want, from now on I'll call the baby a girl."

"I've got a good idea; you keep on calling the baby a boy, and I'll call the baby a girl."

Dan sealed Sally's offer with a kiss and then sat down next to her and received some first-class snuggling as a reward. They talked about Mildred and where she might have gone, but no good leads resulted from their discussion.

Chapter 46

Judge Jones signed the Search Warrant early in the morning. Joey said it was one of the easier petitions he had ever brought to the judge. While Julie and her Forensics team searched Mildred's house, Dan began the process of retrieving Mildred's bank and credit card accounts.

One thing about working in Chicago, the large banks headquartered in the Loop occupied some very large impressive buildings. The Northern Trust certainly fell into that category. Located on LaSalle Street, it was in the center of the Financial District. Of course the problem with big banks was they were big, and finding the right person to talk to presented a problem. After the receptionist tried two different people, she finally hit pay dirt, and fifteen minutes later Dan was talking to Ralph Jackson in the legal department. After passing muster with the bank's lawyers, Ralph contacted Missy Granger who was able to pull up Mildred's account information from her computer. She printed out the last years' worth of information, including photocopies of all of the checks Mildred had written. She handed him her business card and told Dan to call her directly if he needed further assistance.

Dan found a Starbucks off the building's lobby, ordered a double espresso and a cinnamon scone, and sat down near the window overlooking Monroe Street. Several things immediately popped out. First, Mildred had withdrawn $20,000 from her savings account over the last three months, five thousand dollars at a time, all in cash. Second, Mildred didn't write many checks, only forty-seven in the last year. As Dan already knew, she was an online person.

He began studying the photocopies of each check, separating the ones to individuals from the ones to legitimate companies. At the end of this process, there were only nine checks written to individuals. Three were to Bill, Bobby, and Janet, and the words gift appeared in the notation section at the bottom of those checks. Two were made out to Jacob Bauer with a notation of painting. That left four checks. Three of those were written to Lisa Biggins, each for exactly ten dollars, and the fourth was made out to Karen Cutter for $678.43. Dan looked at the back of those checks and determined they had all been cashed in Chicago.

Back at the precinct, he asked Shirley to locate both Karen Cutter and Lisa Biggins. She had been gathering Mildred's credit card information and handed Dan a years' worth of Mildred's Visa and American Express account information in exchange for her new assignment.

Using a yellow Hi Liter Dan prepared to mark any suspicious transactions on the Visa account. There was only one problem; there were none; lots of food stores, restaurants, and the occasional purchase at some store, but not much else. Mildred evidently led a very low-key lifestyle.

Mildred used her American Express card almost exclusively at Costco. All the transactions had been out of their Lincoln Park location. Dan knew the location well. He and Sally were Costco members and shopped at the same location all the time.

Dan noticed Shirley standing behind him looking over his shoulder. She was smiling, a good sign. She handed him a notepad with the telephone numbers and addresses of the two people she had been researching. She said, "Both these women live near Mildred Fowler's house."

"Good work Shirley; when are you going to have her telephone account information?"

"They promised in a few hours. I'll let you know as soon as it comes in."

Dan dialed the first number. "Ms. Biggins, this is Detective Dan Lawson with the Chicago Police Department. I'm calling to see if you know a Mildred Fowler?"

"Sure Detective, she's in our book club."

"I notice that she has written three checks to you in the last few months. What were they for?"

"That's our monthly dues for the club. Sometimes she pays by check. What's this all about?"

"Mildred Fowler is missing, and we think she may have left the city. Do you have any idea where she might have gone?"

"No, we're not really good friends; she just happens to be a member of our club."

So much for that possible lead. Dan then called the second person. "Ms. Cutter, this is Detective Dan Lawson with the Chicago Police Department. Do you know a Mildred Fowler?"

"Sure Detective; she's a good friend of mine."

"I notice she wrote a check to you three months ago for $678.43. What was that for?"

"We split the cost of the Chicago Symphony Orchestra series. That was for her half of the tickets."

"Ms. Fowler is missing, and we believe she left the city. Do you have any idea where she might have gone?"

"Why would she leave town? I thought she was taking care of her son and grandson."

"She was, and then she unexpectedly left town. That's why we're looking for her."

"Well, I have no idea of where she might have gone. She certainly never mentioned anything to me about leaving."

Dan gave her his phone number and asked her to call him immediately if she heard anything. Two dead-ends. It was time to pay a visit to Costco and check the records of some of Mildred's recent purchases.

The Costco just off Clybourn Avenue was no different than most others. Fortunately, Dan knew the manager due to working on other cases in which he needed to check on a suspect's purchases. Luckily, Gail Jameson was in her office talking to one of her colleagues. She looked up and gave Dan the here we go again rolling of her eyes. The person she was talking to, sensing the need for a private conversation, left the office.

"Well, if it isn't my favorite detective. I know, you're here to buy the new car sitting out front; right?"

Dan smiled, "I'm a little short on cash right now, and I don't think there's enough money in your ATM."

Dan handed her his Search Warrant and said, "I'd appreciate it if you could look up the purchase history of Mildred Fowler."

"Okay, you know the drill. I have to FAX this to the legal eagles. Go get a soda and I'll find you as soon as they give their approval."

"I'll do better than that. I think I'll stock up on some things."

Dan called Sally, and after a short discussion, he grabbed a cart and started walking the aisles. He chose a rotisserie chicken and fresh asparagus for their dinner, and picked up a large package of toilet paper and some laundry detergent. After paying for the items, he bought a Diet Coke, sat down at the small food court, and waited for Gail.

She arrived a few minutes later and led him back to her office. "It's been approved. How far back do you want me to go?"

"One year will be just fine for right now."

Gail entered her computer and looked up the name Mildred Fowler in the Costco database. Four Mildred Fowlers popped up, but only one in Chicago. Ten minutes later, Dan left the store with a printout listing all of Mildred's purchases during the last year.

As he unlocked his car, Shirley called him on his cellphone. "The telephone records for her landline and cellphone just came in. What do you want me to do with them?"

"Great Shirley, why don't you e-mail them to me? I'll look them over tonight. I'm heading home now."

"Will do. How's Sally doing?"

"She says she can feel the baby move."

"That's great news. Are you going to find out the sex?"

"Yep, but Sally says not for another couple of weeks."

"Okay, give her my best."

Traffic was the usual mess for the late afternoon rush hour, plenty of time for Dan to study the Costco printouts while waiting for lights to turn green. Mildred certainly wasn't a dedicated Costco shopper. She visited the store about once a month, and then only stocked up on the usual necessities. In fact, there was only one interesting line item in the purchase history; six prepaid cellphones were bought one month ago.

The conclusion to be drawn was obvious; Mildred Fowler's future telephone calls would not be traceable. She was doing everything in her power to remain hidden, and that was not a good thing for Dan.

Chapter 47

Sally had already printed the e-mail sent by Shirley, thirty-six pages of telephone numbers, fifty-five numbers on each page, a little under 2000 total numbers to analyze. She smiled her I'm smarter than you are smile. "See if you can find it; I'll bet you can't."

With Sally reheating the rotisserie chicken, and preparing the asparagus in the microwave, Dan sat back at his desk. Sally was always better at separating the wheat from the chaff, and she could do it without any help from a computer. Dan, on the other hand, used a computer sorting program given to him by Benny a few years ago. First, he used the computer program to filter out Bill's landline and cellphone numbers. That eliminated about eighty numbers; big deal.

He then entered a computer command to list all numbers outside of the Chicago area codes. The electrons whirled around the computer, and out popped one-hundred-twenty-six numbers, almost a manageable number of calls.

He looked at the list, and using another software program on the FBI website, found the names and addresses associated with each of the long distance numbers.

Sally interrupted his analysis and called him to dinner. "Find it yet?"

"Not yet, but I've only just begun."

"It took me nine minutes and eleven seconds; I timed it."

"Well if it isn't goody-two-shoes trying to show me how smart she is."

Sally stuck out her tongue, her usual way of ending a losing argument. During dinner Dan reviewed all of the day's activities. Other than the prepaid cellphones from Costco, nothing of significance had risen to the surface.

After dinner, Dan went back to his analysis of the telephone numbers. It took him a little over one hour to find what Sally had found. "I think I've got it," he yelled from the library. Sally showed up a few seconds later with a smirk on her face. "It's the call to the MIT administration office in Boston, right?"

"Yes, the same school where Mildred received her doctorate degree."

Dan said, "I remember the date on her diploma, and you know what, this year would have been the fiftieth anniversary. Maybe she called about the reunion? Maybe she has some old friends from her schooldays. It's certainly worth exploring, and I'll do it first thing tomorrow."

"So what's next?"

"I want to talk to Bill. I want to find out everything I can about Mildred's life. That information might help me figure out where she went."

Dan called Bill and they agreed to meet immediately. They sat once again in Bill's library. Dan had seen the look on Bill's face many times before. It came when another family member was guilty of a terrible act: a feeling of personal guilt, denial even in the face of overwhelming facts, bitterness, and most importantly a lack of understanding of how the person could possibly have acted so out of character.

Bill felt all these things, but the feelings were also tempered by the fact that he knew he was close to killing Gloria himself. Fortunately, fate had intervened, and she was dead before he could act.

"Have you been able to locate her," Bill asked. "I need to talk to her and apologize."

"Nothing yet. The reason I wanted to talk to you is that I need your help. I want you to tell me everything you can remember about Mildred; from the time she was a child until present day. I think someone is helping her, and it must be a friend.

Bill hesitated, not from wanting to hide anything, but rather from not knowing where to start. "Mom grew up on a farm in Pennsylvania, just southwest of Happy Valley. She was the youngest of two sisters. Her mother died from cancer when she was about five years old, so her father raised her all by himself. Her sister died in an accident when she was in high school."

"Did she have any good friends when she was little?"

"I don't know. She lived on a farm so except for school she probably didn't see many people."

"Then she went to college?"

"Yes, Penn State on a scholarship. She got a B.S. degree in Electrical Engineering. I remember she said she was the only woman in her graduating class. I guess there weren't many women in the sciences back then. Then she went on to MIT and got her PhD degree in Computer Science."

"Did she have friends at Penn State or MIT?"

"I don't know. She never mentioned anyone."

"Did she belong to any sororities?"

"Are you kidding? She was dirt-poor. She always had jobs at school, even with the scholarships, she could barely make ends meet."

"I'm assuming her father's dead."

"He died back in 1993, and she sold the farm as soon as he died."

"Do you know the address of the farm?"

"No, but you should be able to look it up in state records. Her father's name was Melvin Blume. She and her father never got along. We never visited the place."

"What happened then?"

"After getting her PhD, she began working for a company in Boston. I think the name was Cambridge Consultants, and then IBM bought them up. That's when she met Barry. He was working in IBM's Boston Office. They married a couple years later and were eventually transferred to the Chicago Office.

"She finally left IBM to take a job with Antivirus as their CTO, and she remained there until she retired about, let me think, about fifteen years ago."

"It sounds like she didn't have many friends."

"She didn't; nowadays they'd call her introverted; back then she was always described as shy. But the thing is, she had a fantastic mind. She had a reputation for writing the most efficient software code imaginable. That was her claim to fame, and she got a lot of patents in her name, all of them involved in fighting computer viruses."

"Do you know whether she attended a class reunion at MIT this year?"

"She did. She said she wanted to visit the school again. It came as a surprise to all of us, because she never talked about college."

"What else can you tell me?"

Bill thought for a few moments, biting his lower lip as he thought about his missing mother. I can't think of anything. I still can't believe she would do this. She was such a private person."

"Tell me about her ability to shoot."

"Her dad taught her all about guns. She's an expert shot. She belongs to some gun club on the Northside, and she always wins first place in their annual competition."

Dan had been busy taking notes. He closed his notebook and looked up at Bill. "Are they going to send you back?"

"No, I talked to Colonel Kincade. He said he's going to have me serve out the remainder of my tour at the armory helping out with logistics. That way, I'll still be able to take care of Bobby and Janet."

"How are the kids reacting to all of this?"

"Bobby can't believe it, and he thinks it's his fault because he talked to her. Janet, even though she hated her father, now hates Mom. The whole thing is just terrible for the entire family."

Bill seemed to be reflecting on the whole thing. "We've got to find a way to get closure on this, and I'm not sure how that's going to happen."

Dan started to leave and Bill put his arm on Dan's shoulder. "Thanks for not saying anything about my being AWOL."

"Bill, you've leveled with me when we first talked. I don't know what my talking to the army would have accomplished. Let me know if Sally or I can help in any way."

Dan left the Fowler house feeling terrible about what Bill and his family must be going through, but at least he did have a few clues to follow up on concerning Mildred. He reviewed Bill's biography with Sally. "Now, I've got to follow up on the MIT reunion, the gun club, her old company, and the place where she grew up, but first I need to check in with Forensics at Mildred's house."

Chapter 48

Dan stopped at a nearby Dunkin Donuts and bought two coffees, and a small box of donut holes; always keep the Forensics people happy. Unfortunately, when he arrived Julie had bad news. She had absolutely nothing to report. "The lady's definitely smart. Here's what she did. She had several external hard drives; there's absolutely nothing on her "C" drive. It's like a brand-new computer just out of the box."

"So where does that leave us?"

"I've gone through everything except the garage. I even checked the attic to see if anything was hidden up there. One thing's for sure, she's a well-organized and detailed person."

"So let's do the garage together. Sometimes a detail type person can't help but save things, and there's no place like a garage to store all the old mementos."

Mildred Fowler's garage was no different than any other person who had lived in the same place for forty years, with one exception. Everything was neat and very well organized. The two-and-one – half car garage had held only one car. That left a lot of room for storage, and Mildred was a saver, so the whole place was filled up. Mildred had a unique storage system. Everything was boxed up by year. Some years had more than one box, but there were a total of over sixty boxes, each labeled with the year the box was created.

After looking around for a few minutes, Dan, with Julie's help, opened the most recently filled box. Last year's memories. Dan set up a card table and two deck chairs and dumped the contents of the first box on the table. "What are we looking for?" Julie asked.

"I'm not sure, but hopefully something might give us a hint as to where Mildred is hiding."

A large manila envelope labeled taxes was at the top of the pile and Dan immediately opened it and looked at the return. It was a TurboTax packet. Dan used the same software program. He studied each page, looking for clues. "Mildred must have done pretty well in business. In retirement, her annual adjusted gross income was a little less than two-hundred-thousand dollars, and then there was another $67,000 in tax free municipal bonds. Clearly, Mildred was a saver.

Dan continued to study the return while Julie sifted through a pile of paid bills and other receipts. Mildred's return was pretty simple, no unusual sources of income, just her investments and Social Security. There were only a few receipts for some donated clothing and other charitable contributions. Other than that, there was nothing of interest.

Dan reached into the pile and found a checkbook transaction register, and from what he could remember, the checks written were in agreement with the bank's records he had already seen.

He pulled a day-planner from the remaining items and began thumbing through the pages.

There were weekly appointments at the beauty shop, monthly meetings of the book club, several babysitting nights to help Bill while he and Gloria were busy at company functions, and every other week, appointments for nails and a pedicure, and from time to time key birthdays to remember. Bill, Bobby and Janet were there, and then there was a new name that Dan had never seen before, Carla. Her birthday was on August 26th.

Dan quickly opened up the box from the previous year and found the same type of day-planner. There it was again, August 26th, Carla's birthday. He opened ten more years of boxes and in every instance, Carla's birthday was highlighted on August 26th.

Dan took out his cellphone and called Bill. "Bill, I'm looking at Mildred's day-planners for the last ten years, and in every instance she has made a note of a birthday for a Woman named Carla on the 26th of August. Do you know who Carla is?"

"I've never heard of her before. Mildred never mentioned her, but then again, she never talked about any of her friends. She was just a very private person."

Julie asked, "What are you thinking?"

"I'm thinking this Carla is a very special person in Mildred's mind. The kind of person she might seek help from in her time of need. I'm thinking I need to find out who this Carla is."

Dan again took out his cellphone and called the MIT telephone number Mildred had called earlier this year. "Good morning, Massachusetts Institute of Technology Administration Office, Betty Hill speaking; how may I help you?"

"Good morning Ms. Hill. This is Detective Dan Lawson with the Chicago Police Department. I would like to talk to someone who would be able to tell me about a fifty-year reunion that was held this year."

"Oh, that would be our Alumni Reunion Desk. Let me connect you."

There was a thirty second pause and then, "Alumni Reunion Desk, may I help you?"

"Yes you can. This is Detective Dan Lawson with the Chicago Police Department. I would like to find out whether a person by the name of Mildred Fowler attended a fiftieth reunion at the school two years ago."

"I'm sorry Detective Lawson, but we consider that information private."

"I have a Search Warrant allowing me to have access to that information."

"You'll have to FAX it to my attention and then I'll have to get the Legal Department to approve your request."

Dan took down the FAX number and asked the woman to call him as soon as the lawyers approved his request. He stressed the urgency of the matter, and the woman assured him that as soon as she received the Search Warrant, she would walk down the hall and get the lawyers to look at it.

Dan used Mildred's FAX machine to send a copy of the Search Warrant and a second page showing his badge and credentials to the MIT office. True to her word, Ms. Lakeland called back within ten minutes. Detective Lawson, I have Reggie Billings with me. He's in our legal department. I've got you on speakerphone."

"Good morning Detective Lawson, how may we help you?"

"I'm trying to find out whether a Mildred Fowler attended a reunion this year. She would have received a PhD in Computer Science. It would have been her fiftieth reunion."

"Ms. Lakeland is searching her computer records right now."

"Yes Detective Lawson, I do have a record of a Mildred Fowler attending the class reunion."

"Do you have a record of someone with the first name of Carla also attending that meeting?"

"Reggie Billings interrupted, "I'm sorry Detective, but your Search Warrant is specific to Mildred Fowler. That information is private."

"Well how about this Mr. Billings? You tell me whether someone with the first name of Carla attended the reunion, and if there is someone with that name who attended, then I'll get another Search Warrant that directs you to disclose the full name and address of that person."

Billings thought about the request for a few seconds and agreed. Meanwhile, Ms. Lakeland must have already been searching the database because she immediately responded. "I have no record of anyone with the first name of Carla attending the reunion."

Dan thanked them both for their help and told them he might get back to them with a few more questions.

Julie had been listening to the conversation. "You guys are all the same. You have no idea how women think. Women need to establish and maintain relationships. Men only care about exchanging information. Carla was such a good friend that she marked the date in her calendar. Women buy birthday presents for those types of friends. Men just say happy birthday, if that."

"You've got a point. So you think she bought Carla a present every year, and assuming Carla doesn't live in Chicago, she must have mailed it to her."

"Or, just as likely, she bought the gift at a store that would ship it for her. That would be a lot easier."

Dan didn't like his manly logic being upstaged by a person who knew better than he what Mildred would have done, but Julie was right. He fished the bank account information out of his car and identified the information on Mildred's Visa and American Express accounts.

Dan considered the August 26th birthday and decided to first look at the statements for July and August. A few seconds later he was studying the August Visa statement. To get to Carla on time, the purchase was probably made the first half of August or perhaps even as early as July. August had two purchases identified for the first two weeks of the month; something bought at Macys' for $56.23 on August sixth, and a second transaction at Nordstrom's on August seventh for $46.78. Julie, who was looking over Dan's shoulder said, "Both those places would send the package to Carla, and they would both probably still have a record of the shipment in their computer."

"Which one should I try first?"

"Mildred impresses me as a Macy's kind of girl, and the chances are better of Carla having a Macy's near her than a Nordstrom's if she wanted to exchange the gift. I'd try Macys' first."

As Dan left on a new mission he thanked Julie who said, "I'll be done here today, so if you need the key, I'll put it in the evidence locker; and by the way, if I'm right, you'll owe me big-time, I mean really big-time."

Rather than do this over the phone Dan decided to talk to the people at the Michigan Avenue store where the August purchase was made. He parked his car on East Pearson Street in an illegal spot, but placed a Chicago Police Department placard on his car's dashboard to indicate to any cop on the beat that he was on official city business. He found Customer Service on the seventh floor, showed his badge to the person staffing the counter, and asked to speak to the manager.

A stylish woman in her mid-fifties led him back to her small office. She reacted like this wasn't the first time she had dealt with the Chicago Police Department. She examined his Search Warrant, badge and credentials and looked in her internal telephone directory on her computer. She then picked up her phone and talked to another person. "What specific information do you need Detective Lawson?"

"On August sixth of this year, a woman named Mildred Fowler made a purchase in the amount of $56.23. I need to know if the item she bought was shipped to someone, and if it was, what was the address of that person?"

The lady, her nametag read Jane Timmons, relayed the information to the person she was talking to and after waiting a few seconds, ended the conversation.

"Let's see what we can dig up from our database. She first looked at the information printed on the Visa bill and identified a Macy's transaction number. She then looked up the transaction number and said, "The purchase was a porcelain bowl. Now let me check if it was shipped."

She entered another database and keyed in the transaction number. She waited a few seconds for a new screen to appear on her monitor. "You're in luck detective, the bowl was sent out by UPS to Carla Thomas, 5217 Potts Lane, Tyrone, Pennsylvania, 16686."

"Well, thank you Ms. Timmons; you have no idea how helpful you've been."

Jane Timmons smiled, clearly happy with her own performance, "Well thank you Detective Lawson; I always enjoy a little detective work."

Dan left Macy's and headed home. On the way, he called Julie. "Hey Julie I struck pay dirt. Carla Thomas, that's her name and she lives someplace in Pennsylvania called Tyrone."

"So what do I get as my reward?"

"What do you want?"

"Lunch at Ralph Lauren on Chicago Avenue."

"You've got it babe, just as soon as I can wrap up this case."

Dan knew this was the break he needed. He was certain; somehow, someway, Carla Thomas was helping her good friend Mildred Fowler. The afternoon traffic was heavy, but Dan hardly noticed. He called his boss. "Joey, I think I just got the break we need on the Fowler case. I think Fowler is hiding out with a friend of hers by the name of Carla Thomas."

"So what do you want to do?"

"I think I need to visit Carla Thomas. After I talk to her, she's probably going to contact Mildred Fowler, and I want to be right there when that happens."

"Okay let me know if you need any support. By the way, how's Sally doing?"

"She says she can feel the baby moving."

"It's a great feeling, isn't it? I remember our first baby. It's so clinically understandable but so mysterious. It really is the miracle of life."

"My God Joey, coming from you that's a really profound philosophical statement."

"I take it back Dan; if you need any help, don't call me."

Both laughed, and then Dan hung up.

Dan finally arrived home and immediately located Carla Thomas's house on Potts Lane. Google Maps showed the location at the end of a country road about twenty-five miles southwest of Happy Valley, Pennsylvania, near where Mildred Fowler grew up. It was rural America, that was for sure; about a nine hour drive. If he left early the next morning, he could make Tyrone by late afternoon, and then search for Mildred the next day. Barring unforeseen circumstances, it would be a three day trip.

He heard Sally's car pull into the driveway, and his number one mother-to-be walked in the backdoor. "I think I found her."

"Not even a hello Honey, or I hope you had a nice day, but you cut right to the chase. Why do I love you so much?"

"You know it's for the great sex, or have you been lying to me all these years?"

"Well, there is that. I guess I'll keep you after all. So what did you find out?"

Dan filled her in on his entire day, and when he announced his upcoming trip to Tyrone, Sally wanted in. Her reasoning, as usual, made perfect sense. They could share the driving, and most importantly, she had the next three days off.

Dan knew the determination in Sally's voice and trying to convince her to stay home wasn't worth the time or energy. "Okay, but we're going to take your car. The radio said there's going to be a heavy snowfall tonight and tomorrow, and I'm betting that means the lake effect will probably be dumping even more snow east of Lake Michigan. Your SUV may come in handy."

Chapter 49

For once, the weather prognosticators had been right. Overnight, the first major snowfall of the year had blanketed the city, and a northwesterly wind kept driving cold moist air over the entire Midwest. Dan and Sally agreed to leave early to beat the usual rush-hour traffic and that meant five o'clock. Luckily, the snowplows had been working all night and the expressways were clear.

The smart people were staying off the road. The pre-dawn traffic remained light as their gold Jeep Grand Cherokee left Chicago and headed east along Interstate #80. Dan took the first shift and Sally slept until they had entered Indiana. Dan found a Cracker Barrel restaurant just outside of Portage and woke Sally as they pulled up near the entrance.

Fortunately, both were dressed for the six inches of snow they found in the partially plowed parking lot. Sally wore a black ski jacket and a pair of Ugg boots, while Dan sported a navy parka and a pair of outdated yellow Moonboots. Snowflakes dancing around the mercury-vapor lights in the parking lot might have created a pretty picture if they had been looking from the safety of their living room window. Unfortunately, they both saw potential delays and other problems, not the beauty of nature. The short walk from the parking lot, along with the smell of cooked bacon, wetted their appetites. Dan ordered his usual manly three eggs over, sausage, hash brown potatoes, and rye toast. Sally, eating for two, ordered the blueberry pancakes with bacon.

While waiting for their orders, they both made trips to the bathroom. Hot coffees were waiting for them when they returned to the table. "So what are you going to do if she's not there?"

"I don't know, but somehow I know when we find Carla Thomas, we'll also find Mildred Fowler.

As they packed down the calories, they watched the Weather Channel on the large TV overlooking their table. The weather guy was talking about up to fourteen inches of snow along Interstate #80. Dan looked out the nearby window in the early light. The falling snow was heavier now. The lake effect was certainly going to make their drive miserable. The nine hour trip would likely turn into twelve.

Armed with large coffees to go, they headed back onto the highway with Sally taking her turn at the wheel. Two hours later, they had only reached Angola, and traffic had been reduced to a single lane. It was definitely a white-knuckle drive. They had settled in behind a snowplow that was cruising along at forty miles per hour, propelling snow up and over the side of the road. No point in passing because the road ahead of the plow would have been too treacherous.

Sally pulled off the road at a rest stop. Baby Lawson had decided Sally needed to pee every two hours. They stretched their tired muscles. The high-stress driving was taking its toll.

Dan took his turn at the wheel, and they were able to pick up speed until they fell into a caravan following the same snowplow they had left ten minutes earlier. By lunch they had made Youngstown where they stopped at a McDonalds. The snow seemed to be tapering off by the time they had finished their lunch. With Sally at the wheel they made good time until a three-car pile-up on the side of the road slowed them to a crawl.

Sally, ever the responsible doctor, pulled off the road and checked to see whether anyone was severely injured. The worst injury was a little boy who had hit his arm on the car's armrest as their car hit the ditch. Sally carefully examined the injury and pronounced him free of any broken bones, but insisted the parents get the arm x-rayed just to be sure there wasn't a stress fracture.

They switched drivers again just outside DuBois, Pennsylvania. At Clearfield, they turned south onto State Route #350. There was over twelve inches of new-fallen snow, but the road had been plowed and salted a couple hours earlier. With light traffic and barely acceptable road conditions, they pulled into Tyrone a little after four o'clock.

Dan had made reservations for them at the only hotel in town, a charming but older B&B. A man in his late sixties, probably the owner, checked them in and gave them the best room he had. Sally asked for a recommendation for dinner. "Well," he said, "given these conditions, I'm assuming you don't want to drive far. There's a fairly nice family type restaurant just down the road. You can easily walk there."

Dan asked, "An older friend of ours was born here. Her name's Mildred Fowler, but her maiden name is Blume. Do you recognize the name?"

"Sure do; the Blumes used to own the farm about five miles out of town. They sold it after Melvin died. I think that was back in 1993. So Mildred's still alive is she?"

"Yep, she's still alive. She asked us to take pictures of the old farm. Can you show us where it is on a map?"

"Sure can." He reached under the counter and took out a rather amateurish map of the town and surrounding area. "The Blume Farm, the Blume Farm. Ah yes, right over here."

He circled a section on the map and said, "You can't miss it. It's got a really tall bright red silo just alongside a green barn. Kind of ugly if you ask me, but Melvin, he always liked the colors."

"Did you know Mildred?"

"No, we went to the same school, but she graduated a good fifteen years before me. She must be in her eighties now."

"She is, I think she's eighty-two years old."

The man handed Dan the key to their room. "Up the stairs; second door on the right. Breakfast's from six till eight."

Up the stairs, two doors on the right. Unfortunately, the man forgot to say don't go in the broom closet. Fortunately, the key they were given, did fit the third door on the right. Unpacking their two small suitcases only took a few minutes. Dan turned on the Weather Channel. The Northeast was going to get dumped on tomorrow, but Pennsylvania was destined for a bright sunny day.

A terrible screeching sound echoed across the front of the B&B. Sally looked out the window as a snowplow began clearing the main street. One good thing about farm country, there was always enough heavy equipment around to keep the streets cleared during a snowstorm.

Neither Dan nor Sally had any desire to get back in the car to search for an upscale restaurant, so they dressed again for cold weather and headed outside to look for the B&B manager's recommendation. It didn't really take much thought to decide what direction to walk; countryside to the left, or a smattering of buildings along North Street to the right.

Walking on the sidewalk was impossible. If there were sidewalks, they were covered with snow. Instead, they stepped over a pile of snow along the road's edge and began walking in the street toward the cluster of buildings about a quarter-mile down the road. Sally pulled Dan's arm to stop him. "Look around Honey. It's like a Norman Rockwell painting."

Dan looked around, and Sally was right; fresh snow clinging to trees, almost twelve inches of snow piled high on roofs, and snowdrifts caused by the blizzard like winds earlier in the day. The wind had died down and now there was only an eerie silence eaten into by the scrapping sounds of the snowplow moving back and forth along the side streets.

Martha's Café was a reincarnated vision of an old-fashioned diner. The aroma of freshly baked bread greeted them as they opened the restaurant's door. They were the only customers in the café. A voice from the kitchen shouted, "Pick any seat, there're no reservations for tonight."

Sally picked out a table for four by the front window. An elderly lady, dressed in a 1950s era waitress uniform, pushed past the kitchen doors and handed them menus. Her nametag read Martha, and she asked if they wanted something to drink. "Do you have any wine by the glass?" Dan asked.

"I've got a nice Chardonnay."

Dan nodded and Sally asked for coffee. Martha left to get their drink orders filled, while Dan and Sally looked at the menu.

When Martha returned, she said, "My cook didn't show up today, so some of the items on the menu might take longer to prepare than others."

Sally asked, "What's easiest for you Martha?"

Martha's smile anticipated a simple order. "I fixed some beef-barley soup earlier today, and the meatloaf's fresh; it's real good, my mother's recipe."

Sally and Dan took the hint. Sally said, "I haven't had meatloaf in years. My best friend's mother used to make it when I was a little kid. I love meatloaf."

With the matter settled, both ordered the soup and meatloaf. Martha walked away to prepare the dinners. She returned a few minutes later with two large bowls of soup and a basket full of fresh-baked bread.

As Dan and Sally attacked the soup, Martha went back to the kitchen to prepare the main-course. Their journey through the snow during the day had worked up big appetites. Martha, spying through a small window in the kitchen door, arrived as they finished their soup to clear the dishes. Sally said, "The soup was wonderful Martha, really delicious."

"Thanks, it's one of my specialties," Martha answered as she walked back to the kitchen.

She returned a minute later and set down their dinners. Several platters were overflowing with large slices of meatloaf, mashed potatoes, and peas; all served family style and more than enough for two people.

Dan said, "Martha, we won't ever be able to finish all of this. Come sit down and join us. I don't think anyone else will be showing up tonight."

"You're right about that. I was surprised to see you. I was almost ready to close up for the night."

Martha brought over a plate and silverware service and sat down next to Sally. "Are you both just passing through, stranded by the snow?"

Dan answered, "We're staying at the B&B down the block. We're just here for the day, checking on some things. Someone we know, Mildred Fowler was born and raised here. Her maiden name was Blume. She asked us to take pictures of the old farm where she grew up. Do you know the name?"

"Sure, we were in the same class at school. I remember her real well. Nobody liked her. I take that back. She had one friend, Carla Thomas. I don't know what Carla saw in her, but they were the best of friends."

Sally asked, "What else can you tell us about Mildred?"

Martha's eyes seemed to be looking back in time as she debated on whether to say something. She finally smiled and said, "She had an older sister, Florence. Florence was very popular. One day, her father found Florence dead in the lake behind the Blume's barn. They couldn't prove it, but we all knew Mildred did it. I don't know what her medical problem was. We all just thought she was crazy. She was always real quiet and then, for the littlest thing, she'd suddenly go berserk."

"Did the police investigate?" Sally asked.

"We're a tightknit community here in Tyrone. It never even got to the County Sherriff's Office. The town elders wanted to keep it hush hush."

Not wanting to focus too much on Mildred, Dan asked, "Over the years you must have seen a lot of changes to the town. What's it been like?"

The young people go off to college and few ever return. The cars are newer and the TVs are bigger. The farming equipment is more expensive, so only the largest farms can survive. I guess the biggest change has been the sale of the smaller farms to the owners of the bigger farms. Now the bigger farmers consider themselves better than the others and the self-appointed leaders of the town."

Sally said, "That sounds like a lot of change Martha."

"I guess so, but I've talked enough. Where are you both from, and what do you do?"

Dan answered, "We're both from Chicago. Sally is a doctor and I work for the city."

This was Dan's usual response to questions about what he did. Working for the Chicago Police Department or FBI usually caused people to shut up, not a response Dan wanted from Martha.

"Oh, what kind of doctor are you?"

"I work in the Emergency Room at Northwestern Hospital."

"I'll bet you see a lot of bad things."

"I do Martha, but I also see a lot of good things. Most people come into the ER either close to death or feeling ill, and usually leave feeling a whole lot better."

"I like you both. I'm assuming you're both married; you act like it. Do you have any children?"

"Just one in the oven," Sally answered proudly, pointing to her stomach with a smile on her face.

"How do you know Mil?"

The front door suddenly opened and interrupted Martha in mid-sentence. It was the snowplow guy. The driver, dressed in a heavy grey snowsuit stomped the snow off his boots and greeted the owner. "Martha, I sure could use a big bowl of your soup and the Day's Special."

"You got it Greg. Sit right down and I'll get you the soup right away."

Greg looked at Dan and Sally. "How you do folks; stranded?"

Sally answered, "No, were just passing through. We're at the B&B for the night."

Unlike city folk, who made it a point to stay out of other people's business, small town culture assumed strangers in town were to be questioned about why they were here.

Martha had quickly moved back to the kitchen to serve Greg's soup and prepare his dinner. Good news for Dan, who didn't want to answer any questions about how they knew Mildred Fowler.

For dessert, Martha sold them both on the apple pie with a scoop of vanilla ice cream. Sally, who now ate for two, raced Dan to see who could finish first, and she easily won.

After saying goodbye to Martha and the snowplow guy, they walked slowly back to the B&B trying not to slip on the freshly salted street. The sky was crystal-clear. With the sun having set, the temperature was dropping quickly.

Back in their room, they both dressed for bed and Dan set the alarm on the nightstand for seven o'clock. After checking the Weather Channel and confirming tomorrow would be sunny and warmer, they found a movie on HBO they both could agree on and watched it to the end. After turning off the TV, they quickly fell asleep. It had been a long hard day.

Chapter 50

The buzzer on the alarm sounded its call to action. Dan reached over and tried pushing the top. The alarm continued until Dan stood up and realized he needed to flip a switch on the back of the device. He shook Sally from a deep sleep and both headed into the bathroom.

While Dan shaved, Sally showered. She screamed suddenly. "The hot water's gone."

"Gee, thanks Honey; just what I was looking forward to, a nice cold shower."

Dan turned on the shower while Sally dried off. The temperature was just fine. "Liar, liar, pants on fire."

Sally laughed. "I just couldn't resist."

The B&B manager's wife had prepared a fantastic breakfast: eggs to order, sausage, fresh-baked biscuits, escalloped potatoes with cheddar cheese, and fresh-squeezed orange juice.

They finally left the B&B and found their car covered in snow a little after nine o'clock. Dan removed most of the snow and the ice coating on the windshield with his snowbrush and ice-scrapper. With a little help from the defroster, the windshield was finally clean and the temperature in the car was almost acceptable.

Following the directions on their Magellan GPS navigation system, they finally turned onto Potts Road. The old deserted street had actually been plowed once, but four inches of snow still covered the road. Dan slowed the car to a crawl and engaged the four-wheel drive. Carla Thomas's house stood at the end of the old country road. The driveway leading up to the main house of the farm had not been cleared, and there was over a foot of snow on the quarter mile driveway leading up to the house. Dan said, "Let's see what this so-called off road vehicle can really do."

He turned onto the driveway and put the car into second gear. He started forward, trying to maintain a steady speed of ten miles per hour; fast enough he hoped to prevent the car from getting stuck, but not so fast as to fishtail off the road. Dan was surprised at how easily the jeep maneuvered in the deep snow.

He stopped the car near the main house. Dan was thankful for his old-fashioned Moonboots as they shuffled through the deep snowdrifts. With Sally standing next to him, he rang the doorbell and waited for Carla Thomas to answer the door. Immediately after ringing the bell a second time, a voice from inside shouted, "I'm coming, I'm coming!"

The door opened and a grey-haired woman close to sixty years old appeared in front of them. She was way too young to be Carla Thomas. Dan took out his FBI badge and credentials and introduced himself and Sally to the woman who studied everything carefully. "Sorry to bother you ma'am, but we'd like to speak to Carla Thomas."

"I'm sorry Special Agent Lawson, but that won't be possible."

"Why is that?"

"My mother now lives in a nursing home."

"Where's the home located ma'am?"

"It's in Tyrone. What's this all about?"

"I'm sorry, but we need to talk about that with your mother."

"If you don't tell me what this is all about, then I'm not going to give you the address."

Dan considered the stalemate. "Do you know a woman by the name of Mildred Fowler? Her maiden name is Blume."

"Yes I do. I saw her yesterday."

It was hard for Dan to suppress a smile. "We need to talk to your mother about her. Do you know where Mildred Fowler is?"

"No I don't. She and my mother talked in private. My mother might know where she is, but I'm warning you, she's suffering from dementia and may not be able to remember her conversation with Mildred."

The woman, whose name was Gail Fisher, was a widow trying to run the family farm, a tough job for one person, let alone a sixty year old woman. She thought her mother might be able to remember more easily if she was there, so the three set out in the jeep.

The nursing home was tucked away on a quiet residential street off the main road, just a half-mile from the B&B. All three signed the guest register. Dan, after showing his badge to the receptionist, studied the guest book. A woman by the name of Sophie Shultz had registered yesterday to visit Carla. "Gail, do you know this person?"

"Never heard of her before. She's certainly not from around here."

Carla's room was located in the Dementia Wing of the two-story building. A nurse sat at a desk just inside a locked door keeping watch to ensure none of the patients in her care accidentally left the area. As she buzzed them in, Gail greeted the woman.

Gail led them down the hall into a small residence near the end of the corridor. Carla Thomas sat in a rocking chair, dressed in a robe, watching the TV, some game show neither Dan nor Sally had ever seen before. Carla recognized her daughter who planted a loving kiss on the woman's cheek. "Hi mom, there're some people here to see you."

Carla Thomas looked at Dan and Sally with uncertainty and suspicion. Her eyes darted back and forth between her three visitors. She stared at her daughter and said, "Who are these people?"

"Mom, they want to talk to you about Mildred Blume. You remember Mildred Blume. She stopped by the house yesterday, and told me she was coming here to see you. Did she see you?"

Carla stared out the window, either trying to remember, or distracted by something. She looked out that window for a very long time. Gail whispered, "Patience."

Carla finally turned to face her daughter and said, "Yes, I know Mildred; she's my best friend.

We were playing in the schoolyard just a couple days ago."

Dan spoke softly in his least aggressive voice. "Ms. Thomas, do you remember where Mildred said she was going to hide?"

The question was almost too much for Carla Thomas to process. She looked out the window again, and finally turned her face toward Dan. "I'm sure it was our favorite place."

Dan continued, "And where would that be Carla?"

Carla again returned to the safety of the view out of her window. She took a very long time to answer, and she started to cry. "I don't remember. Gail, I can't remember."

Gail moved close to her mother. She knelt down and hugged her with all the love she could manage. "It's all right mom. It's not important."

Gail was crying as they left the nursing home. "It's getting worse. I couldn't cope with it anymore. I had to put her in the home."

Sally put her arms around Gail. "I'm a doctor Gail; I understand the stress you must have been under. You did the right thing."

Sally's words had a soothing effect. The tears stopped and Gail was composed once again. Sally said, "Gail, how about some lunch. How about Martha's café."

Gail didn't answer, but nodded in agreement. There were almost a dozen people at the café having lunch. Every worker in the area must have been there. Martha had a smile on her face. It was probably going to be a very profitable day at the café.

After ordering, Dan asked Gail, "Do you have any idea where Mildred and Carla used to play together?"

"I'm trying to remember. Mom and I haven't talked about it for many years. I think it might be near where Mildred lived."

Gail finally smiled. "There was an old cabin in the woods behind the Fowler Farm. I think it was an old hunting cabin built over one-hundred years ago. My mom said they used to play there. They thought of it as their own private dollhouse. They had fixed it up with old furniture."

"Can you show us where it might be located?"

I can point out the general area, but I've never seen it, so I don't know its exact location.

Dan took out the map given to him by the B&B manager. Sally had a pen in her purse and handed it to Gail. Gail looked at the map. She circled the area behind the Blume farm. "Someplace back in here. This whole area is a very old dense forest. It's no good for farming, just a good place to hunt. It would cost too much to clear. I think it's back in this area. I'm almost sure of it."

Dan looked at the map. The area circled was too large to cover on foot. "Gail, do you have access to the internet back at your home?"

"Sure, we're not that backward here. I've got the Dish Network."

"I'd like to search on Google Maps. Can we do that after lunch?"

"Sure, no problem."

Chapter 51

Gail led Dan and Sally to her library, a small but cozy room overlooking the back of the house and the hundreds of acres being farmed. Sally asked, "What do you grow here?"

"We rotate crops between corn and soybeans. We make more money on the corn these days with all the ethanol production, but the soybeans add nitrogen and other minerals back into the soil. Why do you want to see Mildred Fowler? Did she do something wrong?"

Dan answered, "I'm sorry Gail, but I really can't discuss that with you."

Dan entered Google Maps and located the Fowler Farm on the map. He then switched over to the satellite view and began looking for a cabin in the woods. Sally said, "At her age, she wouldn't have walked there, so there must be some type of old access road big enough for a car. She would have driven there before the big snowfall, so the road would have been passable."

The satellite showed a summer view of the forest. Dan located four access roads entering the woods from the northwest. They weren't roads so much as cleared trees in a straight line. Three roads spread out into the woods, but only one came even close to ending near the Blume Farm. Dan zoomed in and at the highest magnification, thought he could see the outline of a cabin's roof. He checked the scale at the bottom of the view. It looked like a mile distance between the Blume Farm and where the road ended. Dan zoomed out and switched back to the roadmap view. "We'll have to drive down to Tipton and then take this side road northeast. That should take us right up to this road leading to the cabin."

It sounded easy enough, but who knew what the quality of the road would be like. They made a pit stop before leaving Gail and headed back into Tyrone. At the main street, they turned right and headed toward Tipton, the next major town. They reached the small farming community and then took another five minutes to locate the correct side road. The road had been plowed once, but in the middle of the snowstorm. A good two inches of snow still covered the road.

Dan once again engaged the four-wheel drive and headed northeast. They were able to make an easy ten miles per hour. Luckily, they didn't have far to go, but Dan wondered how the jeep would perform in the heavy snow leading into the forest. They didn't have long to wait. Dan had estimated they would need to drive about six miles before they reached the road.

Right on cue, at the 5.7 mile mark, the road appeared on their right. Road was a misnomer. It was nothing more than a wide dirt trail cut into the forest. Dan put the car into second gear and slowly entered the snow covered dirt path. Luckily, the trail had been cut straight into the forest.

Creeping along at the pace of a fast walk, they moved along the tree-lined path. The tires made a crunching sound as they compressed the fresh-fallen snow. Two deer looked on in amazement, perhaps having never seen a car. Dan had estimated they had to travel almost four miles before they would reach the cabin. Ten minutes into the forest, they passed over a fallen tree and got stuck in the snow. Dan put the car in reverse, and with the tires fighting for traction, he stopped with the front tires on top of the tree blocking the road. He then put the car back into forward gear and accelerated past the place where they had been stuck.

Four miles along the snow-covered dirt road, they could see a clearing and the faint outline of a log cabin in the distance. Dan said, "She may have a gun. We need to walk the rest of the way."

Dan checked his gun and moved it to the pocket of his parka. They left the car and began the half-mile trek to the cabin. Halfway there, they saw a car covered in snow at the edge of the clearing. Dan didn't recognize the car, but with all the snow, who other than Mildred Fowler would be holed up in this God-forsaken spot.

They slowly approached the cabin. The bright sun reflecting off the pure-white snow was blinding, and their boots crunched in the snow with each step they took. The smell of a recent fire hung in the air, but no smoke from the cabin's chimney rose into the clear blue afternoon sky.

Dan quietly tested the front door to the cabin. There was no lock on the door. With Sally standing beside him, he quickly opened the door and stepped inside. He held his gun with both hands and rapidly scanned the room moving his gun with his eyes from left to right. At first, he didn't see anyone, but then he suddenly saw Mildred Fowler lying on a bed in the corner of the cabin.

At first, he thought she was asleep or dead, but as he approached the bed, he could see her eyes following him as he crossed the room. "Is that you Dan?"

"Yes Mildred. What's wrong?"

"Nothing Dan, I'm just getting ready to die."

Sally stepped in front of Dan and looked at Mildred lying motionless on the bed. She couldn't resist being the healing doctor. She removed the covers. Mildred looked very old and fragile. Her eyes were yellow with jaundice, and Sally could see swollen lymph nodes on both sides of Mildred's neck. She was clearly in great pain.

Sally asked, "Mildred, what's wrong with you?"

Mildred finally recognized Sally and smiled. "I have stage four pancreatic cancer Sally. I was diagnosed a few months ago. Dr. Butler said I had six months to live unless I agreed to have chemotherapy. I said no. I had something to accomplish, and then I wanted to die. It was time for me to say goodbye. That's why I came here. This cabin holds some special memories for me. My friend Carla and I spent time here when we were growing up. I wanted to die in this very special place."

The cabin suddenly felt very cold. Dan added some wood to the glowing embers in the fireplace and soon a fire was radiating heat into the small cabin. He moved closer to the bed. "Mildred, you almost let Bobby get arrested for the murder of Gloria. As a grandmother, how could you do that?"

Mildred Fowler looked up at Dan, tears flowing down her cheeks. "I never would have let that happen. I kept proof that I was the one who killed them both."

"What kind of proof would you have that would be so absolute?"

Mildred laughed a sickly laugh and then coughed. "Look in my suitcase," she whispered.

Dan opened the suitcase sitting on the wood floor, and immediately saw what Mildred meant. Sitting on top of her clothes was a pink flip-flop. The missing flip-flop. It matched the one found on Gloria Fowler's foot.

Dan took out his cellphone and called 911. He explained who he was and stressed the need for an ambulance to get here as soon as possible. At first he tried to describe the location of the access road and finally gave up. Instead, he gave them the GPS coordinates he had found on Google Maps.

Dan knew it would be a long time before help could arrive. Sally fought off the urge to take Mildred to a hospital in their car. The walk to the car would probably kill her.

Dan found a chair and moved it close to the bed. Mildred, you need to tell me the full story. What really happened?

"So, you want my deathbed confession is that it? Well why not. Here's what happened. I hated Gloria from the beginning, and when Bobby told me about what he had seen, I guess that pushed me over the edge. I told him to tell his father when Bill came back, but I had other plans. I decided right then and there that I was going to kill her and then Ray Bussard for good measure. I'm sure you can understand why."

Dan, not wanting to get in an argument with her, didn't answer her rhetorical question.

Mildred continued, "I had one more score to settle and that was with the Raccoon. He was like a national hero. People thought he only killed other bad guys, so he was helping society, but I knew different. He killed my friend's husband who was going to testify at his trial. I wanted to make him pay for that murder."

"Tell me about what happened on the day Gloria died?"

"I knew her schedule. It was always the same. After tennis, she went over to that motel across the street with that tennis pro. I followed her home, and I knew she would shower, she always did. The day before, I had modified the front doorbell so that I could activate it remotely. I snuck into the house while she was taking a shower and waited in Bobby's room."

"What time was that Mildred?"

"I think a little after noon. When she started drying her hair, I activated the doorbell. She walked down the hallway to answer the door, and when she reached the stairs, I ran out and pushed her down the stairs."

"What happened then?"

"I went downstairs and she was dead. I guess she hit her head on the marble floor. She was lying in a pool of blood. That's when I decided to take one of her flip-flops, just in case Bobby was arrested."

Dan pressed her on one point. "How did you know Gloria was really dead?"

"Are you kidding; all that blood; she was definitely dead."

"Did you touch her?"

"Just to get her flip-flop. Then I left by the front door, removed the remote device from the doorbell, and wiped away the fingerprints."

"What did you use to wipe away your prints?"

Mildred hadn't anticipated the question. She hesitated and then answered, "I used a silk handkerchief. It's still in my purse."

"Tell me about Ray Bussard and Freddie Moran."

"I found out where he lived. I had the whole thing planned out. I planted a virus in an e-mail from Janet to Ray. When he opened it, the virus took control of his computer, and sent another virus to Moran's computer. That e-mail then infected his computer, and both computers exchanged messages without either one knowing what was happening."

"How did you kill Bussard?"

Mildred coughed violently for several seconds and a bloody liquid dripped from her mouth. "That was easy. I waited for him to pull into the garage that night. He had his own parking place. I shot him when he got out of his car."

"Where were you standing when you shot him?"

"I was hiding behind a car parked across from his spot."

"What time was that?"

"I don't remember for sure; probably around eleven."

"Where's the gun?"

Mildred looked over at the other side of the room. A nine-millimeter Glock with a silencer lay on the table.

"Mildred, you're not telling me the truth, are you? You killed Ray Bussard, but you didn't kill Gloria did you?"

She looked up at Dan with pleading eyes. She hesitated and then said, "I killed them both Dan, and they both deserved to die."

Sally found a bottle of water and lifted Mildred's head so she could drink the liquid. Mildred closed her eyes and drifted off into a peaceful sleep. Sally checked her pulse. It was weak, very weak. Mildred was getting ready to die.

Dan left to bring their car up to the cabin so the ambulance could reach them. By the time Dan walked back into the cabin, Mildred was gone. Sally, with tears running down her face, hugged Dan. Sally held up a vial of Ambien, a strong sleeping pill. "The vial's empty. She believed so much in what she was doing. She must have been living with all that hate for so many years. Other than the fact that Gloria wasn't dead when she hit the floor, what else didn't Mildred get right?"

"The doorknob was wiped clean with a Kleenex tissue, not a silk handkerchief."

"So the truth rests on a Kleenex tissue. Life's so simple and yet so complicated."

"She got everything right about Ray Bussard, and the computer virus."

"So, what does it all mean?"

"I think Mildred's trying to protect someone else, and I'm afraid to say, it must be either Bill or Bobby. Nothing else makes sense. It's sad, but I'm convinced Bobby or Bill killed Gloria and Mildred decided to take all the blame. But there's another complicating factor; whichever one did it, they planed the whole thing with Mildred. This was all premeditated. That's for sure."

"What do you mean?"

"The virus was inserted into their computers before Gloria was killed. Mildred wanted to make it look like the Raccoon did it. The date of Gloria's death, and the fact that it was made to look like an accident, means whoever killed Gloria was working closely with Mildred. If it's not Bobby or Bill, then who could it be?"

Sally said, "Of course, Mildred, close to death, may have forgotten she used a Kleenex."

"Yes, it's possible, but there is the fact that Gloria didn't die from the fall. However, the rest of her story was accurate, and she was perfectly lucid. The bigger problem is I don't have enough evidence yet to arrest either Bill or Bobby."

The sound of a siren grew in the distance. A few minutes later, they could see the red-colored emergency vehicle pull slowly up to the cabin. Sally and Dan walked outside and met them as they left the ambulance. Sally said, "You can take it easy. I'm a doctor and the person died already."

The two medics walked into the cabin and examined Mildred. After confirming she had indeed expired, Dan flashed his FBI badge and talked to them about why she was at the cabin and the need to close off the entire area as a crime scene. The medics brought in a gurney as well as a body bag, and after Dan took a number of pictures of Mildred and the cabin with his iPhone, he allowed them to remove the body.

The medics gave Dan the telephone number of the local sheriff's office, and Dan spoke with the sheriff while the ambulance crew worked with Sally to fill out the proper paperwork. The sheriff asked Dan to return to Tipton with the ambulance. He would send out one of his deputies to seal off the crime-scene as soon as possible.

Dan agreed and said, "I'm going to take possession of some of her personal effects as important evidence."

The sheriff understood and asked Dan to log it into the new case folder that his office would open as soon as Dan arrived at the sheriff's office.

Dan gloved up and carefully placed Mildred's gun, the pink flip-flop, and the empty vial of sleeping pills in evidence bags. He always kept evidence bags in all the Lawson cars just in case. He then closed Mildred's suitcase and brought both items out to their jeep. Returning to the cabin, he searched for any possible missed clues, shut the cabin door, and started up their car.

Both vehicles slowly headed back down the dirt path toward the main road. Sally was quiet, contemplating what had just happened. She finally spoke. "I should have seen this coming. Mildred has looked terrible for the last few weeks. I should have noticed her symptoms. I shouldn't have assumed it was just stress."

"Honey, at the end of the day, it didn't matter. She didn't want to live anymore. That was clear."

This time, Dan rolled over the fallen tree with a little more speed. The shocks almost bottomed out, but they didn't get stuck. They followed the ambulance into Tipton and stopped at the Sheriff's Office. Sheriff Strauss, who was waiting outside, asked the medics to have the hospital quarantine the body until the coroner could confirm the cause of death.

He then introduced himself to Dan and Sally. Brad Strauss seemed like a regular guy. He led them back into his small building. It was basically one large room with a small lockup in the back corner. There were desks for about four deputies, probably more than enough to maintain a safe environment in the county.

They stopped at the communal coffee urn. Dan knew it was the only constant in police stations throughout the world, and the coffee was just as bad as in his own precinct. It took over an hour for Dan to brief Strauss on the case and he only had one question. "I never met anyone who was both a Detective and a Special Agent for the FBI; how could that happen?"

Dan explained how he and Sally had been asked to work on a special case, and they continued to work for the FBI from time to time. Strauss still couldn't understand but decided to leave it alone. Instead he switched gears and asked, "What do you want me to do with the body after the coroner releases it?"

Dan thought for a moment. "I need to talk to the family first; I'll get back to you. I don't think you need to worry about anybody disturbing things at the cabin, but I would like you to seal off the area as a crime scene. We may need to send our Forensics people in, although I doubt it."

"Well, anything to help you on the case. Things are pretty slow around here, so just give me a call if you need anything."

With that statement of support, Dan and Sally left the Sheriff's Office and headed back to Tyrone.

Chapter 52

Dan checked in with Joey and Jimmy as soon as they returned to the B&B. Dan thought about contacting Bill to give him the bad news, but decided against doing it now. He wanted to be there when he talked to Bill, and he wanted Bobby there at the same time. It was all about seeing how they reacted to the news.

Dan then called Gail Fisher and updated her on the demise of Mildred Fowler. Gail promised to tell her mother when the time was right, and Dan understood the time might never be right.

Now it was time for a dinner and Martha's café beckoned once again. Martha's was crowded with the early dinner crowd; a few families, but mostly young single men wanting some good home-cooking before they returned home for the evening.

Martha greeted them at the door and seated them at a table near the kitchen. Martha had significant help tonight, two servers; and from the sounds of pots and pans crashing in the kitchen, at least two cooks. With time to relax and enjoy the evening meal, Sally asked Martha what she recommended. "The chef says the prime rib looks very good, and all our beef is prime and the cattle are raised in the area."

Dan remembered with great fondness the first meal Sally had ever prepared for him; It was prime rib, and since that day, it had become his favorite. Sally too remembered their first dinner. She didn't have a clue of what to fix, but she wanted to impress, and the local butcher convinced her to prepare a prime rib.

So, prime rib it was for both Dan and Sally. Dan ordered a half liter of the house Merlot, and Baby Lawson requested a Diet Coke. While waiting for their salads, Dan said, "It's going to be easier to prove Bill did it than Bobby."

"Why is that?"

"Like I said earlier, this whole thing was well-planned. If Bill and Mildred conspired to kill Gloria and Ray, then they must have been in contact while Bill was in Afghanistan. He'd only have a few options. He could Skype her, use e-mail, or just call her from a phone. There would have been no time for snail-mail. If they Skyped, then Bill must have used the base computer, and there would be a record of that. Mildred might even have left a record on her own computer, but I doubt it. If they used e-mail, then Benny can probably recover the messages. I'm betting on Skype."

"What if you can't find any record of Bill contacting Mildred?"

"Then Bobby did it, and right now all I have is circumstantial evidence. I'm going to need to find something else to prove he did it, and right now I don't have a clue of how to find it."

"Well assume he did it. From what you've told me, it would have been on his lunch hour."

"Right."

"So, how did he get from the high school to his house?"

"He probably took Bill's car. He's been driving it almost every day."

Dan suddenly smiled. "And if he drives his car to school, where does he park it? The school must have all kinds of rules on who can drive a car to school, and where they can park. I guess I'm going to have to make another visit to the high school. Thanks Honey, once again you helped me think outside the box."

"It's okay Detective Dan. That's why I get paid the big bucks."

The salads arrived, followed by the prime rib with baked potatoes and a medley of garden vegetables. They ate in silence; Sally thinking about how sad it would be if Bobby was the one, and Dan going over in his mind the steps needed to find out which of the two did it. Dan looked at Sally and gave his usual Prime Rib statement. "It's okay Honey, but not as good as yours."

Sally knew it was bullshit but happily accepted the compliment anyway.

Over dessert, Sally finally spoke. "Whatever happens, their family has been totally ruined. It's hard to imagine the sadness the remaining innocent person will have for the rest of his life. The scars will never heal. Life sometimes can dish out some real shit."

"That's true Honey, but you're forgetting Gloria didn't ask to get killed. She definitely lived on the edge, and her risky behavior eventually led to her death, but that's no excuse for murder. If Bobby did it, I could understand why, if he had done it in a moment of passion when he saw them screwing, but he waited several weeks, and passionate outrage turned into premeditation.

"If Bill did it, then it was clearly premeditated. He cooks up this complicated plot with his buddy. You know, I would be inclined to think it was Bill, but the timeline just doesn't add up. Amber told me there was only a one in a hundred chance her death could have occurred after 1:30 p.m."

"That doesn't make it impossible, just unlikely."

"That's why I need to gather more evidence. There's just not enough to convict either one of them right now."

Sally suddenly smiled and grabbed Dan's arm. "I could feel the baby move, just for an instant."

Dan kissed her hand and smiled back. "I can't wait to find out if Baby Lawson is a boy or a girl. Then, we can decorate the room."

"But we haven't even decided which room to make into a nursery."

"I'm thinking the room overlooking the deck. We'll have to move some things around, but it's got the most space."

Sally thought about the room and then smiled again. "For once I agree with you. I think it will make a great nursery."

After dinner, they walked slowly back to the B&B. Dan couldn't resist making a snowball and throwing at a streetlight across the street. It struck the ground short and to the right. Thus began an epic contest between the two to see who could hit the post first. It took almost five minutes of laughing, shouting of demeaning four-letter words, and a few well-timed shoves of the thrower's arm before Dan finally hit the post and strutted his stuff in his yellow moonboots.

They kissed in mutual celebration and then walked arm in arm back to their hotel.

Chapter 53

They departed Tyrone after another great breakfast, and worked their way back to Chicago. After a stop for gas, Sally drove and Dan contacted Sergeant MacClosky on the Bluetooth. "Sergeant, this is Detective Lawson. I'm afraid I'm going to need your assistance once again."

"I'll try to help Detective."

"I'm going to need to talk to the Military Police on Bill Fowler's base in Afghanistan."

"What's this all about Detective?"

"I'm afraid I can't discuss that with you, but rest assured, it's important that I speak with the person in charge of your MPs."

"I'll talk to Colonel Kincade, and I'll call you back in a few minutes."

While Dan waited for MacClosky's call, he looked at the farmland stretching from horizon to horizon. The fields were covered with the snowfall from two days ago. The only signs of life other than the cars on the road were the birds skimming across the white landscape searching for food and thin wisps of smoke rising from farmhouse chimneys near the highway. Except for the cars moving along the highway, it was certainly a Norman Rockwell moment.

Dan's foray into the world of art was interrupted by MacClosky's call. "The name of the guy you want to talk to is Major Dustin. He's in charge of the MPs on the base. Colonel Kincade is going to have him contact you. He'll try your cellphone first, and if that doesn't work, then he'll try to reach you at your office. It's on your business card, right?"

Dan also gave him his home phone. The Sergeant said Dustin might call back within an hour if he was on the base and reachable. "Thanks for your help Sergeant; I'll expect Major Dustin's call."

The call from Dustin came in two hours later while Dan and Sally were eating lunch at a Subway near the highway. It took Dan almost thirty minutes to bring Dustin up to speed on the case. "So what can I help you with Detective Lawson?"

"I need to find out whether Bill Fowler contacted Mildred Fowler in the last month. It could have been a Skype conversation, an e-mail, or telephone call."

"Well, that's a simple request and a complicated search. We've got about one-hundred computers on the base, any of which could have been used to Skype or e-mail Chicago. Also, there're about sixty phones capable of making an international call. I'm assuming it would be a pay phone and that a credit card wasn't used. Of course, it could have been a prepaid phone card. A lot of the guys over here have those. I think we can rule out any off base communications. We're far enough away from any town to make an off base call highly unlikely."

"Major, I think I've reached the right person to help ferret out the information."

"Detective, I'll have a couple of my people get right on this. It could take us two to three days to check everything out. I'll get back to you as soon as we've completed the investigation."

"Thank you Major. You've been a big help."

It was Dan's turn to drive. After getting back on the highway, he set the cruise control to 80 mph and thought about the army. They certainly appeared to have their act together; no nonsense, not much bureaucracy, just a desire to complete the mission.

They reached the outskirts of Chicago a little after three o'clock. Dan stopped by the precinct and while Sally kibitzed with Joey, he brought his evidence bags to Julie. "I've got a surprise for you."

Julie gloved up and opened both bags. She saw the pink flip-flop and Glock and laughed. "Well, I'll be Detective Lawson. Haven't you been busy. She carefully lifted the flip-flop from the plastic bag with a tweezers to avoid spoiling any latent prints and placed it carefully in a Tupperware container. She then placed a label on the top of the container with the case number, date, and a brief statement of how the evidence was obtained. She did the same for the gun. "Dan, e-mail me the report number for your trip so I can cross-reference the evidence to your report."

"Better than that, I'll bring you the report tomorrow morning."

Dan left Forensics and found Sally sharing a cup of coffee with his boss. Sally was trying her best to convince him to have hip surgery. He had been complaining for over five years, and as his osteoarthritis became worse, his refusal to have the surgery had slowly softened. Sally handed him a piece of paper with the name of a doctor. "Joey, she's the best. If I needed the surgery, I'd insist on Dr. Hillman."

Joey stared at the piece of paper. Mulling over the need to make a decision, He finally said, "I can't live with the pain anymore; I'll call Hillman."

"What's this; you're actually going to do it; my God, does that mean we won't have to hear about your bad hip anymore. Believe me, the precinct will be a better place without your constant whining."

Joey fought back, "No, Dan, I'll just be complaining about something else. It's in my nature. Just ask my wife."

They left the precinct and finally arrived home at about four o'clock. Dan called Bill Fowler. Both he, Janet and Bobby were home and available for a meeting. Sally wished Dan good luck as he headed next door.

Chapter 54

They met at the kitchen table. Janet wasn't paying much attention; she wasn't interested in any more bad news, so she just sat there apparently lost in her own thoughts. In contrast, Bill and Bobby were both on edge and very attentive.

Dan had their undivided attention. "I'm afraid I have some very bad news. Yesterday, I found Mildred in a cabin near the farm where she grew up. She had gone there to die, and passed away while Sally and I were with her. She had just taken an overdose of sleeping pills."

Dan stopped to measure everyone's reaction. Janet had a sardonic smile on her face. After all, Mildred had confessed to killing both her parents. Bill's reaction was quite different. He buried his face in his hands and began to cry. Bobby looked stoic, but tears were dripping down his face.

Bill finally looked at Dan. "I'll never be able to apologize or say goodbye. Why did she have to die? What happened?"

Dan knew the answer to Bill's question would be the key to judging both Bill's and Bobby's body language. Did either of them know Mildred was dying of cancer? "When Sally and I found her at the cabin, she was close to death. She told us she had been diagnosed with pancreatic cancer and was given six months to live. She refused chemotherapy."

Dan let his words sink in. Bill's eyes looked very large. "Why didn't she tell us? Why would she keep it a secret?"

"Bill, I don't know the answer to that question. She never told us."

Dan was looking at Bobby. His facial expression remained unchanged. Tears were continuing to flow down his cheek, but nothing changed. Was he in shock, or did he already know his Nana was going to die shortly. It was impossible to tell. Was Bill just a great actor, or did he really have no idea his mother was dying of cancer. Dan waited for the next question.

He didn't have long to wait. Bill asked, "What else did she say? She must have told you other things.

Dan knew this question would come up, and he had debated with himself on how to answer it. "She told us a number of things Bill, but I can't tell you about them now. What I can tell you is she admitted to shooting Ray."

Janet, who had been listening, finally asked, "But what about my mother. Her letter said she had killed my mother."

"I'm sorry Janet, but at this point I can't talk about that."

Janet fought back. "But she admitted to doing it. She did it, right?"

"I'm sorry Janet, I can't talk about it."

Bobby remained stoic and Bill thoughtful. Bill asked, "Are you saying my mother didn't kill Gloria?"

"Bill, I'm saying Mildred told us other things and I can't talk about what she told us at this time."

Bobby spoke for the first time. "So, are you closing out the case?"

Dan stared at him. "Bobby, I can't close the case at this time. I'm still investigating."

Bill said, "If you can't close out the case, that means you don't think Mildred killed Gloria. If my mother didn't do it, then who did?"

"I'm sorry, but I can't talk about that. Bill, the coroner will probably release the body tomorrow. I told the local sheriff that I would call him to let him know what you wanted done."

Without thinking too much, Bill said, "We'll use the same funeral home I used for Gloria."

"Sally and I offer you our sympathy. I wish I could have brought better news."

Dan started to leave. He hadn't worn a jacket even though it was getting pretty cold. After all, it was only a fifty yard walk between the two houses. Bill cornered him in the driveway.

"You think I did it don't you?"

"Look Bill, we're good friends, but I really can't talk about it anymore. If you keep pumping me for information, then I'm going to ask my boss to be pulled off the case, and I guarantee, the person who replaces me will be giving you a lot less information than you've been getting from me."

"Okay, okay; but I'm going to talk to my lawyer; I want to take the lie detector test."

"My advice Bill is to do what your lawyer says; too many innocent people fail lie detector tests."

Dan left Bill standing in the driveway and walked the fifty yards back to his own house. Sally met him in the kitchen with a hug and a kiss. "How did it go?"

"About as bad as could be expected. Joey was right, I'm too involved with the family. I should give the case to someone else."

"No you shouldn't; in the end, whoever remains in the Fowler household will learn to appreciate what you've done."

Sally sealed her support with another kiss.

"How's Baby Lawson doing?"

Sally smiled. "Getting more active. In a couple weeks, I'll get the ultrasound and start the genetic testing. That's the next big hurdle."

Sally had found some leftovers in the freezer, and after nuking them in the microwave, they sat down at the kitchen table and watched the evening news. Dan's own troubles paled in significance to the problems in Pakistan and Afghanistan.

Chapter 55

Dan started his day at the high school. Elsie Feingold, the principal, was able to immediately meet with him. "Detective Lawson, nice to see you again. What can I do for you today? I hope it's not something bad about Bobby Fowler."

"I hope so too Doctor Feingold. I should have asked you sooner, but I'd like to take a look at your security cameras on the day that Gloria Fowler died. I hope you still have the data."

"My dear Detective Lawson. We have entered the digital age, a time when gigabytes of memory are cheap and potential lawsuits are many. I'm sure we have all the video evidence saved for the last ten years. That's what our lawyers said; save everything for at least ten years."

Feingold called someone on the phone and a security guard dressed in a reasonable facsimile to a police uniform entered the principal's office a few minutes later. "Detective Lawson, this is our head of security. Reggie Fields. He's an ex-cop, and I'm sure he can help you."

Reggie Fields led Dan down into the basement of the main building. They passed through a storage-room filled with pallets of toilet paper, various housekeeping supplies, and thousands of cans of the types of vegetables high school students hate eating.

They entered a small room near the back of the warehouse. "How do you like my digs Dan?"

"Well Reggie, it's only one small step above my office at the precinct. At least you have total privacy."

Reggie Fields laughed, "You're right about the privacy. I guess I should consider myself lucky. What can I do for you today?"

Dan reviewed the case briefly with Reggie, including the date of Gloria Fowler's death. "First, I want to look at your security camera coverage for the date she died. Bobby Fowler says he had lunch at the Dawg House that day, and I want to confirm he left school during lunch and walked toward the Dawg House."

Reggie laid out a picture of an overhead satellite view of the campus on his desk and pointed to the location of the security cameras. The cameras were set up to cover the entrances to the main building, the Fieldhouse, and the football stadium. "If he left by the front door, then we should be able to pick him up on camera five."

Fields walked over to a large grey metal file cabinet, the cheapest of the cheap. It screeched in protest as he opened the drawer. He located a CD for the appropriate date and camera number and brought it back to his desk. He booted up his computer and placed the CD in the proper slot. "What time do you want to start?"

Dan thought for a moment. "Let's start at eleven o'clock."

A few seconds later, Reggie had advanced the video to eleven o'clock, and the main entrance to the school was clearly visible on the computer monitor. Teenagers of every imaginable description passed through the main entrance, mostly leaving, but a few were entering the building. Dan sat back in an orange plastic chair and looked for Bobby to emerge from the building. Meanwhile, Reggie walked over to his own private coffee pot sitting on a back shelf and poured himself a cup. "Do you want a cup? It's actually pretty good. I wouldn't be able to stomach the crap they serve in the teacher's lounge."

The coffee smelled fresh and enticing, and Dan readily accepted the offer. Dan was tempted to fast forward the video, but wanted to make sure he didn't miss Bobby's departure. At 11:51 a.m., Bobby rushed through the front door. Dan paused the video and looked at Bobby. He was wearing his Letterman Jacket with a blue sweatshirt underneath. Dan wrote down the time and asked Reggie. Do you have any cameras that might show Bobby heading for the Dawg House?"

"Camera sixteen might show something. I'll get it."

While Reggie looked for the other camera, Dan fast forwarded the video to 12:45 p.m., and continued watching the monitor. He wanted to determine what time Bobby returned to the high school. Reggie, what time would his lunch period have ended?"

"One o'clock Dan, that's when his next class would have started."

Sure enough, two minutes before one, Bobby Fowler once again appeared at the front door. Dan once again wrote down the time. Bobby had been gone a total of sixty-seven minutes.

Reggie placed another CD in the computer slot and fast-forwarded it to 11:54 a.m. One minute later, Bobby was walking quickly, almost running past the camera.

Dan fast-forwarded the video to a little before one. At 12:57 p.m., Bobby Fowler passed the camera running to the school's front entrance at a full all-out sprint.

Dan thought about the videos. Kids are running all the time. He could understand why Bobby was running back to class. Every teenager in the world waited to the last minute, but almost running as he was leaving the school seemed a bit strange. Could Bobby have gone home, murdered his stepmother and returned to the school within forty-nine minutes

Dan turned to Reggie who was sipping his coffee. "Reggie, I need these two CDs. I'll have Forensics make you copies. On a separate issue, I'm assuming Bobby drove to school that day. Where would he have parked his car?"

"We control student driving. Only Upperclassmen are allowed to park their cars within four blocks of the school. Since Bobby is a Senior, he would have been issued a parking permit for the student lot."

"And where's that located Reggie?"

Reggie pointed to the map of the school and a parking lot one block away from the school. The lot held parking places for about eighty cars. "Does he have an assigned space?"

Reggie entered his computer and quickly located a spreadsheet with the assigned spaces in the student lot. "He's been assigned spot # 47."

For some reason, Dan wanted to look at the space, so Reggie led the way out the front door toward the student parking lot. Walking toward the area, Dan asked, "The cameras showed Bobby running in this direction. Is this also the way he would have gone to the Dawg House?"

Reggie pointed up the street. "It's two blocks ahead. He probably would have walked this way. A light fluffy snow was falling. About two inches already covered the ground. They cut across the lot making their way to spot #47. Bobby's car was parked in the spot covered in a thin veil of snow. Dan looked at the car, then up the street in the direction of the Dawg House.

A car pulled into the lot area and a gate rose to allow access. Dan asked, "How do the cars gain access to the lot?"

"Cars approved for access are given a specific bar-code decal that they put on their right rear window. When they approach the gate an optical scanner reads the bar-code and opens if they're on the approved list."

Hopefully, Dan asked, "Does the system keep a record of the car entering the gate?"

Reggie excitedly answered, "Yes, yes it does."

They both hurried back to Reggie's office. Reggie entered a program on his computer and found Bobby's authorized bar-code number. He then entered another section of the program and printed out a record of every time Bobby's car entered and left the parking lot since the beginning of the school-year.

Dan looked up the date of Gloria's death. There were four events recorded. The first was at 8:50 a.m., the beginning of the school day. The second event was at 11:59 a.m. The third was for 12:55 p.m., and the fourth and final event recorded for the day was at 4:39 p.m., probably after the end of Bobby's football practice.

Reggie asked, "You've got him don't you Dan?"

"I think I do Reggie, and I feel terrible. I live next to the Fowlers, and we're friends of the family. Life sucks, especially today."

Chapter 56

Dan threw the case file down on the living room couch, scattering the papers all over the floor. He walked over to his liquor cabinet and poured himself two fingers of scotch. He swallowed the entire amount in one gulp. His throat burned, and he cussed this case for the one-hundredth time since he left the high school.

He filled his glass again, set the bottle down on the kitchen table, and collapsed in the chair. What was the next step? Was it time to arrest Bobby for the murder of Gloria or did he need more evidence. The weight of the decision was anything but trivial. Luckily, an additional bit of information would make his decision an easy one. His cellphone rang. It was Julie.

"Dan, I wanted to call you immediately. I pulled two prints off of Mildred Fowler's flip-flop. One is Mildred's and the other is Bobby Fowler's."

Silence followed. Julie finally asked, "Dan, did you hear me? I found Bobby Fowler's fingerprint on the flip-flop."

"I heard you Julie. I'm sorry; I was just thinking about the implications. Now I've got to arrest Bobby Fowler, and I was thinking about how it's going to destroy Bill Fowler. I can't imagine how it feels to lose your wife and then find out your own mother and son did it. It's a real bummer, that's for sure."

"I see your point Dan. Sometimes I get too wrapped up in the technical things and forget there're people's lives at stake. I wouldn't have a clue how to break the news."

"That's what's going through my mind right now. I've got to think this whole thing through. Listen, thanks for the good work on this. Without your help, we wouldn't have a case."

"Just doing my job Dan, but thanks anyway."

Dan knew it was time to pay a visit to the District Attorney. The evidence was not conclusive, but the case against Bobby had built to the point where it had passed the reasonable doubt threshold. Of course, a good defense attorney would have an explanation for each bit of evidence, but the aggregate sum of the evidence would probably convince most jurors.

The key question for Dan was should he confront Bobby with his fingerprints on the flip-flop and his car trip on the day Gloria was killed? He had already timed his drive from the high school to Bobby's house. It had taken only nine minutes. Assuming twenty minutes for the round trip, that left thirty-six minutes to enter the house, hide in his room, ring the front doorbell remotely, and push Gloria Fowler down the stairs.

The only problem with the case was that all of the evidence was circumstantial. Sure, it was compelling, but at the end of the day, it was just circumstantial.

Sally walking through the backdoor interrupted his thinking. Sally looked at the bottle of scotch on the table and said, "The shit must have hit the fan!"

"You've got that right."

Dan reviewed his day. Sally sat next to him at the table absorbing everything Dan was saying. Tears were flowing down her face. Bobby was like a brother; Bill was a close friend; life had taken a terrible turn for the Fowlers, and now things were going to get even worse. They were witnessing the total disintegration of a family, nothing less.

"What are you going to do now?"

"Tomorrow, I'll review the case with Joey and then it will be time to call in the DA. They'll have to make the decision of whether to arrest Bobby."

Sally stood up and sat down on Dan's lap. She wrapped both arms around his neck and pulled him into her chest. She then looked him in the eye and said, "I was wrong. You should never have taken the case. You're too involved personally."

"You're probably right, but I felt I had a better chance of figuring out what happened than another detective who didn't know the family. Let's forget about the Fowlers for right now. How's Baby Lawson doing?"

Sally looked down at her bump and smiled. "Just about as good as can be expected."

During dinner and even sitting down watching TV afterward, Dan still couldn't put Bobby Fowler out of his mind. He didn't look forward to meeting with the DA. It was going to be a bad couple of days; that was for sure.

Chapter 57

Joey listened quietly to Dan's presentation of the evidence on Bobby Fowler. "I'm thinking like you Dan, the fingerprint on the flip-flop is incriminating, but everything is, as you point out, purely circumstantial. Let the DA decide if the case is good enough for a conviction."

Dan sat down at his desk and began writing a formal summary of the case to date. He left nothing out and tried to be as objective as possible. On the last page, he listed with bullet points the key evidence: Bobby witnessing his stepmother having sex with her ex-husband, his admitting to hating Gloria, his leaving school in his car at the time of the murder, the fingerprint found on the pink flip-flop, and Mildred's attempt to confess but not knowing the doorknob was wiped off with a Kleenex. And of course, Gloria died from asphyxiation, not her fall. In total, the evidence, even without a smoking gun, was very convincing.

Dan had called the District Attorney's Office earlier in the day and a meeting was scheduled immediately after lunch. The case had been assigned to Norm Feldman. Dan had worked with him on earlier cases and respected his judgment.

Norm normally had that legal look about him, but not today. The office had gone to business casual except when in court, and Norm pushed the limit of acceptability. He silently reviewed Dan's summary and then puffed up his cheeks and exhaled quickly. "What a bizarre case Dan. We both know Bobby did it, but the question is whether a jury will agree. Here's the deal, a good lawyer will be able to cast reasonable doubt. Bobby Fowler might have driven his car to meet some girl; and he might have handled the flip-flop the day before the murder. Then too, you've got the letter of confession from Mildred Fowler, and the Defense will argue that given her age, she just forgot she used a Kleenex to clean the doorknob."

"So where do you think we should go from here?"

"I think we've got two alternatives. Either we get more evidence or we get Bobby to admit that he did it."

"The Fowlers hired Phil Jacobs, and you know Phil, he's not going to let us question Bobby without his being present."

"But Dan, you've caught Bobby in a big lie, and then there's the fingerprint. I can ask him some questions that might get him to tell even more lies. Let's do this. I'll prepare a line of questioning I think might trap Bobby Fowler, and you try to dig up some more evidence. Let's meet tomorrow afternoon and see where we're at."

Dan left the District Attorney's Office feeling depressed. Norm Feldman was probably right, and Dan was probably taking things too personally; but Bobby Fowler was guilty of murder and needed to pay for the crime.

Returning to the precinct, Dan poured a cup of coffee and sat down at his desk. It was hard to concentrate with all of the commotion; drug dealers being brought in from the street, a variety of people pleading their personal issues at other detective's desks, two drunks being lead to the lockup, a mother with her two little children crying in the corner. It was no environment in which to be able to think, let alone solve a case.

With all of the distractions hovering around him, Dan opened once again the Fowler case folder and studied the contents; a report from the coroner, another report from Forensics, and finally all of his own notes taken over the last few weeks.

A teenager screaming at the top of his voice interrupted his thoughts. He looked at the handcuffed young man being led to the lockup. He was wearing a high school Letterman Jacket, similar to the one Bobby Fowler wore. Dan looked on with some amusement as the kid was dragged away. He kept on staring at the spectacle, and for some strange reason focused in on the boy's jacket. What was there about the jacket? Dan had seen thousands just like it, but in his subconscious mind, he knew there was something about the jacket that related to the Fowler case. What was it?

The jacket; something about Bobby's jacket. Finally, it came to him, not as a flash of insight, but rather a slow-building realization. Dan had not seen Bobby wear his Letterman Jacket for weeks, and the more he thought about it, he realized he hadn't seen him wear it since Gloria's death. His eyes moved from staring at the office wall back to his desk and they finally fell on the two CDs from the high school security camera.

He booted up his computer and inserted the first CD. He found the picture of Bobby leaving the high school at 11:51 a.m. Bobby was wearing his Letterman Jacket. Dan fast forwarded the CD, and at 12:58 p.m. Bobby Fowler once again came into view. This time, however, he was not wearing the Letterman Jacket. Dan interlocked his hands and brought his index fingers up to his lips. Why, why, why? Why would Bobby Fowler not wear his jacket after he pushed Gloria to her death?

Dan pondered the question, and it didn't take long to come up with a possibility. Something had happened to the jacket, something that Bobby didn't want anyone to see, something implicating him in the homicide. Maybe Gloria had fought with him at the top of the stairs and ripped the jacket as she fell to her ultimate death. But that would mean there was a struggle and the undamaged furniture at the top of the stairs seemed to preclude that possibility.

Dan thought about Gloria lying on the marble floor in a pool of blood and Bobby leaning over her, finding out that she was still alive, and then pinching off her nose and holding her mouth shut until she died. Dan could envision Bobby leaning over the body and perhaps his jacket dipped into the pool of blood. Dan quickly opened up the Forensics report and turned to the pictures of Gloria.

The pool of blood surrounding her head looked like a crimson halo. Dan took out his magnifying glass and looked at the deep-red liquid. It glistened in the camera's flash. The pool of blood looked undisturbed except for a slight disturbance on the surface near Gloria's head. Dan could picture Bobby leaning next to Gloria asphyxiating her and the sleeve of his jacket touching the blood.

Dan needed to get hold of that jacket. He looked at his watch; it was almost four o'clock. Football season was over and Bobby was probably already home or would be shortly. Bobby was a minor so Dan needed to proceed with caution. It would be best if Bill was there. Bill would need to hand over the jacket.

Dan grabbed his Search Warrant from the case file and headed down to see Julie. He explained his latest theory and Julie listened intently. If you can get your hands on the jacket, and there's blood on it, we should still be able to get a DNA match with Gloria's blood. Julie handed Dan a large evidence bag and wished him good luck.

On his way home, he kept thinking about the jacket, and the more he thought about it, the more he realized the jacket might very well be the proverbial smoking gun. He pulled into his driveway and checked his gun. He didn't know how Bobby or Bill might react. The end was approaching and either one of them might suddenly become violent.

He knocked on the backdoor and waited. Bill, wearing his army fatigues, answered the door. He looked at Dan and sensed Dan's concern. "Not more bad news?"

"No Bill, I just had a question that I'm hoping Bobby can answer. I hope we can do this without a lawyer, but it's up to you."

"Well, I guess that depends on what the question is."

"Is Bobby back from school yet?"

"He's upstairs doing homework."

"Can you ask him to come down?"

Bill left the kitchen, walked over to the stairs and shouted up to Bobby. A minute later Bobby was standing in the kitchen looking at Dan with a sense of impending doom in his eyes.

"Bobby, I've noticed that you haven't been wearing your Letterman Jacket since Gloria died. Why is that?"

"Bobby pointed to a scar on his left wrist. I cut myself last week and got blood on the sleeve of my jacket. It looked kind of ugly, so I decided to get it cleaned. It's at the cleaners now."

Dan asked, "May I have the dry cleaner's receipt?"

Bobby dug into the back pocket of his jeans, pulled out his wallet, and handed Dan the dry cleaner receipt. The ticket said Centennial Cleaners. "Is this the one on Lake Street near Harlem Avenue?"

Bill was glaring at Bobby as Dan left their house. It took only ten minutes to drive to the cleaners. Luckily, they were still open. Dan pulled out his badge and the ticket and explained to the manager that the jacket was brought in with a blood stain.

"Oh yah, I remember it. It was a Letterman Jacket. I told the kid who brought it in we'd have to send it out to our main plant. I normally don't touch blood stains. I don't have the right solvents for the job."

Dan said, "I need to get that jacket before it's cleaned. Do you think it's been cleaned yet?"

"I don't know. Let me call the plant and they can tell me what the status is."

The manager got on the phone and called the main plant. He asked to speak to Florence, and after waiting a couple of minutes said, "Hey Flo, it's Jake over at the Oak Park site. I sent in a blood stained jacket about two days ago. The police are here and want to get hold of the jacket before it's cleaned. What's the status?"

Jake read off the ticket number and waited. Finally, Jake turned to Dan. "Flo said it was sent down for cleaning just this morning. She's going down right now to try and pull it before it hits the special solvent bath. She said she'd call back in about ten minutes."

Dan asked, "Where's the main plant located?"

"Over on Ashland just south of the United Center."

Jake wrote down the address and Dan gave him a business card and asked Jake to call him as soon as Florence pulled the coat. He needed it whether it had been cleaned or not.

Dan headed over to the main plant on Ashland Avenue with his blue light flashing. While dodging cars, Jake called and told Dan that Florence had been able to pull the coat just before it was treated. The coat would be waiting for him at the back entrance to the plant, at the guard's desk.

It was past five o'clock before Dan found the back entrance to the Centennial plant. As promised, the jacket was hanging at the guard's desk, protected with a clear-plastic wrap. He thanked the guard and placed the coat in the back seat of his car and headed back to the precinct.

Dan called Julie on the phone and explained he was coming in to deliver the jacket. The afternoon traffic was building as Dan maneuvered his car around a fender-bender at the intersection of North Avenue and Western. He finally arrived at the precinct and found Julie working at a lab-bench looking in a microscope.

She inspected the jacket. Dan explained, "Bobby said the blood was from a cut on his wrist. I saw the scar and there definitely would have been a lot of blood, but I'm thinking he dripped his own blood over Gloria Fowler's thinking it would hide any evidence."

"Well lucky for us, Bobby Fowler is wrong. I'll have the blood type by tomorrow, but it's going to take about two weeks for the DNA analysis to come back. The good news is, Gloria Fowler's blood type was AB-, and less than one percent of the population has that blood type."

Dan drove slowly home, thinking about the look on Bobby Fowler's face when asked to produce the coat. Dan could only imagine the subsequent discussion between Bill and Bobby. Even Bill probably now suspected his son might have actually killed Gloria. Knowing Bill, he would probably blame himself for what Bobby had done, and why not. After all, if Bill had the courage to divorce Gloria earlier in their marriage, she still might be alive today. The whole thing stunk.

It was after seven when Dan finally pulled into the garage. He had called and left a message for Sally. He told her he'd be late and to eat without him, but there she was, sitting at the table looking at some medical charts, waiting for her favorite man. "You shouldn't have waited."

"No problem, I was just writing some reports."

Sally had broiled some chicken breasts, and with the addition of some broccoli and baked potatoes, the dinner looked special. "The dinner's great Honey. What possessed you?"

"I thought you needed to relax tonight. The case is getting to you. You're taking it personally. I know you can't help yourself, but it's taking a toll."

"I'm sure Bobby did it. Today we took possession of his Letterman Jacket. It has blood on the sleeve. He says it's his, but I think it's Gloria's and he then cut himself and added his own blood on top of hers. Julie says she'll be able to sort out the two types of blood without a problem. I think the jacket is the smoking gun."

Chapter 58

The call came in at a little before nine o'clock. It was Julie. "I thought you'd want to know, I found two blood types on the jacket, AB- and O-. I'd say you've got your smoking gun. I asked the lab to expedite the DNA testing, and they said they'd try to get it done in ten days."

"And you're sure?"

"Yep, it's absolutely definitive."

"Well thanks Julie. Once again you've come through in the clutch."

After talking to Julie, Dan briefed Joey and then scheduled an immediate meeting with Norm Feldman. He left the precinct with a definite feeling of closure. From what Julie had said about how rare the AB- blood type was, her expectation was that the DNA match to Gloria's blood would only be a formality.

The Gods of the four seasons had officially decided winter had arrived. A howling northwesterly wind took falling moisture-laden snowflakes and turned them into flying micro-bullets. Dan was glad to reach the protection of his car in the precinct parking lot. Surely, they had enough evidence now to bring Bobby Fowler to trial. Only the lack of a DNA match of the blood to Gloria Fowler would free him from a long prison sentence.

Norm Feldman smiled as Dan entered his office. "What's the rush; I thought we were going to meet later in the day?"

Dan explained the detailed story behind the bloody Letterman Jacket. Norm listened carefully and slammed his fist on his desk when Dan explained just how rare an AB- blood type was. "We've got the son of a bitch!"

Norm thought for a moment and said, "We need to wait for the DNA test results to come back just to be sure, but it definitely looks like we've got him."

Dan said, "So how do you want to handle this once we get confirmation of the DNA match?"

"I've been thinking about this since we talked yesterday. We've basically got a conspiracy between Mildred and Bobby Fowler. A key question for the jury will be who's the principle instigator. Was it Mildred or Bobby? Bobby may have talked to Mildred about what he had seen, but I think Mildred planned the whole thing. The computer virus and the shooting of Ray Bussard seem to be all tied to Mildred.

"A good Defense lawyer, and Phil Jacobs is one of the best, will try to make it look like Bobby, as a minor, was just under the control of Mildred. A jury will find him guilty, but probably out of sympathy might want to find him guilty of only Second Degree Murder. Bobby's age will mean this will be tried in Juvenile Court, and that means the judge will tend to err on the side of leniency."

"So what are you thinking?"

"I'm thinking we don't arrest him yet, but we bring him in for questioning. With his lawyer present, we get him to confirm his side of the story. After he goes on record with his string of lies, we begin to confront him with some of the evidence, but we make it clear to Jacobs that there's even more evidence we're holding back. After he's arraigned, I'll approach Jacobs with a plea deal. We'll see if he goes for pleading guilty to Second Degree Murder and a shortened sentence. I think he will."

"I like it Norm. I don't think Bobby Fowler deserves to spend the rest of his life behind bars. He's basically a good kid who made one very bad decision."

Back in his office, Dan called the Fowler's lawyer. "Mr. Jacobs, it's Detective Lawson. I'd like to bring in Bobby Fowler for questioning and I thought the best thing to do, because he's a minor, was to work it out with you."

"What kind of information do you want Dan?"

"I'm trying to establish exactly what Bobby did on the day that Gloria Fowler was murdered. There're a few inconsistencies in his story, and I thought the easiest way to get it resolved was to get him to answer a few questions."

"Who's going to be there?"

"Well, from our side, Norm Feldman, a court stenographer, and me; and whoever you'd like to be there is okay with me."

"Will he be under oath?"

"Well, I'd like it, but I can understand why you might object, so let's just leave it as we'll have a permanent record but he won't be sworn in."

"What if we say no?"

"If you say no, then I'll probably take the only step open to me, and you won't like that."

Phil Jacobs knew the next step meant arrest and all of the legal steps leading up to trial. He weighed the pros and cons and finally said, "We'll agree, but only under the condition that I can stop the questioning at any time."

Chapter 59

Bobby Fowler walked into the precinct at ten o'clock with his father and Phil Jacobs. He was dressed in a dark-blue suit, white shirt and a tie. He looked more than presentable. In fact, Phil probably set Bobby's dress code in anticipation of Bobby having to appear in court in the near-future.

Bobby had a nervous twitch on the third finger of his left hand, and a thin film of dampness appeared as a moustache above his upper lip. Norm Feldman, Bobby, and Phil sat around a small conference table. Lois Lane, Dan couldn't believe her name, sat to the side of the table ready to record the meeting for posterity. Dan sat next to Bill on the other side of the table.

Norm started the meeting by announcing that they were now going on the record. "Thank you for agreeing to meet with us today Bobby. Let me first identify the people present at this meeting. I am Norm Feldman the District Attorney representing the State. Mr. Robert Fowler is here with his attorney, Mr. Phillip Jacobs, and Mr. William Fowler, Robert Fowler's father is here as well as Detective Dan Lawson, the lead investigator in the death of Gloria Fowler."

"Bobby, we're here today to try and understand the exact sequence of events on the day of your stepmother's death. In particular I would like to understand what you did on that day from the time you left the house to go to school until you arrived home after school. I know these questions will seem rather detailed and may even seem a bit unimportant, but I can assure you that all of my questions are important in trying to reconstruct the events of that day. Are you ready to begin?"

Bobby nodded yes. Jacobs explained to Bobby that since there wasn't any video camera recording the meeting, he would need to give verbal answers to all questions. Bobby then said, "Yes, I'm ready to begin."

"Bobby, let's start out the morning of your stepmother's murder. Do you recall what you were wearing?"

"Bobby said, "I think jeans and a sweatshirt."

"And what type of shoes?"

"Nike shoes. I always wear Nikes."

"Do you recall what you had for breakfast?"

"Not really, usually I have cereal, but I don't remember for sure."

Phil interjected, "Bobby if you don't remember, then just say I don't remember. It's perfectly okay to say I don't remember. After all, it was many weeks ago."

"Okay Bobby, so after breakfast what happened?"

"I left for school."

"Did you wear a coat that day?"

"Yes, my Letterman Jacket."

"How did you get to school?"

"I drove my dad's car. When he's in Afghanistan, I use his car."

"Did you drive there alone, or did you pick anyone up on the way to school?"

"I drove there alone."

"Do you remember what time you got to school?"

"I wasn't late or anything so probably about ten minutes before first period."

"What time does First Period start?"

"Nine o'clock."

"Where did you park your car?

"In the school parking lot. There's a section that the Seniors can use."

"Did you attend all of your classes that day?"

"Yes."

"Do they take attendance in all of your classes?"

"Yes, they do."

"What were your morning classes on that day?"

"First Period was English; Second Period was Advanced Algebra, and Third Period was Study Hall."

"And what time did Study Hall end?"

"11:45."

"What's after Third Period?"

"I have lunch."

"And how long does lunch last?"

"Until one o'clock."

"And what did you do for lunch?"

"I already told Dan what I did."

"I know Bobby, but please answer the question anyway."

"I had lunch at the Dawg House."

"And how did you get there?"

"I don't know what you mean."

"Did you drive there, or walk, or ride a bike."

"I walked there."

"What streets did you take to get there?"

"I walked south on Scoville Avenue to Lake Street, and then turned right on Lake Street and the Dawg House is on Lake Street."

"Did anyone see you walking to the Dawg House or at the restaurant?"

"I don't know. I didn't talk to anyone."

"What did you order for lunch?"

"A large Italian Beef, fries and a Coke."

"Did you eat there?"

"Yes, I sat at a counter."

"And nobody saw you?"

"Well, lots of people saw me; I wasn't invisible or anything, but I didn't recognize the people I sat next to."

"Tell me about the two people sitting next to you."

"They were just two guys."

"White, black, young, old, tall, short; what did they look like?"

"They were both older, maybe in their fifties. One had a beard and smelled bad. The other guy was fat."

"There's a church across the street. Did you hear the church bell ring?"

"I don't remember."

"Did you walk right back to school after lunch?"

"Yes."

"You didn't take your car anywhere."

Phil Jacobs looked like he was going to say something but Bobby answered too quickly. "I already told you, I walked right back to school.

"Okay Bobby, let's skip to the afternoon. What classes did you have?"

"History, Physics, and Spanish."

"What time did school let out?"

"Three o'clock."

"And what did you do then?"

"I had football practice until 4:30."

"And then what did you do?"

"I got in my car and drove home."

"Did you go in the front door?"

No, I went in the backdoor."

"And what happened then?"

"I threw my backpack on the kitchen chair and that's when I saw Dan. I saw my stepmother on the floor. Dan stopped me and said there was an accident and she was dead. I asked if she fell down the stairs, and he said he didn't know what happened."

"Then what happened?"

"Dan took me to his house and Sally took care of Janet and me."

"Thanks Bobby; I only have a couple of more questions for you. You're doing a great job. When did your grandmother tell you she had cancer?"

Bobby didn't expect the question, and he waited almost ten seconds thinking about the question and how to answer it.

"Detective Lawson told us all after he got back from Pennsylvania."

"Were you surprised when you heard the news?"

"Yes, but she did look kind of sickly the last few weeks."

Dan now carefully studied Phil Jacobs. Feldman and Dan had agreed on the order of questions, and Dan knew the next set of questions were likely to prompt reactions from Bobby, Bill, and Phil, but Phil Jacobs was definitely the key. His reaction would indicate whether Bobby had told him the full story, or as Dan suspected, withheld some critical pieces of information.

"Bobby, Detective Lawson took your Letterman Jacket as evidence. There was blood on it. How did the blood get there?"

"Like I told Detective Lawson, I accidently cut my wrist, and I bled on the jacket. That's why I took it to the dry cleaners, to have it cleaned."

"And how exactly did you cut your wrist?"

"I was in the kitchen cutting an apple and the knife slipped."

"And you were wearing your jacket?"

"Yes."

"Bobby, Detective Lawson was able to find the jacket at the cleaners before it was cleaned. He brought it back to the Forensics Lab for analysis. They found two different blood types on the sleeve. The top layer of blood was O-, but there was another layer of blood under the top layer, and it was AB-. Do you know how it got there?"

A pale looking Jacobs jumped to his feet. "Bobby don't answer that question. Gentlemen, this interview is over. Bobby won't be answering anymore of your questions. After all, you haven't charged him with anything."

Dan stared at Bill Fowler, who looked absolutely devastated. Clearly from his expression, Gloria's blood on Bobby's jacket came as a total surprise. A tear streamed down his face as the Fowlers and their attorney left the conference room and walked out the precinct door.

Chapter 60

Back in Norm Feldman's office and behind closed doors, Norm and Dan recounted the testimony. "We need to wait for the DNA results, but as soon as they're in, you can arrest young Mr. Fowler."

"I was looking at his father and Phil when you popped the question about Gloria's blood," Dan said. "I could tell, neither one of them knew about her blood. If they had, Phil would have stopped you before you asked Bobby how the blood got there."

"You're right; and I think Bobby knew about Mildred Fowler's cancer before he said he found out. All in all, I think it was a very good day for the Prosecution. Phil will never put Bobby on the witness stand, but when he eventually sees all of the evidence we have, he'll go for a plea bargain, I'm sure of it."

Dan returned to the precinct and sat at his desk with mixed feelings. Bobby Fowler was going to spend some time in jail for a crime he committed, and that was a good thing. But the Lawsons and the Fowlers were friends, and nobody likes to see their friends get hurt. Dan knew his friendship with Bill was at an end, and that was the price to be paid for working the case. Joey was right, he shouldn't have taken the case. Dan held the thought, and the more he thought about it, the more he realized most other detectives wouldn't have been able to solve the homicide. His knowledge of the family had been instrumental in getting to the bottom of Gloria Fowler's death.

He hoped Bobby's attorney would agree to a plea bargain down to second-degree murder. That way, Bobby could still have a productive life after serving his time.

Dan didn't look forward to the trial. His testimony would probably be key to the case. Of course, Jacobs would bring in the young girl at the school who thought she might have seen Bobby, and there was the matter of Mildred's written confession; but the amount of evidence tying Bobby to the death of Gloria had mounted to the point where a reasonable jury would find him guilty of her death. The problem of course was all jurors were not reasonable. One bad apple, so to speak, could spoil the whole bunch. He had seen it up close and personal too many times.

Toward the end of the day, he was e-mailed the transcript of the morning's meeting. He printed a copy, and while the pages spewed forth from the printer, he grabbed another cup of bitter brew. He was seriously thinking of petitioning for one of the new upscale coffee machines. He knew he could count on at least ten others splitting the cost of the machine, but one could only dream.

He clipped the twenty-five pages of double-spaced legal paper together and sat back at his desk reading the official version. The stenographer had done a good job keeping up with the dialog. He finished reading the document once and then sat back sipping his coffee. He closed his eyes and thought about the facts as presented in the transcript. He had this feeling many times. He knew it well. His subconscious was uncomfortable with something in the transcript, and he could almost taste the incorrect fact, but not quite.

He began reading the document, but this time more slowly, studying every answer Bobby gave to Norm's questions. He finally got to the section on Bobby's arrival at his home the day of the murder. The transcript read, "I threw my backpack on the kitchen chair, and that's when I saw Dan. I saw my stepmother on the floor. Dan stopped me and said there was an accident and she was dead. I asked if she fell down the stairs, and he said he didn't know what happened."

Dan tried to recall exactly what had happened, and it was definitely as Bobby had remembered the incident. Still, there was something about his answer, something that didn't make sense. Dan carefully studied the words. "I threw my backpack on the kitchen chair, and that's when I saw Dan. I saw my stepmother on the floor. Dan stopped me and said there was an accident and she was dead. I asked if she fell down the stairs, and he said he didn't know what happened."

"I saw my stepmother on the floor." "I saw my stepmother on the floor."

The obvious was staring him in the face. He was an incompetent idiot. Sally told him that all the time, but this time he really meant it. He rushed from his desk and headed home. The answer was right there in front of him and he was too stupid to see it. A good detective would have solved the case that first day. On the ride home, he thought about the floor plan of their own home. It was the mirror image of the Fowler house, built by the same builder during the same year. That's the way it was in their neighborhood. Years ago developers bought up a half-dozen lots on a block and built the same style house with minor changes to each.

He pulled into the driveway and left the car near the backdoor. He would park it later. He stood in the kitchen and moved a kitchen chair to where the chair would have been located, the one Bobby threw his backpack on. He stood where he had stopped Bobby and looked at their own foyer.

No shit Dick Tracy; there's no way Bobby could have seen Gloria's body from that position. Of course he would have to verify everything with actual pictures taken in the Fowler house, but it was absolutely clear, if Bobby Fowler couldn't see the body from that position, then how could he possibly ask the question "Did she fall down the stairs."

There were only two ways he could have known she was lying near the stairs; either he had peeked into the foyer from a front window just before entering the backdoor, or he had previously seen the body; and that meant he had been in the house earlier in the day, and the only time could have been during his lunch hour. Of course, he'd have to check with the football coach to make sure Bobby was at the football practice the entire time, but Dan already knew the answer to that possibility because Bobby's car had only left the parking lot during the lunch hour and at the end of the day.

Dan reached Norm Feldman on his cellphone. He was driving home. It took Dan about five minutes to explain his theory. Norm, with a rare excitement in his voice said, "Tomorrow get Forensics to get a bunch of pictures of their house. Make sure one of them is taken from the exact position where Bobby was standing when you stopped him. Also, check with the football coach. If the facts checkout, then arrest him, read him his Miranda rights, and book him for first-degree murder. Great job Dan; I'm going to have a double martini when I get home to celebrate."

Dan called Julie and left a message for her to send out her best photographer to the Lawson house first thing in the morning. He then called Bill, and after a harsh greeting from Bobby's father, Dan explained that their Search Warrant was still valid, and Forensics needed to take some more pictures of the crime scene. Bill reluctantly agreed.

Chapter 61

Sam Waters arrived at the Lawson house just in time for some coffee and cinnamon rolls. Dan explained the situation. "There's only one picture that's important. It's a view from the kitchen looking into the foyer. When we get in their house, I'm going to stop exactly where I want you to stand and face in the exact direction I want the picture shot from. I'll ask you to begin as soon as I'm in the spot. But here's the thing, I want you to walk all through the first floor taking pictures, over fifty would be good, especially of the foyer. I want pictures from every angle, including from the top of the stairs. The key is, I don't want any of the Fowlers to figure out which picture is more important than the others."

Sam smiled at his clandestine assignment. "My, my, my, Detective Lawson; aren't we getting a bit dramatic?"

"Perhaps Sam but we must disguise what the important shot really is."

"Where's the good doctor?"

"She's on the early shift this week."

"I heard you guys are having a baby; congratulations. I'll tell you from experience, there's nothing like a first child to change your life. Getting married is nothing compared to the first baby."

"Well thanks for those encouraging words Sam. You're not the first to give us that advice."

With the cinnamon rolls washed down with a second cup of coffee, Dan and Sam walked next door. Dan rang the back doorbell and Bill, who had been waiting in the kitchen, let them in.

Dan walked slowly to the spot in the kitchen where he had stopped Bobby the day of the murder. He turned to Bill. "Thank you for letting us take the pictures Bill. I know our relationship has become strained, and this must be very difficult for you."

He then faced the foyer and said, "Bill this is Sam Waters from our Forensics Lab. Sam, why don't you begin."

Dan moved off the critical spot on the floor and casually led Bill past the foyer and into the living room. He looked at Bill, whose face displayed utter contempt. "This will only take about five minutes."

Dan sat down on an easy chair and Bill remained standing. The message on his face was clear, get out of my house now. Sam walked into the foyer and began taking pictures focusing on the place in the foyer where Gloria had been found. After taking about twenty pictures, he moved into the living room and then the library. Then he moved into the kitchen and took several shots, including the key photo. He finally walked up the stairs and shot a couple of pictures of the foyer from the second floor.

"That should do it Detective Lawson. Sorry for the interruption Mr. Fowler."

They stopped out in the driveway as a light snowfall descended from an ugly dark sky. "I took a couple of shots from the spot with several wide-angle lenses. I'll e-mail you the pictures as soon as I get back."

"Thanks Sam, You did a great job."

Dan started his car and followed Sam out of the driveway. Sam headed back into the city and Dan turned in the opposite direction so he could pay a visit to the high school and interview the football coach.

After talking to Elsie Feingold again, a student escorted Dan across the street to the field house where Coach Wilson was conducting a gym class, trying to teach the finer points of basketball dribbling to a bunch of sleepy teenage boys.

The student walked up to Coach Wilson and explained the interruption. Wilson screamed at the tallest boy in the group. "Jackson, take over the class. Set up a dribbling drill; two lines; the losers run a half-mile."

As the group formed up into two lines Wilson shook hands with Dan and they exchanged introductions. "Coach Wilson, I'm sorry to interrupt your class, but I need some information. Bobby Fowler is on the football team, and I need to confirm he was at practice several weeks back."

"Let's go back to my office. I keep the attendance records there.

The office area was located in the back corner of the Field House. Wilson sat down at his desk and turned on his computer. "What date are you interested in?"

Dan gave him the date of Gloria Fowler's death and in less than a minute, Wilson had confirmed Bobby Fowler was present at the practice. Dan asked, "Could he have arrived late or left early?"

"No, I would have noted it in the computer. He was here for the entire practice. Is this good news or bad news for Bobby?"

"I'm sorry coach; I can't talk about it, but thanks for your help."

Dan headed back to the precinct and then immediately opened the Fowler case file. He looked at a picture of Gloria's body taken from the top of the stairs and set his ruler on the picture lining up the edge of the kitchen doorway with her head. The line extended to a hinge on a closet door near the front entrance. Dan knew if he couldn't see the hinge from the picture Sam had taken, then there was no way Bobby could have seen the body from where he was standing when Dan stopped him.

Dan found Sam's e-mail and opened the file. A broad smile broke out across Dan's face as he looked at Sam's picture. He couldn't see the door's hinge, and there was no way Bobby could have seen Gloria.

Norm Feldman gave Dan the go ahead to arrest Bobby Fowler. Dan walked over to Amy Green's desk. She looked up from her computer and said, "It's you again. What do you want this time?"

"It's show time Amy. How do feel about making an arrest in the Fowler case today?"

"Well it's about time Detective Lawson. What have you been doing all these weeks; just goofing off?"

Amy jumped up and checked her gun. "Let's go big shot; I need to be home for dinner."

Dan looked at his watch. It was eleven o'clock. If they left now, Bobby would be ready for lunch by the time they arrived at the school. If Bobby stayed true to form, he'd be having lunch at the Dawg House.

The ride to the school was made in silence. There was something about an arrest on an important case that forced self-contemplation. Dan thought about the Fowler case from beginning to end and considered all of the ways he had failed to see the important clues. Hopefully, he could learn from the experience. After all, that was all one could hope for; to learn from your failures.

Epilogue

The case never came to trial. After seeing all the evidence against Bobby Fowler, Phil Jacobs convinced him to plead guilty to a lesser charge. The DNA match on Gloria Fowler's blood, and his not being able to see her body from the kitchen were the clinchers.

In exchange for the plea bargain, Bobby Fowler finally explained what had really happened after he had told Mildred Fowler about what he had seen. She had planned the whole thing, but he had insisted on shoving Gloria down the stairs. He had used a remote device Mildred had built to ring the doorbell, and when Gloria Fowler tried to answer the door, he had followed her down the hallway and delivered the big push. He had checked for a pulse and then pinched off her nose and closed her mouth to suffocate her. That's when he accidently dipped his sleeve in her blood. Then, he removed the remote device and wiped everything clean with a Kleenex tissue.

He said Mildred was the one who thought up the scheme to kill Ray Bussard and plant the virus to pin it all on Freddie Moran. Everything was just as Mildred had said except for her protecting Bobby in the death of his stepmother.

So Bobby was sentenced to twenty years, with the possibility of parole after ten years. Janet Bussard decided to move out of the house and in moved in with some of her colleagues at work.

Bill Fowler was a different matter. He never spoke to the Lawsons again. He put the house up for sale as soon as Bobby left to serve his prison term, and moved to an apartment in the city.

Oh, and by the way, just last week Sally Lawson gave birth to a little girl. She and Dan changed the name a hundred times during the last month of her pregnancy, but on the day of the birth, Sally introduced Debbie Beth Lawson to Dan as he looked on in wonder at the miracle and perfection of their first child.

Made in the USA
Columbia, SC
23 November 2018